I0588262

LADY DARLING INQUIRES AFTER A KILLER

NEW YORK TIMES BESTSELLING AUTHOR
COLLEEN GLEASON

Praise for Books by Colleen Gleason

"Gleason is really on a roll!"

— Publishers Weekly

"Exhilarating...Sure to please."

— The New York Times Sunday Book Review

"Wonderfully witty...deliciously dark and delightfully entertaining."

— The Chicago Tribune

"[This] novel is a well-oiled machine...the authentic historical framework... the compelling personalities."

— School Library Journal

"Sexy, violent, electrifying...[An] edgy, page-turning series...Brilliantly conceived and executed."

— Library Journal

Praise for Colleen Gleason writing as Colleen Cambridge

"...Totally delectable entertainment for fans of light-hearted detective fiction."

— *The Washington Post*

"If a murder mystery can be delicious, this one is."

— *The Sunday Denver Post* on *Mastering the Art of French Murder*

"This cute and clever mystery is perfect for historical fiction buffs."

— *Buzzfeed* on *Mastering the Art of French Murder*

"Utterly charming...Cambridge also does an excellent job of creating a cast of suitably quirky suspects and side-characters."

— *Historical Novel Society* on *Murder by Invitation Only*

"Dame Agatha would be proud."

— *Publishers Weekly* on *A Trace of Poison*

Chapter One

London, 1898

Irene Colchester, née Whitney, The Most Honorable Marchioness of Darling, had come to the conclusion that a married-off child was the best sort of child to have. Especially if that child was a daughter.

Irene loved her four children. Every single one of them was a joy and a source of maternal pride, albeit in different ways and for different reasons. They ranged in age from twenty to twenty-seven and were sensible, attractive, and kind. Some were wittier than the others, some were more generous or more patient or more tolerant than their fellow siblings, but at heart, they were all decent people.

Irene had cooed and mooned over them as infants, enjoyed them when they were young—even doing the unthinkable by the standards of the London peerage by actually spending time with them in the nursery: playing with blocks or reading stories, dressing dolls or serving them tea, or, in some cases, crawling over the floor as she set up an army of miniature tin soldiers representing the French, in a vain attempt to stave off an attack by the always victorious English (her youngest, Jane, was a rather bloodthirsty sort)—in lieu of attending balls or making social calls or meeting with a modiste about the newest fashions.

Irene had watched her offspring learn to ride horses and bicycles, cheering them on vigorously (to the dismay of her very proper, rather quiet husband).

Edward, Lord Darling, was a born and bred, stiff and unbending peer, while Irene...well, she was very much not.

But the two of them...*oh*, they'd loved each other deeply and had shared great passion during their time together.

They had braved the sneering, cold shoulder, and in some cases, cut direct, of the *haute ton* when the marquess chose to marry a woman who not only lacked a title, but whose family was *in trade* (not to mention being incomprehensibly rich).

Despite their different approaches to life, they'd been happily, even joyously, married for nearly twenty years. And then Lord Darling succumbed to an illness of the heart at the age of fifty-three, nine years ago.

Irene mourned her husband deeply. There was no doubt she suffered his loss greatly. But she also took advantage of societal mores by eschewing London and the world of the aristocracy for over three years, staying at one of the Darling country estates under the guise of seclusion, conveniently taking a cue from none other than Her Majesty the Queen.

Despite grieving the loss of her husband, Irene had been at her most happy there in the country—away from the rules and strict class structure of the peerage and London society... including the requirement to wear a corset and the skinny, hobbling skirts that had, thank Heaven, recently gone out of style.

At last, she'd had no choice but to return to the city and launch her daughters into Society. She loved the three of them (and her son, too, of course, but men children were different, especially if they were marquesses), but it was high time for the girls to be married off so they could start their own families and run their own households.

And so they could cease mollycoddling their mother, who needed nothing of the sort. Yes, she grieved her husband...but her own life had not ceased and she intended to enjoy what was left of it.

Now that all four of her children had been happily and advantageously wedded (Edward, the eldest of them and the new marquess, had been the last, only five months ago; for, as previously noted, men children *were* different), Lady Darling's life was suddenly as wide open as the ocean her father had loved so much.

Due to her son's marriage, Irene was now the dowager marchioness, and she had no responsibilities, no family members to care for, no large households at various properties to manage, no one to criticize her actions...

Well, that was not quite true, as Violet was never shy about giving an honest—and often unasked-for—opinion over her mother's wardrobe, accessories, mode of transportation, type of pastime, or choice of pet.

"And so you ask, dear Mr. Timms, why would I have agreed to do such a foolish thing and take *on* a task such as this when I've been enjoying doing absolutely *nothing* but puttering in the garden, reading novels, and redecorating my lovely dowager house," Irene said, tossing onto the cushion next to her the letter that confirmed said foolish task. "And you would be well within your rights to chide me for it."

Mr. Timms tilted his head, looking at her with his bright, dark eyes, and squawked, "Why? Why?" His scarlet tail flicked as he fluttered up and bounced onto the cushion, eyeing the letter—or, more accurately, eyeing the shiny gold ribbon that had been tied around it in a fanciful adornment.

"No, that is not for you," Irene admonished him. "You are

supposed to be lecturing me about my soft heart and loyalty to friends and whatnot, not eyeing Mrs. Bedwith's seal as if it were edible."

She reached for the top of a petite silver dish on the table next to her. At the familiar clink of the lid being lifted, Mr. Timms swiveled his attention to her, tilting his head with interest. Irene scooped out a small handful of pumpkin seeds and pine nuts and opened her palm to offer the treats to him.

Mr. Timms squawked again—"Thank you, Darling"—and hopped onto her lap. He carefully nipped up the seeds with his powerful parrot beak. She felt the gentle buss of its front curve as it harmlessly brushed her skin, and she smiled affectionately at him. Though his beak could break a small bone or slice through a piece of leather hide, Mr. Timms was always delicate and careful with her.

"I suppose I'd best have Jilly turn out a room for Miss Bedwith soonest, shan't I? You'll have to learn her name too, Mr. Timms. Priscilla. Priscilla. Can you say 'Priscilla'?"

But Mr. Timms was too busy nudging the curve of her hand for more nuts. She stroked a finger down the back of his soft, gray head and said, "Between you and Watson and Beatrice—not to mention the Josephs—I really need no other companions, do I? But here I am, about to be thrust into another season of stuffy balls and interminable musicales...good Heavens, I do hope the Spangler sisters have all been married off by now and I won't have to sit through any of their recitals, but there are ever so many of them one can't be quite certain" —she grimaced— "and there will be garden parties and soirées and the theatre..."

It also meant visits to Monsieur Claude not only for her own wardrobe but for Miss Bedwith's as well. That would be the only part of this whole undertaking Irene would truly enjoy. She loved hats and frocks and lace and flounces almost as much as she loved her menagerie—although she detested corsets and, to Violet's horror, did without as often as possible (hence Irene's extended stay in the country).

But Priscilla Bedwith's mother, Geraldine, was an old and dear friend, and Irene simply couldn't say no to her request. The poor, poor woman simply didn't have the constitution to navigate Society and find a husband for her daughter.

Watson, who'd been snoring on his cushion near the hearth, had started awake at the sound of his name. He lumbered to his feet and shambled over to her, then rested his head on the lap of her skirts as his feathery tail wagged happily. As he was nearly seven stone, the weight of his head was not insubstantial, nor was the event without incident, for, as now, he tended to drool quite a bit.

"Yes, I know, Watson. But it *is* rather difficult to take you along to the musicales," she said, patting his head, then lifting his chin so as to place a protective handkerchief between his damp canine jowls and her skirts. "Especially since the time you decided to join in with the third—or was it the fourth? one simply can't keep them all straight—Miss Spangler as she played the piano to her own vocal accompaniment." Watson had either been compelled to add his voice to the young woman's in an attempt to make it a duet, or (more likely) to drown it out.

Either way, Watson had not been invited back to the next Spangler musicale.

Sadly, Lady Darling had been, and she couldn't invent an excuse not to attend, for that had been the Season she was planning to marry off the twins—a plan at which she had, of course, succeeded.

It had been quite a coup: both daughters, each marrying a young, handsome, and wealthy titled man (Rose, the elder by a mere ten minutes, had wed an earl; Violet, a viscount), in a joint wedding that everyone agreed had been The Event of the Season. Even the Prince and Princess of Wales had attended.

Yes, indeed. It was no wonder Geraldine Bedwith had requested Irene's assistance in marrying off her daughter.

The dowager Marchioness of Darling certainly had a reputation for accomplishing things. The peerage as a whole might not agree with the way she went about conducting her affairs, but no one could deny that Lady Darling accomplished whatever she set her mind to do.

And she was going to find Priscilla Bedwith a proper husband—as quickly and efficiently as possible—so she could return to the country and be left to her own devices.

～

Priscilla Bedwith was going to marry a duke.

Or an earl. Or a viscount.

Or *someone* with a title. She'd even settle for a *baron*, although that would have to be a last resort. And, hopefully, whoever he was would also have pots of money (although nowadays, that delightful combination of title and funds was not assured).

Priscilla was determined to do this in her first season, no matter what. She *had* to, before that troublesome Hugh Bafferty returned from his European tour.

She'd be married, or at least engaged, before he set foot on English soil again. And then she'd never have to think about him ever again.

She uncurled her fists and nodded to herself. Yes, that would just set him back now, wouldn't it? Him coming home to find her with a wedding date set?

It was just that she wasn't very sure about how it was all going to unfold, with her being foisted off onto this old friend of her mother's.

Priscilla had heard *plenty* about Lady Darling, and very

little of it—with the exception of her proficiency in marrying off four children in the span of three years—was comforting. Why, the woman brought her *dog*—who was apparently the size of a small pony—to garden parties and musicales!

And she apparently drank *whisky* instead of sherry. Someone had even reported seeing her smoking a cigar on one occasion, although Priscilla couldn't quite believe that.

Apparently Lady Darling was terribly frightening too, which was not surprising, all things considered.

But Priscilla's mother simply couldn't come to London, conduct her debut into polite society, and navigate her through a season. Confined to a wheelchair and in extremely fragile health, Geraldine Bedwith found country living much easier than going about in crowded, busy, fog-shrouded London. She didn't know anyone anymore, she claimed, except for Lady Darling, whose sister by law's cousin lived nearby, and she was simply too tired to move her household to the city.

And Priscilla's father was far too busy hunting, visiting his gentleman friends, meeting at his club, and going to horse races, to squire his daughter about at balls and the theatre. Besides, Father wouldn't know the first thing about how to outfit her for a Season and trousseau. And she needed a female chaperone anyway.

But the stories Priscilla had heard about Lady Darling made her stick-straight hair want to curl up in shock. But those were stories from years ago, weren't they...although the Enfield Ball incident had been more recent, hadn't it? And some of the stories and rumors seemed to conflict—was the dowager frightening or odd? Was she shockingly uncouth or reclusive? Not much of it made sense.

Lady Darling must be positively ancient and completely creaky by now. Why, she had to be at least fifty—but surely she wasn't quite as eccentric as she might have been. When a person got that old, they just became quiet and sedate. Besides, the stories—as gossip often was—must be exaggerated if they even held a grain of truth at all.

Priscilla's mother had insisted that "dear, dear Irene" would give her a splendid Season, and help her to find a husband.

But Priscilla didn't need help finding a husband. She merely needed to be chaperoned at locations and events that would put her in the proximity of eligible bachelors, and she would do the rest.

Still...it was with some trepidation and quivering knees that she climbed two steps to the entrance of the house where the Dowager Marchioness of Darling lived. Her mother had sent Priscilla on a two-hour journey to this stranger's house with only her maid, a groom, and a pair of footmen to conduct her safely—and now here she was.

The dowager house was a narrow, four-story affair constructed of rich brown brick. Six chimneys sprouted from its roof, and there were five gabled windows across the uppermost floor. It was situated in a quiet neighborhood across from a small park, and was only a fraction of the size of the main London residence of the new Marquess of Darling, where he lived with his recently-acquired wife.

Priscilla heard that the dowager marchioness had moved from the main house with such speed and alacrity that her possessions had been relocated *while* the wedding was actually going on. She couldn't fathom why anyone would want to leave the grand mansion in the middle of Mayfair for this smaller place here, on the quiet side of St. James.

The door in front of her opened before she had even reached to lift the knocker.

A man smiled down at her. He was barely tall enough to be a proper butler, and he was a bit burlier than one would expect for a person in such a position, but he held himself most correctly. His suit was a dark charcoal color, pressed and crisp. His graying, shiny black hair was combed back smoothly and he was clean-shaven except for a pair of neat sideburns. He had smooth skin and brown eyes that crinkled at the corners. They seemed to twinkle with welcome—an emotion Priscilla had never witnessed on the face of a butler. Every other member of that species she'd encountered had a supercilious sort of sneer permanently affixed on his face, and his nose lifted as if he smelt something unpleasant.

"Miss Bedwith, welcome. We've been expecting you. Please come in. Lady Darling is waiting for you in the sitting room. I suppose your maid and other staff have gone round to the back?"

"Yes."

"Your luggage will be collected from the carriage straightaway," he went on, glancing at the vehicle on the street, "and your maid and whoever else came with you will be settled in."

Despite this warm greeting, Priscilla was still nervous as she stepped into the foyer of the dowager house and discovered that it was paneled in pleasant golden oak. Above the panels, the walls were papered in a subtle green and gray stripe. A vase of pink roses sat on a table next to the tray where visitors would place their calling cards.

The tray was currently empty and she wasn't certain what that suggested: A lack of invitations or callers, or ones that had already been perused and responded to?

The foyer had six sides, with two of them leading to hallways and a third being the front door. The others had sconces of cut crystal with gaslights fluttering behind them.

Everything *seemed* comfortable and normal, even pleasant and welcoming...so far.

"This way, miss. May I take your cloak? I'm Josephs, by the by, and m'wife, Mrs. Josephs, is the housekeeper. I don't mind telling you, the woman's delighted at the thought of having a young woman back in the household again and has made certain your room is nice and comfortable. I hope you'll find it quite pleasant."

"Thank you," Priscilla said, taken aback by this effusive explanation. He seemed awfully chatty, and even friendly.

Josephs paused at a set of double doors halfway down the left corridor. He opened the doors with a flourish, speaking into the chamber. "My lady, Miss Bedwith has arrived."

Priscilla's corset felt entirely too tight all at once. She stepped into the room with shaky knees and palms that were clammy beneath her gloves.

The first thing she saw was a big, black shaggy thing. *A bear.*

She gasped and stepped back over the threshold without thinking, for the creature had risen to its feet and was eyeing her hungrily. Her heart shot into her throat and she choked as she tried to swallow, unable to catch her breath due to the corset.

The bear was coming toward her!

"That's only Watson," Josephs said near her ear. "He won't hurt you. He's quite friendly, in fact."

She didn't believe that for one moment. Especially since the beast seemed to be *salivating* over the thought of her, with the drool dripping from his huge mouth.

But before she could take another step either in or out of the room, a loud squawking noise drew her attention. Something gray catapulted across the room, fluttering on *wings*...then came to rest on the top of a tall porcelain vase next to her.

Priscilla reared back again, her heart still wedged in her throat, as she beheld a large gray bird with a nasty looking yellow beak and sly, beady eyes. Its tail was red as blood.

"Bloody hell! Who are you?" demanded the bird. "Bloody hell! Intruder!" He squawked loudly.

"Mr. Timms, *language!* Watson, take your place if you

please. Well, come in then, Priscilla. I promise you, neither of them will bite. It's only Beatrice you'd have to worry about in that regard, and she's in the kitchen hoping for a crust of bread to fall her way."

The voice, a strong, rapid one that gave no suggestion of the quavering or confusion of advanced age, came from a high-backed chair upholstered in sapphire brocade. The woman sitting in the chair was not at all, not the *least* bit, what Priscilla had expected.

First of all, the woman was not *ancient*. She didn't even look *old*.

Mother had given off the impression that Lady Darling was a rickety old thing, and of the same fragility and advanced age as herself. The dowager marchioness might not even *be* fifty—which was still very old and one should rather be finished with Society at that age, if you asked Priscilla—but she certainly didn't appear to be hampered by the weight of those many decades.

Secondly, Lady Darling was a surprisingly pleasant, even attractive, looking person. From her position in the chair, she didn't seem to be terribly tall, and unlike most aged women, she was neither very round nor very thin and brittle. Her hair was still black—a true, ink color—but it was colored with a generous amount of white that mingled with the dark like silvery threads. Her face—which was more of a rich golden hue than peaches and cream or dull gray—was still rather pretty for her age, though her chin and jaw sagged a little, and she did have a few lines at the corners of her eyes and mouth. Her eyebrows were thick and dark, matching her hair, and her lips had not thinned, as often happened with age. But it was her eyes that told the story: they were dark and intelligent and very, very penetrating.

She was studying Priscilla with those almond-shaped walnut brown eyes. "Well, come closer, pet, I'm not going to

11

bite. I need to see what we have to work with—sadly, it's a factor in the marriage mart, looks and presentation, so we must be practical in our plan of attack and make the most of any advantages. Sit there, on the divan."

Priscilla glanced nervously at the large black beast, who had settled on a roomy cushion in front of the fireplace, but did as she was bid, lowering herself slowly onto the edge of the sofa's pale pink cushion. Still, she kept an eye on the bear-like creature in case he bolted to his feet and lunged at her. His dark eyes gleamed hungrily in her direction and he was still drooling.

The gray bird—Mr. Timms?—had fluttered over and was now perched on a sort of hat rack. He tilted his head one way and then another as he looked at her. "Intruder!" he screamed.

"That's Priscilla, Mr. Timms. Now behave yourself. You take after your mother, I see, and that is fortunate," Lady Darling said, and it took Priscilla an instant to realize she'd said this last bit to her and not the bird. "She was quite comely in her day. It's a shame that the look of a person's face can make or break their marriage prospects, but *I* am not responsible for making the rules. I *assure* you, if I *was*, I—ah, thank you, Mrs. Josephs," she said, looking toward the door. "Yes, I'm certain Miss Bedwith would appreciate a cup of tea and perhaps a bite to eat.

"Really, it's rather tiresome to see how a smart and kind or a civil and interesting young woman can be overlooked because she has an overbite or spots on her face or an unfortunate nose. Don't you agree? It's not as if all the men looking for wives are any physical prizes themselves. Not mentioning any names in particular, but there is a certain son of an earl who could learn to clean his teeth better."

Priscilla's head was spinning with all of the information, opinions, and directions that had been pouring out of Lady Darling's mouth.

Mrs. Josephs, who seemed very pleasant and not at all crisp and formal like the housekeeper back home, had the light brown skin of a person from India or somewhere in that direction. She had brought a tray to the low table between the divan and the sapphire blue chair, and now she was preparing to pour the tea.

Priscilla looked back up at Lady Darling and realized the woman was watching her expectantly. As if waiting for her to speak? To respond? Had she asked a question somewhere in that long barrage of words?

"Um," Priscilla said, suddenly understanding why people thought of Lady Darling as scary. It was her manner of speaking, rapid-fire and assured, and those eyes—so steady, so calm, so expectant, almost encouraging...and yet, they delved into you, pinning you like the mounted butterflies she'd seen at the British Museum. "Yes, yes, of course, my lady," she stammered, not at all certain what she was agreeing to, but she'd decided it was always best to agree with a marchioness.

"Very well. Now, I have already made appointments with us at Monsieur Claude's, and then we will also see the milliner and visit Miss Mathilda's for gloves and lace and the like. The Enfield ball is next week, and you shall make your first big public appearance there. You have already been introduced at court, I understand, so at least we needn't worry about that. I do loathe all that pomp and circumstance."

"Enfield? Why, isn't that—I mean to say, weren't you...er, wasn't that..." *Oh dear*, Priscilla thought, and lifted her tea cup to drink swiftly in an effort to stem her thoughtless babbling. Unfortunately, the tea was hot and strong and she hadn't added sugar to it yet, so it scalded her mouth and was bitter to boot. *Good Heavens, what a ninny I am!*

Lady Darling lifted her chin and smiled, her eyes still settled on Priscilla. It was a cool, calm, confident expression that came over her face. "What I believe you are attempting to

13

communicate is that Lady Enfield and I are well-known former friends. Rather steadfast on the former part, I must say, and quite public about it, I admit—particularly considering what happened the last time I was present for her ball.

"But, be advised, you and I *will* be attending Lady Enfield's ball. I expect it shall be quite interesting for me to be stepping over that threshold for the first time in four years. One certainly hopes no one will *die* this time."

Chapter Two

"Despite the plethora of English dukes that might appear in romantic novels, there are fewer of them than the fingers on my hands," Irene said.

She and Priscilla were riding in one of the Darlings' equipages—this one a well-sprung, red-velvet upholstered carriage with the Darling seal on the exterior.

They had an appointment with Monsieur Claude at half three and, unless something unexpected happened, they would arrive precisely on time. Neither Irene nor Monsieur Claude were the sort who believed in being fashionably late.

"And of those, only four are unwed," she went on. "Two of *those* have half a foot in the grave and are not suitable husbands for a girl of nineteen, and another has been in mourning for his wife for three years. There seems to be no suggestion that the Duke of Delfting will return to Society, and certainly not to seek a bride."

At that moment, the carriage turned onto Bond Street with far more verve than it should have done, jolting Irene sharply to the side. She'd forgotten how trying it was to manage a young woman's search for a spouse, and now she had to contend with a new, young man for a driver. Barth, who'd replaced Irene's previous driver when he'd retired to the country, seemed to think the streets of London were a training ground for the Epsom race track.

"And the fourth unwed duke?" Priscilla asked, a gleam of determination and stubbornness in her eyes and blazing across her countenance.

Irene suppressed sigh. She certainly understood determination and stubbornness—she herself possessed those traits in spades—but in this case, she feared the girl's bravado was in vain. Priscilla Bedwith was a pretty girl, but she was no great beauty. She had money, but not *that* much money. She had no title, although her family was of the peerage.

And the Duke of Wessley was the type of man who expected his bride to possess *all* of those traits, and in excess.

Or, more accurately, his *mother* expected the duke's bride to be extremely beautiful, exceedingly wealthy, and to come from a family with a proper title.

It was all good and well to be stubborn and determined, but only if one had good reason to be. She thought fondly of her dear, departed Edward and how stubborn *they'd* had to be in the face of Society looking on their union askance. Of course, that hadn't lasted long, for one couldn't continue to ignore a marquess and his wife.

"The Duke of Wessley is the only eligible bachelor with that title," Irene replied as the carriage swayed and swung on its springs, trundling too quickly over a rough patch of cobblestones.

"Then he is the man I shall marry," said Priscilla.

Irene didn't visibly react to this pronouncement. She had, after all, raised three daughters and fully understood how unreasonable and fantastical a young woman could be.

Nor was it lost on her that Priscilla had declared her intention of marrying the duke—which, of course, must be the hope of every young debutante in the *haute ton* this Season—without ever having laid eyes on Wessley and his weak chin.

"It is admirable to have a specific goal," was all she said.

Priscilla smiled complacently, as if everything was settled and she'd won the duke's hand already.

Fortunately, the carriage jolted to a halt at that moment. Irene's head bumped rather hard against the wall, and she grimaced as she felt her hat shift and her hairpins jam deeper into her scalp. Beatrice, who had been tucked inside her reticule, gave an annoyed little yip and poked her head out from the bag.

"Why—Lady Darling, you brought the *dog*?" Priscilla exclaimed, horrified. "To an appointment with a modiste?"

"Of course. Why not?" Irene replied, reaching over to pat the little beast on her springy head. "She loves Monsieur Claude, and the feeling is quite mutual."

Beatrice was a champagne-colored poodle who was so small she could curl up in a soup plate—which she had once done after licking it clean of beef stew, falling asleep with a full, bulging belly. Her snores had been something to behold.

Prior to meeting a nine-week-old Beatrice, Irene had never seen a dog so tiny and with so much soft, silky, poofy hair, and she'd fallen madly in love with the creature the moment she laid eyes on her.

But now, Beatrice's beady dark eyes glared accusingly at Irene. She did not like to have her naps disrupted...unless it was because there was food involved. And the exaggerated jolting and swaying of the carriage had disturbed her snooze.

There was no choice. Irene was simply going to have to speak with Barth about his driving habits, or Beatrice would decline to go in the carriage with her in the future—and Irene herself would continue to be hitting her head against the wall, knocking her hat and hair askew every time she went out. It was particularly annoying because she had to sit *forever* while her dear and extremely patient Vella fussed about her coiffure and settled the hat just-so atop it.

Irene stifled another sigh, then told herself to buck up. London was not the country. London required complicated coiffures and tight corsets (which exacerbated her aching left hip, for one of the boning slats always pressed right into it), updated fashion and numerous social engagements, stacks of calling cards and invitations, and allowed very little time to muck about in one's garden or play tug-the-stocking with one's pets.

She was here to help a friend—and, true, there was the added benefit that she would be able to see her own children as well. Although Rose and Violet were particularly good about writing to her (Jane was not, and of course Edward would never set himself to writing a newsy letter to his mother—or anyone; she'd be lucky to hear that the new marchioness was with child before the woman was delivered of it), it was not the same as seeing them.

The footman, George, helped Irene—along with her Beatrice-stuffed reticule—and Priscilla down from the carriage.

As she'd feared, they'd stopped nearly a block past the entrance to Monsieur Claude's instead of in front of it. Irene didn't really mind the walk, even though the air was smoggy and flakes of soot filtered about over one's hat and cape, but a driver should be more conscientious about the location of his stops.

Beatrice, for her part, enjoyed being conducted along where she could look out from the top of the reticule and observe without having to exert the energy of perambulating on her own delicate legs.

She was also quite vocal in her criticisms of anyone who might walk past them, across from them, near them, or even who might be simply standing upon a street corner perusing a news-paper. Beatrice took particularly loud exception to anyone wearing a hat with fluttering feathers.

Irene gave instructions to Barth to return for them in an hour. She also kindly suggested he might want to stop in *front* of the shop instead of beyond it.

Bond Street, located conveniently near the posh neighbor-hood of Mayfair, where much of the gentry lived, was crowded by establishments filled with all sorts of luxurious items.

There were modistes and tailors, lace shops filled with silk flowers, feathers, and other trimmings, millineries, jewelry stores, and even an enterprise that sold only gloves made of the finest kid—for both men and women. Small tea shops and bakeries offered the opportunity for repast and relief to those who'd expended much of their energy perusing the dry goods offered for sale.

The sidewalk was filled with pedestrians: other women of the *ton*, a few dandies, and some older gents heading to their respective clubs, newspaper and errand boys darting among and between the others, calling out for work or to sell their wares.

There were carriages, omnibuses, and lorries trundling down the street, each conveyed by a number of hitched-up horses, and Irene fancied she felt the ground shiver beneath her feet and thought it might be the underground train going along...well, under. The world was filled with noise: rattling wagons, clomping hooves, jingling bicycles, people talking, call-ing, laughing—and Beatrice, yapping at anything that seemed a threat. The air was filled with the smells of all sorts of smoke: coal, wood, pipe, cigar, along with the scents of refuse and waste that, even in Mayfair, hung in the air.

"Why, Lady Darling! What a pleasure to see you back here in London! Why, I thought you'd stay in the country *forever!*"

Irene smiled at Lady Pelicourt and even offered her cheek

for a kiss that wouldn't come anywhere near touching her skin. Both she and Lady Pelicourt—a slender, brittle, screamingly unnatural redhead with a nose as pointed as her remarks—were fully aware that the latter didn't find it any sort of pleasure to encounter Irene, and that, ironically, they both wished with equal fervor that Irene had remained in the country.

Still, one must keep up appearances in such public places as Bond Street—especially since Irene had a task ahead of her. After all, she and Lady Pelicourt had known each other for over thirty years. They had ceased *liking* each other approximately twenty years earlier.

"I simply couldn't stay away from the City," Irene lied blithely, patting Beatrice on the head in an effort to quiet her. The small canine shared her opinion of Lady Pelicourt, but she was far less circumspect in expressing it than her mistress. "The dowager house needs updating terribly, and it's no good if I'm not there to oversee it."

"Of course," replied Lady Pelicourt. "But you've missed all of the excitement over the ruination of Miss Ferndale's nuptials! It was ghastly the way it all fell apart, the poor girl, and so suddenly. Everyone thought it was a perfect match, her and Lord Leavington. Oh, dear...I suppose you didn't hear a *thing* about it, being in the country."

"I was in the Lake District, not the Shetland Islands," Irene said with a laugh. "We do get news up there. She cried off—only the day before, was it? Tragic and terrible, I'm sure, the poor girl. I feel terribly sorry for her parents too. But, my dear Lady Pelicourt, more importantly, I must congratulate you on your own daughter's nuptials. What a happy event that must have been."

There was no need to mention that Lady Pelicourt's eldest daughter had been in her seventh Season before landing a husband, for both of them were quite well aware of it.

And, as the daughter had as much of a sour personality and cutting tongue as her mother did, it was no surprise that the man she'd finally married had been up to his muttonchops in debt and was desperate for a means to pay it off. Christiana Pelicourt had had a very large dowry.

"I'm *so* sorry you couldn't attend," replied Lady Pelicourt, lying just as baldly as Irene had done as she arranged her features in an expression of dismay. Her attention slid to the little dog, who continued to express her displeasure with a quiet growl, and she grimaced, then lifted her gaze back up.

Irene smiled at her and nodded, acknowledging what they both knew: that Irene had not even been invited. "I'm certain it was lovely, and that your Christiana was a beautiful bride. Lady Pelicourt, may I present to you the daughter of my dear friend Mrs. Bedwith. This is Miss Priscilla Bedwith, and she is staying with me at the dowager house. I shall be sponsoring her for the Season."

"How lovely," replied Lady Pelicourt, this time arranging her features into a look that was presumably meant to seem welcoming. "I suppose you're looking for a husband, then, Miss Bedwith?"

"Yes, my lady," replied Priscilla pleasantly, giving a brief and appropriate curtsy. "I am very grateful Lady Darling has so very graciously agreed to chaperone me this season."

Irene was relieved the young woman hadn't gone on to announce her intention of wedding the Duke of Wessley. She had half expected the girl to do so, as a way of staking her claim. Perhaps Priscilla wasn't as much of a lost cause as she'd feared.

"Yes, I suppose you are," Lady Pelicourt said, looking down her sharp nose at the girl. Somehow she managed to give off the impression that the task of wedding her off would be challenging at best. "Well, then. I wish you all the best, Miss

Bedwith. I look forward to seeing you next Friday. It's long past time for Lady Enfield to host her ball again—as ghastly as the last one turned out, *I* didn't think she needed to cancel it for *four* years. But, oh dear...I don't suppose you *will* be at the Enfields' for the ball after all," she added with a superior smile. "Of course I'll be there with Christiana—she is now Mrs. Radkey, you know—but what a shame for you to miss it. It's the first big ball of the Season. Simply *everyone*...or everyone who matters...will be there."

Irene felt Priscilla gear up to respond and correct Lady Pelicourt's assumption, but she spoke before the young woman could. "Indeed, it would be a shame," she said with a bland smile. "Now, my dear Lady Pelicourt, we mustn't keep you any longer, and we have an appointment with Monsieur Claude. One does not like to keep him waiting."

"Monsieur Claude?" Lady Pelicourt snickered, pretending to hide it behind her glove. "I see. Well, one can only do what one can do."

Irene gave her a benign smile. "I look forward to seeing you and the new Mrs. Radkey in the near future." She clamped a hand firmly on top of Beatrice's head to keep the little minx from lunging at the unpleasant woman, whose tone was so provoking that the poodle couldn't help but respond. Irene closed the reticule over the dog's fluffy head.

"What's wrong with Monsieur Claude?" Priscilla asked in a hushed, worried voice. At least she'd had the presence of mind to wait until they were out of earshot of Lady Pelicourt. "And why didn't you tell her we would be at Lady Enfield's? Are we truly going, even after—after what happened?"

"There isn't one thing wrong with Monsieur Claude," Irene told her, and decided to leave the topic of what happened at the Enfields' four years ago for another time. "Monsieur is brilliant and there is no one else I trust with my wardrobe. It's only that Lady Pelicourt can no longer obtain an appointment with him. You see, she was once fifteen minutes late." She lifted her brows and smiled as she opened the door to monsieur's shop and sailed inside—exactly on time.

There was a little shriek, followed by what appeared to be a bundle of fabric exploding and cascading onto a table.

"But my magnificent Lady Darling! You have finally returned from the wilds of the Lake District!" cried a tall, spindly man as he rushed toward her, leaving the fabric behind.

His incredible dark brown mustache led the way, wider than his narrow cheeks and full and shiny with wax. Monsieur Claude had light olive skin and a nose as long and spindly as his torso, legs, arms, and fingers. What little hair remained on his head was combed back from his face and over his scalp and fluffed like duck down. Several tape measures, which were slung over his shoulders like untied neckcloths, fluttered as he embraced her. His kisses—one on each cheek—landed there with loud smacks, his wax-stiff mustache brushing her skin.

"Ah! And you've brought the little mademoiselle!" he cried, catching sight of Beatrice, who'd popped back out from where Irene had stuffed her to keep her away from Lady Pelicourt.

Beatrice began barking enthusiastic greetings, and Monsieur Claude offered her a tiny piece of the light, sandwich-like biscuits called *macaron* that were usually reserved for his human clients. Once that was accomplished and the front door was firmly latched, Beatrice was allowed to alight from the reticule so she could explore the shop.

She took off into the depths of the place, sniffing around for any bit of food—crumbs of said client biscuits—that might have been dropped and forgotten.

Beaming, Monsieur Claude took Irene's gloved hands in his

and looked down at her. "I have missed you so, my dear madame! Welcome back, and let me see what it is you are *wearing* beneath that cloak."

As Irene allowed him to remove her outerwear, she caught a glimpse of Priscilla's expression. It was one of shock that quickly turned to horror and affront. Apparently, monsieur's familiarity and informality with a marchioness did not sit well with her. Irene swallowed a smile and gave an internal shrug. Miss Priscilla Bedwith had much to learn.

"But what is this? What is *this*? I cannot—but this—this is a *horror*! Ah, Lady Darling, it is *right* that you have come to me. But, you cannot be *seen* in such a disaster! I cannot know what you have been thinking!" Monsieur was gaping at her simple frock that was several years out of style. It had been comfortable and, due to the cloak, well-hidden to anyone on the street. Irene had specifically chosen to wear it for comfort—and the certainty that he would react just as he was doing. Even a man as confident and boastful as Monsieur Claude needed to feel needed.

"That is why I'm here, of course, monsieur," she told him. "I am dreadfully hopeless without your guidance and talent. And, I have brought someone new to you. May I present Miss Priscilla Bedwith."

Priscilla shot her another gaping look (likely because Irene had presented her *to* Monsieur Claude, a mere tradesman, instead of the other way round), but inclined her head in greeting. "It's a pleasure to meet you, monsieur," she said—and managed to sound sincere.

Irene gave her credit for that, at least.

"Miss Bedwith is going to be my chaperone this season," Irene told him, causing Monsieur to roar with laughter.

"Ah, yes, that is so. That is quite so, and you, mademoiselle, you will have your task—what is it they say? Cut it out for you?" He was still chuckling, his mustache fluttering like a window shade over his upper lip. "If there is anyone who is in need of a chaperone, it is the Lady Darling.

"Now, come, come, let me see what it is I have to work with, mademoiselle. You," he said, giving Irene a pointed look, "I shall have Monique and Tatiana update your measurements, although they do not look as if they've changed much since the young marquess's wedding, and you shall leave *everything* to me. But you..."

His practiced and objective gaze swept over Priscilla. "*Bien*, you have a more than adequate figure, Miss Bedwith. And the shade of your hair—why it is so very lovely, and it is smooth. It will be quite versatile with many of the colors that are showing this season. The new buttercup yellow is quite stunning—not for you, madame," he said, spinning sharply when Irene's eyes lit up.

"But I do love a good buttercup!" Irene protested.

"In your garden, madame, but not on your person. You are one who must wear the dark, the rich colors, the ones that are—"

"Loud?" Irene chuckled.

"No, no, *no!* The colors that, what is it...that *speak*. That make an attestation, a—a notice, you see? You are bold and beautiful and you must dress that way. You may wear the rich gold or the ochre, but not—*never!*—the weak and simple buttercup."

Irene was laughing by now. By Providence, it was *good* to see Monsieur Claude. He was one of the few things she loved about being in London. "Bold, perhaps. But beautiful? Ah, those days are long over. And between my aching hip and crackling knees...I don't even feel all that bold any longer."

Monsieur Claude began to protest, but she waved him off. "Very well, monsieur. I shall leave my entire wardrobe in your hands—for you can see how I fare when I do not." She gestured to her frock.

He gave her a skeptical look, knowing she was teasing him. "Off with you, then, my lady. Monique! Tati!"

A curtain that hung in a doorway fluttered and a tiny, round woman with brown skin appeared. She wore a padded band on one pudgy arm with the heads of numerous straight pins projecting from it, as well as her own collection of measuring tapes.

"Madame Darling! *Bonjour!*" Monique's face lit up with a smile, and she gestured for Irene to follow her back behind the curtain. Beatrice, who'd quickly determined the shop was sadly lacking in crumbs, bounded out from beneath a fabric-swathed table and trotted after her mistress.

Tatiana was behind the curtain there as well, wearing an apron with a number of appliances slipped into specific pockets: gleaming fabric scissors, a packet of needles, marking chalk, pencil, tweezers, and tiny embroidery scissors. As soon as Tatiana saw her, she fell upon Beatrice and scooped up the little dog, making cooing and crooning noises.

The three chattered in French—gossiping about all sorts of happenings in town—as the two seamstresses helped Irene out of her clothing, stripping her down to pantaloons, corset, and chemise. Monique took Irene's measurements as Tatiana made the notes. Beatrice decided to settle in for a rest on a little cushion while she supervised their activity.

They caught up on each of their children—Monique had three of her own, all recently married as well, and Tatiana had a litter of kittens that were as close to being offspring as she would ever have—and discussed whether Irene should blacken her eyebrows since the silvery-gray was popping up there and causing these lighter hairs to disappear from sight, especially on the outside edges.

"And then there is *this*," Irene cried, and thrust her chin toward Tatiana. "It was not there when I looked in the mirror before I left the house, but here it is now, suddenly! A sharp, dark hair, coming out from nowhere—like that of a crone!"

"*Tch, tch, tch,*" Tatiana said, and with a quick, sharp movement, used her handy tweezers to yank the offending hair from the side of Irene's chin.

"Thank you," Irene said gratefully, rubbing her chin. "I simply don't understand how those things just *pop* out like that."

"Ah, well, when one becomes older and wiser, it becomes far more difficult to contain one's wisdom and experience, and it must pop out somewhere, *non*?"

"Yes, but what explains the pain in my hip and the fact that my knees creak every time I stand up?"

The three of them laughed over this as Irene was redressed. Then it was Priscilla's turn to be measured, and that left Irene and Beatrice with Monsieur Claude in the front room.

"And how are you, truly, my lady?" he asked, taking her hands in his slender, cool ones.

"I am quite well, despite being dragged back to this fogged-up, loud, crowded, smelly city you love so much," she responded, squeezing his hands with hers. "And you?"

"I am well, of course." He thrust out his chest and grinned behind his broad mustache. "I am too busy to even spend the time gossiping, eh? But I will do all of it for you, of course."

"Ah, of course, and I thank you so very much for making time for me."

"Any time, my dear marchioness." He patted her hand.

"Now, Claude, I shall need something magnificent and stunning for the Enfield ball next Friday," Irene told him with a little smile and a tilt of her head.

His eyes met hers and his brows shot up, but there wasn't a hint of judgment or skepticism in his face. Instead, there was interest and curiosity. "It will be the first time the ball will be held since that terrible night. It was how long...three years ago?"

"Four. It was the year before Violet and Rose came out."

"And you plan to attend?" He was still looking at her closely.

"Yes, and so of course you understand why I must have something brilliant."

"Of course you shall, *ma chére*," he said, patting her hand and resorting to a less formal address as they often did in private —something that would horrify Priscilla Bedwith but that Irene was quite content with. After all, until she'd married Edward, she'd been just plain old Miss Whitney.

"I heard about poor Miss Ferndale," said Irene. "Is there anything else scandalous I should know about so that I don't put my foot into anything untoward?"

Monsieur Claude gave a little shrug of insouciance. "Eh, you know, there is always the scandals, the gossip, twittering. That's one thing I do like about you, my dear madame—you have little time for it. No, there is nothing important."

At that moment, Miss Bedwith flowed through the curtains in the doorway and put to an end the more intimate and informal portion of Irene's conversation with monsieur.

They finalized a number of frocks and gowns, leaving much of the fabric and trim choices to the modiste, then bid Monsieur Claude farewell. Beatrice was tucked back into the reticule where she promptly fell asleep. Snuffling out crumbs in an entire shop and supervising the work therein was an exhausting business.

"That was rather interesting," Priscilla commented, once they were on the street. "If nothing else, the man certainly has a beautiful array of fabric choices."

"Monsieur Claude is a genius," Irene assured her as she looked up the street for the carriage—which was not in sight. Frowning, she checked the small timepiece she had pinned to her bodice. They had been only slightly more than the prescribed hour in monsieur's establishment. Barth should have been here by now.

At that moment, the carriage came jouncing wildly around the corner a block away. Irene was watching the road, waiting for her ride to come screeching to a halt when Priscilla gasped and bumped into her as she took a step back.

"Mr. Bafferty! What—what are you doing here?" Priscilla said in a squeaky voice. She was apparently so overset that she didn't remember to apologize for bumping into Irene.

Irene turned to see a man standing on the sidewalk, facing the young woman. Her attention went from him—a young man dressed as a gentleman in a fine hat and frock coat—to Priscilla —who was clearly shocked and...

Hmm.

Irene couldn't tell whether Priscilla was delighted or dismayed by this encounter. Her ward had a hand clapped to her chest and her cheeks were flushed a pretty pink. Irene was leaning toward her charge being delighted—based on the pretty pink flush rather than a dark red one—but not wanting to show it.

"Miss Bedwith." The man, presumably Mr. Bafferty, removed his hat and gave a flourishing bow. "What a lovely and welcome surprise to encounter you. I've only just returned from the Continent—a bit earlier than planned." He turned to Irene and bowed again. "Forgive me, my lady, for any impertinence, but may I presume you are Lady Darling?"

Irene felt rather than heard Priscilla's sharp intake of breath as she stood next to her. "You presume correctly, sir. I'm afraid you have the advantage of me."

"Oh, goodness, forgive me, my lady," said Priscilla, shocked into action. "Lady Darling, may I present Mr. Hugh Bafferty. He...his estate is near ours. I've known him since we were children." There was an odd note in her voice.

"It's a pleasure to meet you, Mr. Bafferty," Irene said smoothly. She was aware that her carriage had rocked to a halt in front of them, but she was more interested in the little by-play happening between Mr. Bafferty and her charge.

Her developing impression was that Priscilla was surprised to see the man, and that he elicited neither fear nor anger from her but quite possibly reluctant pleasure. It seemed also that Priscilla was a bit nervous, which was quite interesting, and her expression had turned to one of uncharacteristic aloofness.

For his part, Mr. Bafferty—once having properly greeted Irene—seemed unable to take his eyes from the young woman. "I hope you will allow me to call on you while you are in London, Miss Bedwith. I learned from your kind and lovely mother that you were here."

"Oh, but...well, Lady Darling has kindly agreed to sponsor me into Society," Priscilla replied, lifting her nose a trifle. "I am staying with her, and I am certain we shall be very busy."

Exceedingly curious and certainly not one to remain uninvolved in such an interesting situation, Irene stepped in. "You are quite welcome to call at the dowager house, Mr. Bafferty. It is in St. James."

His eyes shot to her, gratitude and hope shining in them, confirming what Irene had suspected. This young man had learned that Priscilla Bedwith had come to London to find a husband, and he was determined to present himself as a candidate, or to interfere for some other reason.

"Lady Darling, I would never impose upon your hospitality to Miss Bedwith, but I should very much like to call at the dowager house. I am most grateful for the invitation, and for your permission."

"Indeed. Now, Priscilla, you see that our carriage has arrived. Mr. Bafferty, I do hope you have a fine day, and perhaps we shall cross paths again soon."

Irene turned and swept toward the carriage. George stood at its open door, waiting to help her climb inside.

"Miss Bedwith, I...mean to say, you are looking very well," said Mr. Bafferty quickly. "I will call soonest."

No sooner was the door to the carriage closed than Priscilla exploded.

"Why, that *man!* The incivility of him is—is—is simply unforgivable! To approach a young woman on the *street*, without a by-your-leave! I'm so very sorry, Lady Darling, for that rude encounter. Of course you were kind enough to invite him to call, but surely you can inform Hugh—Mr. Bafferty, I mean to say—that we are simply too busy to entertain callers." She threw herself back into the corner of her seat and folded her arms over her middle. Her cheeks were flushed dark pink and her eyes glittered, quite possibly with tears.

"I haven't any idea where to send such direction, Priscilla, even if I was of the mind to do so. Which I am not. What on earth has that man done to you to cause such a stir?" Irene asked.

"Why—why—why he is simply... He was in France! And Germany! He wasn't expected back for months," she went on. "And now he is returned, and he has badgered Mother into telling him where I am. And then he hunted me down and *accosted* me on the street!"

"It seems to me that if a person has known someone since they were children, it would be quite forgivable—even acceptable—for one to greet them should they encounter each other on the street. In fact, it would be rather impolite not to do so."

The fact that Priscilla had referred to Mr. Bafferty by his familiar name, then quickly corrected it, told Irene quite a bit about the situation. "If Mr. Bafferty should call, rest assured I will be present, and I will ensure that no harm will come to you, Priscilla."

"Oh, yes, of course, Lady Darling. I don't mean to suggest that Mr. Bafferty would be inappropriate or would actually *harm* me in any way," Priscilla said quickly. "It's only...well...he is...well, he's no duke, you see."

"I see."

Yes, indeed: Irene most definitely saw.

Chapter Three

"I'm not certain why I—we—should take the time to attend a small dinner party where the highest rank is a viscount," Priscilla commented, rather sullenly for Irene's taste, as they settled into their seats in the carriage. "The Duke of Wessley won't be there, so it seems a waste of my time."

Irene held back a sharp comment about the girl's low prospect of actually capturing the hand of Wessley, and replied in an extremely mild, even voice that, had any of her children been present would have caused the hair on their arms to lift, and fearful glances be exchanged.

"Mrs. Tripley is a longtime friend of mine, and this is an important occasion for her. She and her husband are unveiling the portrait Mr. Dicksee has done of her, and they have taken the excuse to have a dinner party as part of the event."

"A portrait?" Priscilla sounded unimpressed.

Irene stifled a flicker of impatience. "Frank Dicksee is a very accomplished painter, and he has become known for doing portraits of fashionable ladies. For Mrs. Tripley to have been chosen as one of his subjects is quite a compliment to her. She and her husband are very proud of this honor.

"Priscilla, dear...you ought to think of the dinner tonight as an opportunity. You will make the acquaintance of several other interesting people of the *ton* before the ball. Imagine how, thanks to having already been introduced to a select group, word about the pretty, eligible Bedwith girl might precede your entrance at Enfield House." Irene gave her a meaningful look.

"Oh." Priscilla's expression rearranged into a thoughtful, pleased one. She settled back into her seat again, likely in order to fantasize about the ripples of conversation—all glowing and envious, all about her—rushing through the ballroom as she appeared on the threshold the night of the ball.

Irene tucked a smile away. There certainly would be ripples of conversation at the ball—whispers behind fluttering fans, gossip, side-eyes—but they wouldn't be about Priscilla Bedwith. It would be Lady Darling's appearance at Enfield House that would capture the interest of the gossips of the *ton*.

The carriage ride to the Tripley residence didn't take long, and it seemed that Irene's gentle remonstrances to Barth had taken hold, for after the carriage trundled up the drive, it stopped with only the slightest of jolts.

Once the butler ushered Irene and Priscilla into the parlor, Harold and Trudy Tripley greeted Irene with pleasure. Mrs. Tripley gave her a kiss on each cheek, and Mr. Tripley pressed one to the back of her gloved hand.

"Why, you oughtn't have a challenge at all with her," Trudy said to Irene in a low voice. She had greeted and cooed over Priscilla so much the young girl had begun to preen. "She's pleasant enough in looks, and she's a reasonable dowry, yes?"

Irene nodded, keeping her reservations about Priscilla's chances—and determination—to herself. Instead, she said, "I am so *thrilled* to be here for the unveiling. Are you terribly pleased with the way the portrait turned out?"

"Indeed!" Trudy's cheeks flushed pink with delight. She

was a beautiful woman of forty with soft, round features that made her appear delicate and lush at the same time. Her blond hair, set off by glittering sapphires and dancing ostrich feathers that would have sent Beatrice into hysterics, shined in the gaslight. "Harold was not at all pleased when I first proposed the idea—and he was horrified at the cost—but now that it's done, he's about to burst, he's so proud. He insisted we hang it in his study so he can look at it whenever he likes."

"That's wonderfully romantic," Irene replied, feeling a little pang of loss. Edward hadn't been the most romantic of men, but he had had his moments that turned her heart to pudding.

"We shall unveil it once everyone has had their sherry and whisky after dinner. Mr. Dicksee is truly a genius!" She turned to Priscilla. "Now, Miss Bedwith, let me take you round to meet everyone. Lady Darling, I trust you'll find a comfortable seat whilst we do."

There were twelve people at the dinner party; six men and six women, of course. Of the six men, all five of them were eligible bachelors and therefore, husband material. Despite what Irene had told Priscilla in the carriage, the biggest reason she'd insisted on bringing the girl tonight was because she had in mind that Mr. Matthew Feverley would be an excellent candidate for the chit's husband. His sister was a particular confidante of her daughter Rose, and Irene had met the young man several times over the years.

He was kind and seemed intelligent, and, although a little reserved and awkward in social situations—not unlike Miss Austen's delicious Mr. Darcy—he had a comfortable income from the small estate entailed by his father's line. He would be an excellent match with Priscilla, and Irene had prevailed upon Trudy Tripley to make certain the two were seated next to each other.

This was, of course, before Irene had met Mr. Bafferty and

realized there was some sort of past between him and Priscilla. She would reserve judgment on that young man and his appropriateness for Priscilla's hand after she spent some time in his presence. And if the girl had more than one potential husband from which to choose, all the better.

But for tonight, Irene's main purpose was to observe how Priscilla conducted herself in a social situation, and to throw her and Mr. Feverley together as much as possible.

Dinner was a pleasant affair. Irene was an expert conversationalist—meaning she allowed her dining partners (a man on either side, as was proper) to do all of the talking, with an occasional question or compliment designed to keep him verbalizing. It was never a trial to get a man to talk about himself, his horses, his dogs, his wine or spirits collection, or anything else— including his opinions— important to him.

This tactic enabled Irene to listen with half an ear whilst observing Priscilla in a social environment. She did not see anything that concerned her. The girl was pleasant and demure, and even caused Mr. Feverley to laugh at one point. She balanced her conversation between her two dining partners, switching halfway through the meal, as custom dictated.

Perhaps Irene's task would be accomplished sooner than she'd hoped and she'd be able to escape to her own devices before the end of the Season.

"I understand you're planning to attend the Enfield ball," Trudy murmured to Irene as dinner broke up and the men went off to the billiard room for their cigars and whisky.

Irene watched them file out of the dining room, wishing desperately that she could follow. Whisky and soda was far more her preference than the watered down, sweet sherry that was in her near future with the other women in the sitting room.

"That is my intention," Irene replied with a little smile.

Apparently, Mrs. Pelicourt had been busy spreading the word. Although Irene and Trudy Tripley were friends, they'd never really spoken about what had happened four years ago.

"That will be quite...interesting," Trudy replied, looking concerned. "Are you quite certain it's a good idea?"

"Lord Milbright is gone"—she couldn't bring herself to add the expected "God rest his soul"—"and Lady Milbright seems to have quite recovered from the...tragedy. She's been living abroad, as you know." *Thank Heaven.*

"But, you and Lady Enfield—"

"We are both mature, and dare I say, *wise* women, and at our age, I am of the mind that bygones, at some point, must become bygones," Irene replied firmly, but with a smile. "It was a terrible thing that happened that night, but of course it was an accident. Ah, Priscilla, how was your dinner?" She took her ward's arm and joined the other ladies as they paraded out of the dining room to the sitting room, where they would be served sherry and tea.

Irene suffered through thirty minutes of sherry and banal conversation, the latter of which focused for far too long on whether ostrich feathers should ever be dyed, or if they should be left in their natural state. Since Irene (and, quite possibly, Beatrice) was of the opinion that feathers should remain in their natural state—that is, attached to the avian's body from whence they'd come—she had little to add to this discussion.

At last, she could take it no more, and rose. "I must excuse myself for a moment, Trudy," she said.

"Oh, but it's time to meet the gentlemen." Mrs. Tripley smiled and also rose. "I must admit, I'm a bit nervous about it all. The unveiling, you see."

"But you have nothing to be nervous about," said Irene, taking her arm. "It is going to be spectacular!"

The women gathered in the corridor outside of the study, where the portrait was to be unveiled. The door was closed, which was a mild surprise, and seemed to confuse Trudy Tripley as well.

"I can't imagine where Harold is," she murmured to Irene as they stood at the door. "And why he's got it all closed up. Perhaps he's got some sort of surprise planned. And where is Smayle?" she said, speaking of the butler. She squinted toward the hall, but no one materialized.

"Well, I suppose we ought to just go on in. Harold promised to be ready by half-nine, and I trust he'll bring the gentlemen along soonest. They've likely got all caught up in their billiards and whisky and whatnot. I'll ring for Smayle and send him to collect them."

Irene glanced at the hall clock and saw that it was past half-nine already. "I'm so looking forward to the unveiling," she said in an encouraging tone, hoping to get things moving.

But when Mrs. Tripley went to open the study door, she discovered it was locked. "What on earth...?"

She shook the door gently, and it rattled in place but didn't open. Irene pushed closer and bent to look through the keyhole. It was blocked; presumably by the key.

"It appears it's been locked from the inside," she said, frowning.

"That's terribly odd," said Mrs. Tripley. She knocked on the door. "Harold, *do* let us in! Are you in there?" She turned to Irene and murmured, "This is quite embarrassing. I can't *think* what he's about."

At that moment, Smayle appeared, looking grim as only a butler can do.

"Madam," he said. "Is something wrong with the door?"

"I can't get it open. It seems to be locked—from the inside."

"Locked?"

"And I've knocked, but no one is in there—or at least, they're not answering if they are..." Her voice trailed off into confusion. "I don't understand."

Smayle was surely just as disconcerted as his mistress, but he was a butler and would not deign to show such an emotion. "Huntley!" he said sharply, and a footman appeared as if from nowhere.

"Yes, Mr. Smayle?" said the footman.

"The door appears to be locked from the inside. Go round to the terrace and come in through the doors there, and let us in."

"Of course, sir," he said, and hurried off.

"I can't *think* what's keeping Harold," said Trudy again, looking down the corridor as they waited.

Irene knew the billiard room was down a different hall that connected to this corridor, and near the back of the house, thus putting the gentlemen out of earshot and so their cigar smoke wouldn't permeate the rest of the house. She was about to suggest that she might go off and try to hurry them on when she heard running footsteps.

It was Huntley, the footman. He was slightly out of breath and slowed to a more sedate pace as he approached. "Mr. Smayle, madam, I'm sorry but the doors to the terrace are locked as well. I couldn't get in."

"Why...why, that's so very strange," Mrs. Tripley said, looking around, clearly at a loss.

"Do you want I should break open the door, madam?" asked Huntley eagerly as he eyed his target.

"Why, I...I think we ought to get Harold—I mean to say, Mr. Tripley—first," she said. Irene noticed she was wringing her hands and that her cheeks had turned dark pink. It wasn't unusual for a pampered woman of Society to be indecisive and discombobulated when faced with something unexpected, and Trudy Tripley was, if nothing else, pampered. "This is highly unusual. Very strange. I'm beginning to worry."

"Oy—I mean, yes, 'course, madam. Do you want I should—"

The sound of male voices approaching from down the corridor halted Huntley's offer. Irene saw the tension melt away from Trudy's face and carriage as quickly as the eagerness to do something destructive faded from the footman's.

"There they are. Finally," Trudy said, relief in her voice. "I'm certain Harold will know what to do. Perhaps he has another key, or—or..." She frowned, staring down the hall as the group of men approached. "Where's Harold?" she said, starting toward them.

Irene followed, the top of her scalp prickling. There was something strange...something off...about all of this.

"Where's Harold?" Mrs. Tripley said, more stridently this time.

"Why, ain't he here?" replied Lord Garington.

"Said he'd meet us here," added Mr. Bentley-Bodham.

"I was finishing a billiard game and didn't see him come in," said Mr. Feverley, looking around as if expecting Mr. Tripley to materialize in a puff of smoke.

Everyone fell silent, looking about in confusion.

"Smayle, find Mr. Tripley," said Trudy in a tense voice. "Huntley, I suppose you ought to get us into the room there."

"You want me to break in the door, then, madam?" Huntley looked the sort to do it, too, Irene noted, with his burly shoulders and tall frame. He looked more like a man who belonged in the boxing ring than a footman. Not that Irene would ever admit to knowing what sort of man would be in a boxing ring. But she did happen to know that they had broad shoulders and muscular arms.

"I suppose so," said Trudy, still looking down the hall in hopes of seeing her husband.

Mr. Tripley did not appear.

Huntley eagerly set about his task, hauling himself back, then lunging toward the door, shoulder first. The heavy thing jolted in its frame, hardly budging. Surreptitiously rubbing his broad shoulder, the footman geared himself up again and barged toward it once more, and then a third time.

At last, there was the quiet sound of a splinter and a serious creaking—but only just barely. The door was far sturdier and heavier than one might have imagined.

Mr. Feverley pushed forward through the little crowd. "I'll help," he said, and the footman agreed. Clearly, Huntley didn't want to fail at the task he'd been so eager to take on, and Matthew Feverley, although not nearly as broad and tall as the footman, was certainly no will-o-the-wisp.

Mr. Feverley, Huntley, and even Lord Garington lined up together to launch themselves at the door. Irene suspected part of their enthusiasm was due to the audience of three comely and eligible young women, including Miss Bedwith.

It took two more tries with the three men using blunt force to attempt to jolt the door from its moorings.

In the end, it was the lock that gave way. It separated from the wood of the door, and the loose doorknob was jiggled free.

Irene glanced at Trudy Tripley, who'd stood by silently during the entire process. Her hostess's attention had shifted from the long, silent, *empty* expanse of the corridor to the violent activity of an attempt to gain admittance to the study and back again, over and over. Trudy's expression was drawn and her face slightly gray—almost sickly, compared to the rosy glow she'd worn earlier. Irene, too, was concerned about the missing Harold Tripley. Where on earth could he have gone?

With the door to the study now open, the members of the

small crowd—fifteen of them—spilled into the room, chattering softly among themselves. A fire burned quietly in its hearth inside the chamber, which was unlit except from that illumination spilling from the grate. The huge portrait, still shrouded, hung above the mantel and was the first thing one noticed upon entering the room.

Three armchairs were arranged in a semi-circle at the fireplace, with a small hearth rug in front of them. A large divan sat off to the side with a low table in front of it. On the wall to the right of the fireplace were the French doors that led to the terrace, currently mostly covered by floor-length draperies so that the night was closed off.

To the left of the fireplace and portrait was a long wall covered with shelves filled with books and cases and trinkets. In front of it was a large, heavy desk.

Irene froze when she noticed the feet.

They appeared to extend from behind the desk, on the floor. One shod, obviously male foot was mostly straight up and the other tilted inward. She stepped closer, peering into the dim light that was growing brighter as Smayle and Huntley lit the lamps and sconces. The prickling on the top of her scalp grew stronger and was joined by an unpleasant churning in her belly.

Silently, Irene started toward the desk. Just because there were unmoving feet on the floor didn't mean the worst.

But in this case, she was wrong.

Irene caught her breath and moved closer. Her heart pounded so loud it seemed as if it had leaped into her ears.

Harold Tripley lay crumpled on the floor behind the desk. What appeared to be a cord—such as for a curtain—lay across his neck...and in the gleam of the newly-lit gas lamps she saw a small, silver handle protruding from the center of his chest. A patch of red seeped into the shirtwaist and waistcoat around it. She didn't have to crouch (thank goodness, for neither her knees nor her corset were forgiving enough to easily accomplish that); she could see from standing next to him that there was no hope for Mr. Tripley.

Good Heavens.

Good Heavens, you poor man.

Irene collected herself. She'd seen dead bodies before—although not ones that had been made thus so violently and purposefully—and there was nothing that could be done for Harold Tripley now...except to treat his memory with respect.

"Smayle," she said in a firm voice that carried over the low buzz of conversation, "contact Scotland Yard. Immediately. Mr. Feverley, please help Mrs. Tripley to sit down. We'll need a doctor as well, I think. Send for one if you please, Huntley. *Now.*"

"What is it—good...good H*eavens!—Harold?*" cried Trudy Tripley, stumbling to a halt at the corner of the desk. "Oh my God, *Har...ollld...*" These last syllables came out in a sort of wailing, breath-like huff.

Thankfully, Mr. Feverley was the sort who had a clear head in the case of an emergency, and, even more valuable, seemed to have no hesitation when being given orders by a mere woman. Those assets had quite certainly been instilled in him by whichever woman—mother or nanny—had raised him.

Mr. Feverley was at Mrs. Tripley's side by the time Irene turned. Taking the woman's hands, she spoke clearly and succinctly: "I'm so sorry, Trudy. He's dead."

The other woman froze, her mouth working silently, her hands pulling away from Irene's and going to her bosom as if to protect her heart. She staggered, then her knees gave out and her eyes rolled back into her head. She collapsed into Mr. Feverley's waiting arms.

As Mr. Feverley, along with the Viscount of Garington, eased the unconscious Mrs. Tripley over to the divan, Irene gave more orders to a room of people who had mostly fallen silent. Some of them held back, watching with wide eyes. But most of the others pressed forward, afflicted by the age-old human condition of fascination in the presence of a tragedy not their own.

Still, the room was horribly, terribly, taut with silence.

Irene remained next to Mr. Tripley. Despite the tragic sight and the horror that went along with knowing a man's life had been snuffed out like a candle, she found herself compelled to examine the situation. Someone had done this, here, tonight...in a house full of people.

Who? Why?

The poor, poor man. Her heart wrenched again, for he'd always been nothing but kind and charming to her, and she felt a wave of sympathy for Trudy Tripley. It was terrible enough to lose a husband, but this was no accidental or natural death. Yes...someone had taken his life, violently, and in the sanctuary of his own home.

The most important thing now was for the one who committed such a horrifying act to be identified and brought to justice.

She avidly examined the scene as she imagined Mr. Holmes —or, even more realistically, the Scottish physician Joseph Bell —would have done.

Dr. Bell, who Mr. Conan Doyle freely admitted was the inspiration for his famous fictional detective, always emphasized that one must conduct a detailed observation in any situation that required conclusions, diagnoses, or deductions to be drawn. Out of curiosity, she'd consciously employed that tactic at particular times in her life—when her son seemed to be inter-ested in courting three different potential brides; when a bit of her tea sandwich was taken off her plate when she wasn't look-ing; when a particular maid seemed to have fallen down on her task—and in most cases, she'd deduced the correct outcome (which young woman Edward truly fancied, which pet had snatched part of her cucumber sandwich, which footman the maid was mooning over).

Of course, Irene had never imagined she'd be facing such a terrible scene where the skill of observation would come in handy, but here she was.

And, she suspected, due to her level head as well as being the highest rank of anyone in the room, she was quite the best person to be in charge of things—at least until the authorities arrived.

She did hope they would be more competent than the ones portrayed in Mr. Conan Doyle's stories.

The small hilt protruding from the chest of Mr. Tripley looked as if it could have been a letter opener, or some other slender, scalpel-like weapon. It didn't appear to be very big at all, and likely could easily have been secreted in a man's coat pocket or even his boot, which caused Irene to wonder whether this activity had been planned and the weapon brought with the killer.

She wished she could see the entirety of the blade, but of course she would not remove the knife from its position. Even Irene wasn't curious or crude enough to attempt that.

No other wounds or blood patches were immediately apparent on Harold Tripley's person other than deep scratches at the top of his throat where he'd clearly tried to pull the cord away. Nor were there papers on the desk that seemed to have been scattered about due to what must have been several terrible moments of the assault.

Wishing for once that she was required to employ a cane or walking stick that could be used to gently lift the cord that was lying over Mr. Tripley's throat, Irene had to content herself with holding onto the edge of the desk as she bent her knees and carefully lowered herself partway for a closer look. Tight clothing and creaky joints were not assets at a murder scene.

Her knees were becoming uncooperative, so Irene carefully rose back to her full height. She looked at the surface of the desk and committed its contents and arrangements to her memory before she spoke again.

She had conducted this brief but intense observation in a matter of moments, whilst everyone else was still mucking about in shock.

"Priscilla, ring for a maid. Mrs. Tripley needs a cold compress and some smelling salts," Irene said crisply. "And a glass of whisky would be in order. It appears, in case you all haven't yet comprehended, that poor Mr. Tripley has been murdered. Scotland Yard will need to examine the scene."

Mr. Bentley-Bodham pushed his way around to the back of the desk, standing next to her. "*Murdered?* Nonsense. Balderdash. Why, he was supposed to meet us in the billiard room. Of course he hasn't been murdered."

But when he looked down and saw the condition of Harold Tripley, he gasped. "He's *dead*."

He started toward the body, clearly with the intent to kneel next to it, but Irene edged quickly in front of him. Although she was far less sturdy and more than a decade older than he, her action had the desired effect. He stopped short of bowling her over, as one would expect of any gentleman.

"Are you familiar with the stories of Sherlock Holmes, Mr. Bentley-Bodham? The ones by Mr. Conan Doyle?" she said.

"Course I am," he replied pompously. His dull blond mustache, which was wide and thin and drooped on the ends rather like a man's personal tool at rest, shivered with indignation. "Who ain't?"

"Indeed, you're quite correct," she soothed, for members of the male species loved to be told they were correct. "Mr. Conan

Doyle has made a solid name for himself. He has also, in the course of writing these tales, suggested—and rightly so, I daresay —that a person ought not tromp about at the scene of a crime or move things about near it."

"Why, that's—"

"So very, very clever, isn't it?" Irene went on smoothly. She beamed up at him as if the whole concept was his idea and not dear Arthur's (who, along with Dr. Bell, was a close friend of hers), then adopted what she privately called her "old lady" expression.

It was a very useful demeanor when a person desired to appear befuddled and slow and aged—and to accomplish some particular result. She fluttered her gloved hands wildly, further adding to the effect, and said in a slightly higher pitch than normal, "Oh, dear, I think I might be feeling a bit off myself, Mr. Bentley-Bodham. It's—it's just *so* unsettling to see a dead person so unexpectedly—in his *own* study!" She swayed alarmingly, confident that his gentlemanly instinct would induce him to catch her before she fell.

She was correct, of course, and she swooned dramatically into his arms. Clutching at them, she continued to be extremely out of sorts and unable to stand on her own. As the reluctant yet dutiful Mr. Bentley-Bodham drew her toward the cluster of chairs, Irene happened to catch the eye of Mr. Feverley.

His gaze danced with amusement, then the levity eased. He gave her a look that assured her he understood her intention and moved toward the front of the desk, presumably to act as sentry to keep the others from going round the back to see the tragedy. Irene concluded he might be a fanatic about Sherlock Holmes or Mr. Poe's Dupin—or, at least, that he understood the concept of leaving the place where a crime had been committed undisturbed for the authorities.

Murmurs of shock and whispered questions swirled through

the room. Irene noticed with approval that Priscilla had done as she'd ordered and was even now assisting with pressing a cool compress to Mrs. Tripley's forehead.

"But the door was locked from the inside! Impossible for the killer get out with the door locked!" Mr. Chessley was saying. "How on earth did he do it?"

"Is there another way out of the room?" asked Mrs. Yorkton in her squeaky voice.

"A priest's hole. Or a passage for the servants?" suggested Mr. Shaw in a drawling voice.

"Good Heavens! Is the killer still *hiding* somewhere in this room?" said Miss Drewsbury in a high, breathless voice as she clutched Lord Garington's arm. "What if he comes out and attacks us!"

When Mr. Bentley-Bodham attempted to deposit her into one of the chairs, Irene refused to release her grip on his arms, pretending that she was still quite overset and frightened. In reality, she was thinking about a number of startling conclusions she'd drawn in the past few moments, for she'd noticed something quite interesting and possibly very important.

"I believe I need some air, Mr. Bentley-Bodham," Irene said, sagging against him and making her voice as thready as possible. The others had questions, and she was beginning to think she might have at least one answer. "Could you...please...?"

"Of course, my lady," he said with great stoicism.

Whether he noticed she had suddenly acquired the ability to stand and move under her own steam now that he was drawing her toward the terrace doors, Irene wasn't certain. Even so, she didn't release her grip on his arms, trusting that Mr. Feverley would deter anyone else from disturbing the crime scene whilst she was otherwise occupied. As it was, some of the gentlemen (all three of the eligible bachelors) had taken it upon themselves to comfort the three young, unmarried ladies. Irene noticed automatically that Mr. Shaw seemed to have attached himself to Priscilla, an development of which Irene approved since thus far, Mr. Feverley had shown no interest in the young woman.

Mr. Chessley stood near the doorway, speaking soberly, and the other women—older but no less dramatic—had eased into the chairs in front of the fireplace.

Drat it—how long until Scotland Yard would arrive?

As she and her escort painstakingly approached the terrace doors, Irene surveyed the exit carefully. Floor-length curtains had been drawn over the double doors, but what had caught her eye was that one of them was off-kilter and wrinkled.

No maid or footman worth her or his salt would draw the curtains over a window or door and leave them less than straight and neat. And, as every other bit of drapery in the Tripley home —from the parlor curtains to the tablecloth to the drapes in the ladies' sitting room—had been straight and neat, this observation led Irene to deduce that someone had disturbed the curtains in the study, a conclusion which then implied that whoever killed Mr. Tripley left the study through the terrace doors, brushing carelessly past the draperies.

The doors had been locked when Huntley tried to open them, which also suggested that the murderer had to have found a way to lock them behind him. That was why Irene suddenly decided she needed air. She wanted to look closely at the terrace door and its locking mechanism without drawing attention to it, but first glanced back. She saw with satisfaction that Mr. Feverley remained at his station in the front of the desk to keep the curious from nosing about.

Mr. Bentley-Bodham gallantly pushed the draperies aside for her, revealing the French doors. They were glass-paned and locked with a simple latch that flipped down from one door and crossed over the seam between them, settling into a little metal notch on the second door. The latch was in place, as Irene had expected it to be based on Huntley's report. Her escort flipped up the latch and yanked open one of the sides.

An evening breeze filtered into a room that had begun to feel close and warm. Irene appreciated the fresh air. It cooled her flushed face and cleared her mind, which, admittedly, was slightly bogged with shock and horror. It wasn't often a person came across someone who'd been murdered. Her fingers trembled and her knees were a little shaky.

Grateful for the reprieve, she stepped outside, just over the threshold. It was dark except for a lantern hanging on the wall near the door to the study, and then another lantern on the wall further down, near another door into the house. She wondered if that door was unlocked and thought it must be, for that was how Huntley had gone in and out.

There wasn't much else to see. The terrace ran along the side of the house and spilled into a small rose garden that was enclosed by a tall stone wall. A single gate led to the small mews that would take one out to the street. Irene wondered whether that gate was locked and if so, who might have access to the key.

In fact, she had a number of questions running through her mind, and hoped that whoever arrived from Scotland Yard would be equipped enough to know to ask them. Like Mr. Holmes, she had a wary opinion of the investigators of the police department.

Of course, in her experience, Irene knew there were times one might consider it an advantage to have an inexperienced or not-so-bright constable asking questions one didn't want asked.

"Are you feeling better now, Lady Darling?" asked Mr. Bentley-Bodham. "Would you like to sit down?" Clearly, he couldn't wait to discharge her onto the divan or a handy chair.

"Yes, yes, I suppose I am," she said, keeping a bit of the

quaver in her voice in case she needed to swoon again. "If you could help me to sit..."

Sit and think, she told herself as her escort assisted her back inside and to a seat. Just as they approached the divan where Mrs. Tripley had been resting, the woman sat up suddenly. She looked right at Irene, her face red and ravaged with grief and shock, and pointed a wavering finger. "*You.* Why do people always *die* when you're around?"

Chapter Four

Priscilla eyed Lady Darling as the older woman climbed into the carriage.

She, Priscilla, had been waiting for her sponsor to join her in the vehicle after they came out of the Tripley house. Instead of allowing the footman to hand her into the carriage immediately, Lady Darling had disappeared into the shadows beyond the drive and the side of the house, on foot. Priscilla had caught a glimpse of the footman scurrying after, trying to keep up with the old woman. It was several minutes later when they both returned, the footman still trotting after Lady Darling in an attempt to keep up.

The dowager's expression was indiscernible in the dim light as she settled into her seat. She rapped on the ceiling, and when the carriage started off with a lurch she sighed and grimaced.

Priscilla had dozens of questions, but didn't dare ask any of them. Almost immediately after Mrs. Tripley had made that loud and terrible accusation about her, Lady Darling acknowledged it was best that they leave so as not to upset the poor woman any further.

Priscilla had no intention of arguing. She'd only caught a glimpse of Mr. Tripley, but that had been enough.

It had been a *horrible* sight—with his wide open, unseeing eyes, gaping mouth, and the *terrible* bloom of blood on his clothing. She shuddered and clasped hands that were clammy beneath their gloves. The memory of it would surely bring her nightmares for weeks.

Still. She glanced again at her chaperone and wondered what the woman was thinking and where she'd disappeared to outside of the house and why.

And Mrs. Tripley's accusation had surely been an exaggeration, wasn't it? Of course Priscilla had heard about what had happened at the Enfield Ball three or four or some years ago... but everyone knew that Lord Milbright's death had been an accident. And surely Lady Darling had been to numerous other societal events where no one had died.

Priscilla couldn't say that she knew Lady Darling all *that* well, nor that she was completely sympathetic to the woman— she was so terribly blunt and formidable and *odd*—but Mrs. Tripley's accusation was patently unfair.

If there had been any other unexpected or mysterious deaths in the presence of the dowager marchioness, surely Priscilla would have heard about them. And surely her mother wouldn't have sent her to *live* with someone who attracted tragedies.

At least, she hoped her mother's desire to have her married off wouldn't be more important than her daughter's safety.

"Well," said Lady Darling at last. "That was quite unexpected. So very tragic." She sounded sad and contemplative, but not the least bit guilty or remorseful. "What a terrible, *terrible* thing to happen to Mr. Tripley. And poor Mrs. Tripley." She sighed with real sympathy. "I simply can't..." She sighed heavily, looking out the window into the darkness. "It's difficult enough to lose a husband...but in such a violent, tragic way. The poor woman."

She was silent for a long moment, her attention trained into the night.

"What do you think happened?" Priscilla asked at last. She simply couldn't comprehend the fact that a man had been murdered whilst she had been sitting only a few rooms away! How was that possible? And where had the killer *gone*? Where had he hidden himself? Had he been lurking in the room, watching all of them? She shivered.

Thank goodness that nice Mr. Shaw had been there. He'd turned out to be more attentive than she'd expected...and she'd rather discovered she *liked* his attention.

He was so much more genteel than that Hugh Bafferty, even though he seemed rather fixated on racing horses. She suspected Mr. Shaw would never, *never* kiss a lady, even in the moonlight under a starry sky among the fragrant roses—

Priscilla shoved away the thought, but the heat had bloomed in her cheeks. Drat that Mr. Bafferty! She turned her attention to her companion, who was answering her question.

"Hmm," Lady Darling said. "As a matter of fact, I have a number of thoughts. Perhaps it might be helpful if I enumerate them aloud. Not that Mr. Holmes works that way—he rather keeps his cards close to his vest until the end, doesn't he? Poor Dr. Watson never knows what the man is thinking until he tells him everything that happened at the scene of a crime—simply by determining the sort of ash that came from a pipe! Quite astonishing and perhaps a bit unbelievable, I daresay.

"Still, I'm no Mr. Holmes, and I suppose since this is my first murder investigation, I can be forgiven for being a bit less circumspect and perhaps even a bit...hmm...loquacious about the situation."

"Um..." Priscilla blinked. "What does Mr. Holmes—are you

—are you speaking of Sherlock Holmes? The...the detective in the stories? What does he have to do with...with this?"

Lady Darling looked up, spearing her with a sharp glance. "Why, *someone* must determine who snuffed out Mr. Tripley's life so quickly and violently. I don't suppose Scotland Yard should mind a bit of assistance and objective observation from someone who was present when the body was discovered. After all, they can use all the help they can get." This last was said with great irony. "And it's not everyone who stumbles across a dead person. It's rather a sense of one's duty, isn't it, Priscilla? To help to bring about justice, I mean to say. To offer one's skills and abilities in the service of right."

"Do you mean to say that you—that *you* are...that you mean to..." Priscilla trailed off. She couldn't quite put into words this new, shocking thought that had dropped into her mind. Surely she misunderstood. Surely Lady Darling didn't intend to—

"Inquire into the situation?" Lady Darling's lips curved up at the corners. "I suppose that is indeed what I intend, isn't it? It will give me something interesting to do—aside from sponsoring you about Society, of course," she added hastily.

"And I daresay, having someone with a cool head who was there at the discovery of the crime can only be considered an asset to said situation. After all, if it weren't for me, Mr. Bentley-Bodham and who knows who else would have trampled all over the scene."

"I daresay," said Priscilla faintly.

"Now, as you *have* asked, I do think it would be beneficial for me to enumerate the details I noticed and to, perhaps, take ourselves through what might have happened," Lady Darling said in a satisfied voice.

Priscilla couldn't find the words to protest. Was she dreaming?

What proper gentlelady would insert herself into a violent,

criminal situation? Did the old woman truly mean to go about and—and *investigate?*

"We all had dinner," Lady Darling began, settling back against her cushioned seat. "There were six gentlemen and six women including the Tripleys and you and I, of course. Do forgive me if I state the obvious, Priscilla, dear, but one does want to be thorough. And I would like to point out that I did, in fact, notice that Mr. Shaw bestowed quite a bit of attention upon you, my dear."

"Oh...well, I suppose." Priscilla lowered her eyes modestly. "But he hasn't a title, and as you know, I am quite determined to settle for nothing less."

"He would be a reasonable prospect for you nonetheless," Lady Darling said in a voice that sounded almost like a warning. "I understand from Mrs. Tripley that he's got fifty thousand a year, and a small holding in York."

"Of course, my lady," said Priscilla, not meaning a word of it.

If only the interfering woman would leave her to her own devices and let her meet the Duke of Wessley. She *knew*...just *knew*...that he would find her fascinating and beautiful and would fall madly in love with her, and everyone in Society would be shocked by the speed with which their engagement was announced.

But Lady Darling kept insisting that she attend these smaller dinner parties and musicales where only the lowest ranking members of the aristocracy were present, and Priscilla was finding it quite frustrating.

Lady Darling gave her a measured look, then returned to a subject that clearly interested her more than Priscilla's marital prospects—something for which Priscilla was quite grateful, even if it scandalized her.

"After dinner, the gentlemen went to the billiard room, and

you and I and the rest of the ladies were forced to be content with watered-down sherry, and to gossip about ostrich feathers and missing sapphire brooches, and the unfortunate Miss Gaudy being left at the altar—the poor dear—as we gathered in the small parlor.

"We ladies then arrived at the door of the study for the portrait unveiling at half nine. But the gentlemen weren't there yet and, strangely, the door was locked from the inside, restricting entrance to the study. The doors from the terrace were locked from the inside as well—which was the first strong indication that something was badly off. I felt it in the top of my scalp, you see," Lady Darling said, gesturing in that vague direction. "I find that sort of sensation is always a portent of something gone wrong."

"I see," Priscilla murmured. The top of her scalp hadn't prickled, but her stomach was certainly doing strange flipping things now.

"And so when we at last gained admission to the study—just as the gentlemen came to join us; rather tardily and missing Mr. Tripley, which was another indication of some sort of foreboding—I was prepared to find something amiss. I certainly didn't expect to find our host dead on the floor..." Her voice trailed off and she heaved a sigh. "Yes, it is quite off-putting to find one's host in a deceased state after billiards and sherry."

There was silence for a moment as Lady Darling seemed to need to gather her emotions, but then she continued.

"I saw his feet right away, and then of course the prickling on my head again indicated this was something more than a man simply having fallen asleep on the floor, or even knocking himself on the head and taking a tumble. When I drew nearer to observe, it was immediately clear that Mr. Tripley was dead and had been made so by the small knife protruding from his chest.

"But there was also a strip of cloth—shortly after, I ascertained that it was a tie-back from the curtains in that very room —wrapped around his neck...he must have been strangled as well..." Her voice trailed off and in the dim light, Priscilla saw her eyes close as if to recall the image in her mind. Then the eyes popped open.

"Hmm. I wonder if perhaps the curtain cord had been used to take him by surprise so that the knife could be thrust into place. Perhaps the miscreant—no, I suppose that's far too weak of a word for a person who's taken the life of another—perhaps the *villain*—yes, that's much better isn't it? Perhaps the *villain* came up from behind Mr. Tripley and slipped the cord around his neck and either began to strangle him or simply used it to take him by surprise or to pull him back so he could stab him.

"Mr. Tripley would, as one *must* do when something has come round one's throat, reach up and try to pull it away. This would leave his chest open and his hands busy." She demonstrated by reaching her hands up to pull at an invisible, strangling scarf.

Priscilla saw that she was correct—a triangular part of her chest, created by the angle of the two raised hands, was unprotected.

"It was, after all, a single stab wound. One thrust and the blade found its mark. That would have been much more difficult to accomplish if Mr. Tripley was facing this villain and saw the intent to strike, and was struggling to fend him off.

"And the strangulation...well, that might have been not only to immobilize Mr. Tripley so the aim would be true, but also to silence him during the—er—altercation." Lady Darling nodded and hmmed to herself again. "Yes, that does make some sense. There was very little blood for taking a man's life, wasn't there? So one would suppose the killer didn't get much or any on himself, unfortunately.

"And, sadly, I couldn't tell precisely what sort of knife had been used. It could have been as small as a letter opener, although I daresay one would have to be quite sharp in order to do the deed so quickly and efficiently." Lady Darling sighed. "I do have a *number* of questions."

She fell silent again and Priscilla was moved to speak. "But how did the killer get away? Both of the doors were locked from the inside! Is there a secret passageway?" In spite of her certainty that inserting oneself into a murder investigation was utterly improper—especially for a gentlelady—she was curious and a bit nervous knowing that she'd been in the same house, perhaps even the same *chamber* as a murderous villain.

"Yes, that is a question, isn't it, pet? I doubt there is a priest's hole in the Tripley house. It's far too modern to have had need of that, you see. I suspect that the killer let himself out the terrace doors and concocted a way to throw the latch behind him. It wouldn't be terribly difficult, I don't think," she went on, drowning out Priscilla's instinctive negation. "Something as simple as a piece of string or thread on the latch that is fed between the two doors and, once one has stepped outside, pull on the string and the latch falls into place." She gave Priscilla a small smile. "Rather elementary, my dear Miss Bedwith."

"But—"

"And the fact that the curtains were awry supports that supposition. Did you notice them, dear? One of them was wrinkled and buckled—not at all neat and straight as it should have been after a maid came in to draw them—and, I presume, ensure that the terrace door was properly locked.

"Indeed, I'm quite certain the villain came out that way and then let himself back into the house through another door."

"Do you mean he *came back into the house?*" This confirmation of Priscilla's greatest fear made her feel light-headed and a bit sick.

"He certainly didn't go out the gate into the mews," Lady

Darling told her. "I checked as we were leaving. There is a lock on the inside of the gate, and it requires a key. It was locked and the key was hanging near the house."

"Are you saying...my lady, surely you don't mean to say that..." Priscilla's tongue felt thick and her whole body was as cold as when she'd plunged into the pond when she was thirteen, and that dratted Hugh Bafferty had had to pull her out.

"I am, in fact, quite clearly saying it: whoever did away with Mr. Tripley *had* to have been one of the dinner guests. One of the gentlemen, to be even more specific."

"But...I don't understand," Priscilla whispered. "Surely it was just someone who—who sneaked in and—and then let themselves out again. A burglar of some sort."

It was bad enough imagining that she'd been in the same *house* as a murderer, but it was inconceivable that she'd been at the same *dinner table* as one. Someone like Mr. Shaw, who'd been undeniably interesting.

Priscilla refused to believe it. Her sponsor was mad to think otherwise.

"Impossible," Lady Darling decreed. "If you set your mind to it, you'll have no choice but to agree, my dear. No one could have simply waltzed into the house and made their way to the study and laid in wait for Mr. Tripley to *happen* upon them by chance—and alone, might I add, when he is *entertaining*? And that is an entirely other topic, might I *also* add, this fact that Mr. Tripley was *in* the study in order to be murdered by someone instead of being with his guests...now, where was I?

"Oh, yes, the ridiculous suggestion that this supposed miscreant let himself into the house and just happened to come upon the master of the house *alone* in his study—during a *dinner party!* I hardly think so—then took the opportunity to kill him, and *then* let himself out onto the terrace and then back into the house and then back out of the house again without being seen! Why, it's preposterous and thus it must be dismissed as a possibility.

"Therefore, the killer simply has to be one of the dinner guests. There is no other explanation. I suppose that means I shall have to speak with each of them as well." Instead of sounding concerned, Lady Darling actually sounded thrilled.

"Speak to them? Do you mean, the gentlemen? Speak to the gentlemen?"

"Why, yes, of course, pet," Lady Darling said, looking at her in the same way Mr. Timms tended to do: with tilted head and bright eyes, and as if to say, *Aren't you a silly thing?*

"But...but...you're a-a *lady*," Priscilla managed to say.

"Much to my dismay," agreed Lady Darling, shocking Priscilla even further. "It's rather a nuisance being a lady most of the time, don't you agree? One *can't* do this, one *daren't* do that, but one must *certainly* do some other ridiculous thing like bind oneself up in clothing that doesn't allow one to bend over or even to *breathe*—thank Heaven fashion has gotten on past those bloody *hobble* skirts!—and so on.

"The only instance in which being a lady comes in handy is when one is required to pretend to be helpless. Then everyone scampers about doing whatever needs to be done so one doesn't have to lift a finger or break a nail." This last bit was delivered with a bit of wry irony. "To be fair, there are times when simply being a marchioness comes in handy as well. One can become quite formidable as needed."

Priscilla clamped her lips together, for fear of what might come out of them. It was simply *not done* for a *lady* to approach a *gentleman* to speak to him—especially about whether he committed a *murder!* She could hardly breathe, imagining her chaperone tilting her head and looking at Lord Garington—a *viscount!*—or the ever-so-proper (perhaps even a bit overly so)

Mr. Bentley-Bodham and asking whether he'd done away with Mr. Tripley.

Lady Darling didn't seem to notice Priscilla's consternation. Instead, she continued her musings as the carriage turned onto the street where the dowager house was located. "I suppose I shall see some of them at the Enfield Ball, but it may be more effective to speak to each of the suspects—oh, I *do* like that word, don't you, Priscilla? It sounds rather official, doesn't it? *Suspects!* —in a less public or social situation. And of course, the biggest question one must ask is, why? *Why* did someone wish to kill Harold Tripley? And why did they take such a risk, doing it in the midst of a *dinner party*? Why, it must be some act of desperation to do such a thing!"

"I-I suppose," Priscilla replied, somehow being drawn into the discussion in spite of her misgivings.

The carriage jolted to a violent halt in front of the dowager house, prompting a vexed sigh from Priscilla's companion.

"I don't suppose it'll make a difference to speak to him again, shall it?" she muttered as the carriage door opened. "But I suppose one must at least make the attempt, otherwise one will have to suffer jolts and jounces."

Priscilla had no idea what Lady Darling was going on about now. She didn't care, either. She simply wanted to get away from the whole idea, the terrifying *fact*, that she'd not only *seen* a dead body, but had eaten dinner with a *killer*. At the same table!

Perhaps—good Heavens, she suddenly felt faint—perhaps he'd even been sitting *next to her*.

With a quiet little moan, Priscilla climbed out of the carriage with the help of the footman and stumbled into the house.

Lady Darling could stew about it so that she had nightmares

for all Priscilla cared. *She* was going to go to bed and put all of those terrifying thoughts right *out* of her mind.

~

Irene was determined to make it out of the house the next day before the hordes of callers arrived. She expected quite a run of them due to the incident last evening. There was nothing that fueled the desire to be social more than having a tragedy or scandal to be gossiped over.

But then her daughters descended.

"Mother!" cried Rose in the sort of tone Irene used to employ when she misbehaved. "Where do you think you're *going* at half past two in the afternoon? You're expected to be home to callers."

"What on earth are you wearing, Mother?" said Violet, her nose wrinkling as she eyed the hat perched on Irene's head. It was a new one, a bright red confection with little tinkling bells that Mr. Timms particularly loved.

"Was there really a *murder* last night?" Jane demanded. "Can't you simply go to a dinner party without everything going awry, Mama?"

Irene beamed at her daughters, all of whom—despite their saucy comments—were smiling and laughing with affection as they greeted her. She gathered the three of them into her arms and squished them all into a hug tighter than their collective corsets as Beatrice pranced around and between their legs, barking and bouncing in a bid for attention, and Mr. Timms dove and glided overhead crying, "Intruder! Where's my hat? Intruder! I need a pickle!"

"I'm so glad you're all here," she said, smacking each of them with a loud kiss on the cheek in turn. "What a wonderful surprise! It's been *ages* since I've seen you."

"It's only been two months," Rose reminded her. Her eyes danced with humor, but she was the one who tended toward the pedantic and proper. "And if you had a telephone, we'd be able to ring and talk to you whenever we wanted! Most everyone has one now, Mama. You really ought to get one."

"A telephone? Why would I want a telephone? Why, then people would *ring* me!" Irene said, shaking her head, laughing. For when Rose said "everyone" had one, what she meant was, most everyone in the upper class—the very people Irene generally preferred to avoid—had one.

"I thought you wanted to stay quietly in the country," said Jane in a voice muffled by her mother's shoulder. "And here you are, attending *murders*!"

"Mother, I love you dearly, but I do think you ought to think again about wearing that hat," Violet said, extricating herself gently. "It's...well, it's a bit *young*-looking for you, don't you think?"

"Where *were* you off to, Mother? It's social call hour. You're supposed to be *home,* to callers." Rose linked her arm through Irene's and began to lead her to the parlor.

"You're the only callers I want today," Irene told them quite happily. Although their unexpected arrival put a dampening on her plans for the afternoon, she was still delighted to see them. She removed the offending hat and advised Josephs that she was not at home to callers for the afternoon, then, with Rose still on her arm, led the way to the small sitting room.

Violet and Jane—the latter of whom reached down to scoop up Beatrice—followed, all of them chattering happily together as they went into the comfortable, informal chamber Irene used for family gatherings. Watson, who must have been deeply asleep not to have heard the commotion of their arrival, woofed and lumbered to his feet as they came into the room. He accepted pats and scratches from each of the girls and Jane even offered a cheek for him to swipe with a kiss.

Mr. Timms was still fluttering and swooping around the room, crying, "Intruder! Intruder! Where's my hat? Where's my pickle?" (No one knew why he said that, but Irene suspected it was something Jane had taught him just to be mischievous.)

"So where is she?" Jane demanded, looking around. "The girl. The one who's taken our places in your heart, Mama." She smiled winsomely at Irene, her seven (the girls had actually numbered them in ink once, many years ago) dimples dancing as she batted her eyelashes.

Jane was the youngest, slightest, and most energetic and outspoken of the girls—not that they weren't all outspoken, at least in their mother's presence. She was also the most stubborn and daring of all of the four children—including Edward, the eldest and only male.

Because of these traits, Irene had been quite delighted to pass on the responsibility of Jane to her new husband, who, in Irene's estimation, was quite suited to managing her daughter's particularly challenging temperament.

It had been a love match (Irene would not settle for anything less for her children than what she'd had herself), and Mr. Charles Kearnley madly adored his pretty wife. He was light-hearted yet practical, and he gave her just enough freedom to keep from dampening her spirit and squelching her curiosity...but not too much that she ran wild and out of control, which Jane was wont to do. He rather reminded Irene of her own darling Edward, who'd tempered—or at least tried to—her own tendencies toward adventure and mayhem. And since Irene had spent most of the first thirteen years of her life traveling the world on various of her father's trade ships, she had very strong tendencies toward adventure and mayhem.

Nevertheless, Irene shuddered at the thought of what sort of children Jane and Charles Kearnley would make. They would surely be beautiful, intelligent, and very headstrong. She was glad she would be a grandmother and not their parent, even though it was completely unfashionable for a parent to have any sort of involvement in raising a child.

"Are you speaking of Miss Bedwith?" she asked as she settled into her favorite chair next to Mr. Timms's treat dish. The parrot wasted no time in fluttering onto a perch next to her in hopes that she'd lift the lid and offer him a sunflower seed, and of course she did. He settled on the arm of the chair and nibbled his treat.

"Yes, of course," Rose said. "We decided we had best see for ourselves who has taken over your time."

"And replaced us in your affections," said Jane.

"And then we heard about the *murder* and decided we'd best make certain you weren't prostrate with shock over it all," Violet added, grinning.

Violet had three dimples, and her identical twin had only two. The only way for strangers to tell the two of them apart was by counting their dimples, should either of them smile. When they were younger and taking advantage of the fact that they *were* identical in the most mischievous of ways, Violet and Rose had quickly learned not to smile when they traded places.

"Clearly I am not prostrate with shock," Irene told them with a flap of her hand. "And in fact, you've interrupted my plan to play Sherlock Holmes."

"Your *what*?" Rose sat up straight, her brown eyes popping wide, her chin lifting sharply, and nary a dimple in sight. In that moment, she looked so much like a disgruntled Edward that Irene's heart gave a little lurch. How she'd *loved* that man so, even during his most priggish and haughty moments.

"My plan to play Sherlock Holmes and investigate the murder," Irene told her as the parlor door opened. "Oh, thank you, Vella," she said with a smile as her oldest friend and close confidante—in the form of housekeeper and companion—came in, rolling a two-tier cart laden with tea. Beatrice bounded off Jane's lap and scampered over in hopes that something might conveniently tumble from the tea tray to land near her tiny paws. Even Mr. Timms looked up, knowing that sometimes little nuts were to fall off scones or biscuits. Watson was snoring on the hearth again.

"Did you hear that, Mrs. Josephs? Mama is planning to play Sherlock Holmes!" Jane said. Her eyes danced with delight and excitement, and Irene thought she'd better be careful or her youngest daughter would insist on playing Watson to her Holmes—or vice versa—and that would *not* do.

"Oh, I did indeed," said Vella with a wry smile. "In fact, I heard all about it last night when she got home." She shook her head and tsked, even though her eyes danced with humor as she began to unstack teacups onto the table. "Your mother has an entire list of suspects, and a plan to inquire after all of them."

"That is true," Irene said, settling back in her chair as her three offspring gawked at her. "I made Vella and Josephs sit up with me for *hours*, listening as I went over everything. We drank whisky and smoked cigars—"

"Oh, you did nothing of the sort, Mother! Don't tease," said Violet, reaching for a currant scone before Vella had even finished pouring the tea.

Irene's eyes narrowed a little and she looked at her daughter thoughtfully. Violet was not usually the first to help herself to a treat; that was more often Jane, who could be a bit greedy over sweets. In fact, Violet had never had a particularly large appetite, nibbling like a bird more often than not. Was her face the slightest bit rounder? Irene smiled to herself and tucked the thought—and the little maternal instinct—aside for now. "Well, we did have whisky, but I confess, only Josephs had a cigar."

"*Mother!*" Rose said, huffing and shaking her head. "If someone saw you drinking whisky—"

"And so what if they did?" Irene replied. "It's not against the *law* for a woman to drink whisky—though there are *plenty* of other things that are against the law for a woman to do," she grumbled. "Such as vote, and hold office, and have equal custody of her children—"

"Yes, Mother, we know, we know," chorused her offspring.

"Now tell us about the girl—" Violet started.

"No, no, that's boring, Vi. Tell us about the *murder!*" Jane said. "Was it terribly bloody? Did you scream? I want to hear about these suspects!"

"Where *is* the girl?" Rose said, looking around as if Priscilla might materialize at any moment. "Weren't you expecting callers?"

"Of course I didn't scream, Jane. Rose, Priscilla is upstairs resting. She was quite...er...overset by the events of last night," Irene replied. "More likely, she's upstairs attempting to avoid a certain Mr. Bafferty, who is, apparently, a friend from her childhood. He's indicated he means to call, and when I met him, he was perfectly polite and civil. And if you three keep squealing and shouting, I daresay she'll find her way down soon enough and ruin our little visit."

"Are you *truly* going to the Enfield Ball, Mama?" asked Violet. Her voice had gone soft and she gave her a concerned look.

All three of the girls were looking at her in that way: their heads tilted to the side, brows lifted slightly.

"Yes, of course I'm going," she replied firmly. "Whyever shouldn't I?"

"It's just that...after last night, are you certain it's a good idea?" Rose said carefully, then yanked her plate aside and up. "Beatrice, *no!*"

But Beatrice had already dived under the divan with a piece of scone in her little teeth. Only the pouf of her tail showed from beneath the sofa. It vibrated slightly—a sure sign that the little beast was well into scarfing down her treat.

"You know better than to let your plate get to Beatrice level," Irene told her eldest daughter (the eldest by ten minutes). "And, incidentally, I see no reason not to go, regardless of what happened last night. I had nothing to do with it," she said.

"It's just that with what happened last night and what happened the last time you were at the Enfield Ball..." Rose began.

"That was four years ago, Rosemary," Irene said in a voice that brooked no argument. "And as you know perfectly well, there hasn't even *been* an Enfield Ball since then, due to that particular event. And most importantly, the murder last night has absolutely nothing to do with what happened to Lord Milbright."

"Everyone will be talking about you," Violet said. "I only—we just don't want it to be uncomfortable, Mama. That's all."

"I am never uncomfortable except when I'm wearing a bloody corset, my darlings, or having to speak with mindless people," Irene told them with a fond smile. She ignored Rose's shocked gasp—*"Mother!"*—at her use of a curse word. If a person couldn't swear in front of her own children in her own sitting room, when could she?

"Which is why I far prefer the country. I'm too old to care what people think, and now that you're all married off and your Papa is gone, I care even less if people gossip about me."

"That's the ticket, Mama!" said Jane so bracingly Irene suspected she was considering when and how to adopt the usage of curse words herself. "I for one am glad you'll be there. I can't *wait* to see the look on Lady Pelicourt's face when she sees you there." Her eyes gleamed like that of a sly cat.

Then the delight faded and Jane's expression grew sad and concerned. "But it truly must have been awful to have a man be murdered practically in front of you. Did you *see* him? How did he die? Was there a lot of blood? Was it terrible? I'm so sorry, Mother. I'm certain it *was* a frightening, horrible situation. I don't mean to make light of it, I promise."

"It certainly was a shock to find Mr. Tripley on the floor with a knife sticking out of his chest," Irene said grimly.

Violet gasped and pressed a hand to her stomach. "Good Heavens, Mother!" Her face had gone pale. "You saw the *knife*?"

"Was there a lot of blood?" asked Jane. She actually sounded concerned rather than morbidly curious.

"Not very much but certainly enough," Irene replied. "There was a large bloodstain on the front of his shirt and waistcoat."

"Weren't you afraid that whoever did it was still lurking about?" asked Rose, her brown eyes wide. "I would have wanted to leave immediately!"

"Whoever did it was almost certainly still there," Irene said, prompting gasps from all three of her daughters. She went on to explain how she'd come to the conclusion that the killer had been a dinner guest. "Which means that I have a finite list of suspects," she said with great satisfaction.

"*Suspects*?" Violet echoed, reaching for a lemon biscuit this time. Her favorite. "You can't be serious about this detecting business, Mother."

"I'm perfectly serious," Irene told her. "And you three can help me."

"What on earth are you talking about?" said Violet as her twin retorted, "*Absolutely not*, Mother."

Violet frowned as she set the lemon biscuit aside after a tiny nibble. She reached for another of the currant scones. "You simply aren't going to drag us into this scheme of yours, Mama."

"Help you how?" asked Jane, her eyes sparkling.

"By telling me everything you know about my suspects," Irene said. "One of them had a reason to kill Mr. Tripley. In order to determine who, I have to know about them. And as you know, I've been hidden away in the country and I'm not up on all the current *on dits*."

Rose gave her skeptical look. "That's all? Just tell you what we know?"

"That's *all*," Irene said firmly, giving her youngest daughter a quelling look. "I'll handle the rest of it myself."

Jane merely smiled as she lifted her cup to sip. For the first time, Irene began to regret mentioning her detecting plan to the girls.

"Well, Mama, who are they?" Jane asked. "These suspects?"

"Lord Garington, Mr. Bentley-Bodham, Mr. Harry Shaw, Mr. Chessley, and Mr. Feverley. What do you know about any and all of them?"

"Do you mean Matthew Feverley?" said Rose, sitting up straighter. "Amanda's brother? Why, that's ridiculous. He's always been so civil and charming. He's definitely *not* a murderer."

"I was under the impression he loathes social gatherings," Violet said. "Do you mean to say he was at the dinner party? That's rather odd, though, isn't it?"

"He doesn't *loathe* social gatherings," Rose corrected her twin. "He simply avoids them when he can."

"Whatever the reason, Matthew Feverley was present. He was also level-headed and very helpful in keeping people from trampling all over the crime scene," Irene said. "I tend to agree with you, Violet. He's a suspect only because he was there, but I simply can't imagine he would do such a thing. His mother simply wouldn't stand for it."

"Charles loathes Mr. Bentley-Bodham," said Jane thoughtfully, speaking of her husband. "The man cheats at cards, and he always leaves a mess on his table at the club. Ashes everywhere; it seems he doesn't use an ashtray. He's just an unpleasant man all around. He told me I ought to simply sit quietly in my chair because I was much more attractive when I didn't speak. I do hope it's him," she added with a malicious grin.

"Cheats at cards, does he?" Irene murmured, thinking of how pompous and dismissive he'd been last night when she announced that Mr. Tripley was murdered. As if she couldn't tell a victim when she saw one. "That's interesting. Is there anything else to recommend him for the role of killer besides the fact that he's an arse?"

"Mother!" Rose's reprimand wasn't quite as forceful this time. "You simply can't go round saying things like that!"

"Why not? It's only the three of you here. You're not going to repeat it, are you?"

"Of course not," Rose replied with a huff. "Lawrence hunts with Lord Garington and they're often at the club together. He's never said anything about him that suggests he might be willing to *murder* someone. He's never really said much about him at all, now I think of it. They know each other from Cambridge, I believe."

"David doesn't care for Lord Garington," said Violet. "I'm not certain why; he's simply told me not to invite him to any of our gatherings. I could try and find out more," she added. "David was at Eton with him."

"That's the spirit," Irene said, pleased. "Just ask your husbands and listen to any gossip about these four—well, five—men, for we really must be thorough and cannot simply write off a suspect because we know him—and pass all of the information on to me. Now, what about Mr. Harry Shaw and Mr. Chessley?"

"I don't know much about either of them," said Jane. "Mr. Shaw is nice enough looking and he's always been civil to me. He was courting Lily Bloomfield last I heard."

"Oh, you're behind the times, Janey. Miss Bloomfield just got engaged to Mr. Bentley—not Mr. Bentley-Bodham, just Mr. Bentley," Violet clarified.

"Well, goodness—what happened there? I thought they were practically *engaged*," said Jane.

"I'm not quite certain, but I got the impression Miss Bloomfield found out something she didn't like about Mr. Shaw. Something unpleasant enough for her to give up fifty thousand a year, I suppose," said Rose.

"Perhaps she just realized she didn't love him," said Jane with a bit of a moony expression that suggested she was thinking of her husband. Rose rolled her eyes.

"That's a relief," said Irene. "I mean to say, it's a relief that Mr. Shaw's not courting Lily Bloomfield, for he seemed rather taken with Miss Bedwith last night. I should like to know what it was that had Miss Bloomfield turning him off, however, in the event he pursues Miss Bedwith. If she isn't going to settle for this Mr. Bafferty—goodness, *so* many B names!—I may direct her toward Mr. Harry Shaw."

"But Mama, he's a *suspect*!" Violet said, horrified.

"Mr. Shaw likes his horse racing," said Rose. "One time I was seated next to him at dinner and the entirety of the conversation was about his racing horses. I even tried to discuss the weather to change the subject, and he just went right back to his dratted horses and jockeys and all of that nonsense."

"So we have a cheater at cards in Mr. Bentley-Bodham, a viscount who is an all-around arse" —Irene looked right at Rose when she said this, and her daughter didn't *quite* roll her eyes, but she did look up at the ceiling in exasperation— "along with Mr. Shaw, a man obsessed with racing horses, and a charming and civil man—Mr. Feverley, of course—whom none of us would believe is a killer...and then there's Mr. Chessley. What do we know about him?"

"Not very much," replied Violet. "I've never met him, I don't believe."

"Wasn't he the one involved with that carriage accident?" Rose said. "Or was that Mr. Chess*ler*?"

"Carriage accident? When was this?" said Violet.

"Why, I don't exactly recall, but I believe he was injured somehow."

"But, Mama, you're forgetting the servants. Everyone always forgets about the servants," Jane said, leaning forward with sparkling eyes.

"Of course I didn't forget about them—how could I? But I simply rejected the idea out of hand because it makes absolutely no sense that any of them would have wanted to kill their employer. By all accounts, Mr. Tripley and Mrs. Tripley are quite reasonable people—Mrs. Josephs told me so last night. She knows Mrs. Canefield, the housekeeper, very well. And besides, the only one who could have had the opportunity was the butler, and he was busy serving us ladies. All the other staff was downstairs eating their dinner. No, it is definitely one of the five men."

Josephs suddenly appeared in the doorway to the sitting room, ending the conversation.

"Excuse me, my lady, but there is an Inspector Burgess from Scotland Yard at the front door. He wishes to speak with you."

Chapter Five

"Oh!" squeaked Violet, her eyes going wide. "Mama!"

"He's not here to arrest you, surely," whispered Rose, glancing toward the door.

"Of course not. He's here to ask me what I saw and noticed last night," Irene said with great satisfaction. She had expected a representative from Scotland Yard to arrive far sooner than this, and she'd rather hoped it would be Burgess.

After all, they did have a history of sorts and she was quite aware of his investigative process. And, really, it was far better that he'd shown up *now* than earlier today when she was having a bit of a lie-in. Sadly, she didn't handle her whisky as well as she used to. "Show him in, Josephs, if you please."

"In here, my lady?" On a good day, Josephs was terrible at hiding his thoughts behind a stoic or austere expression, but with murder in the air, there was no hope for it at all. His face showed bald shock and worry as his gaze flitted from her to the girls and then back again.

"Of course. But please have Vella come in and take Mr. Timms and Beatrice away first." Irene smiled complacently and settled back into her chair. She was debating whether to adopt the helpless old lady mien or the airs of a peremptory marchioness for the benefit of the policeman.

Inspector Burgess was as sharp and bony a specimen of a man as she remembered. He wore a thick black mustache that swept up into a pair of mutton chops. He had eyes that darted about like those of a ferret searching out a vole, and he was not, Irene had previously discovered, an admirer of intelligent women.

"Good afternoon, Inspector," she said when he came into the room. Watson, who'd bestirred himself at the sound of an interloper, had been ordered to stay in his place on the hearth. He eyed the newcomer from beneath the fringe of his canine brows. To his credit, he didn't growl, although his lip was lifted in a silent warning.

Irene didn't rise at Burgess's appearance, as was her prerogative as an older woman of high rank, but her daughters did.

"Lady Darling, thank you for seeing me," Burgess said, holding a hat in his hand. His attention barely skimmed over the girls, and due to this ignorance, the trio of them sat back down as soon as it was proper to do so, exchanging irritated glances with each other over such dismissiveness.

Irene had considered offering the inspector a seat, but rejected the idea. Instead, she merely looked at him from her comfortable chair and said, "I expect you're here about poor Harold Tripley."

"Yes, my lady," he said. "I was hoping you'd answer a few questions about the incident. If, I mean to say, you're not too terribly overset about it all. I'm sure it was quite shocking for someone of such a delicate constitution."

Irene had been about to opt for the helpless and mildly confused old lady persona, but this statement nudged her in the opposite direction. It also made her wonder whether he remembered her after all. Probably not—after all, she was "delicate" and a woman. Not at all worth remembering.

"My dear inspector," she said in a cool voice, "a man—the husband of a friend—is dead, and violently so. I certainly feel a great deal of grief and regret over that, but I am not prostrate with terror nor clutching my smelling salts. *I* am not in any danger of being murdered." She swore she heard a snicker from the direction of Jane. "Poor Mr. Tripley is in far worse shape than I, and of course Mrs. Tripley is surely in a terrible state—and understandably so. I will of course be of every assistance possible to you in your efforts."

"Thank you, Lady Darling—"

"I'm assuming that by now—as it is more than twelve hours after the tragic event—you've determined how the killer got out of the study whilst leaving it locked from inside. A very simple process, really, for a person to go through the terrace doors and pull the latch down behind oneself—and quite obvious too. And, one hopes you've realized that there are exactly five suspects who could have done the deed. No more, no fewer. I'm afraid I can't tell you very much about any of them as of yet except for Mr. Feverley—who is not actually a suspect—but I intend for that to change."

Inspector Burgess blinked at this onslaught of information (which, really, none of it should be *new* information to him). "Blimey, me lady. I mean to say, perhaps...only five suspects, you say? I...but there were eleven people at the dinner party. Besides the victim, I mean."

"Yes, indeed. But there were six gentlemen and all of them went into the game room for cigars and billiards. During that time, one of them somehow managed to lure Harold Tripley into the study on his own, do away with him, and then rejoin the others without anyone the wiser. There wasn't enough blood to have left a trace on the killer, sadly, and so I believe you'll have to solve this crime through observation, deduction, and conclusion rather than bloodstains, but since there were six men including Mr. Tripley and he is dead, that means there are five left and one of them must be the killer. I have no reason *why* someone would want Harold Tripley out of the way—at least, not yet—but clearly someone did. It will be most instructive and, I daresay, challenging to determine the motive.

"I'm rather inclined to strike Mr. Matthew Feverley off the list," Irene went on, "as he was quite instrumental in assisting me in keeping the scene of the crime from being—oh, what is the word? contaminated, I suppose—and I daresay if he were the culprit, he would have been far more eager to have things mussed up and moved about and so on. However, I of course shan't do that as of yet—strike him off, I mean to say—because one never knows, does one? Sometimes it is the nicest, most genial people who hide the most terrible and frightening secrets."

"Er...yes, my lady, I see."

"None of the women could have done it—surely you're quite aware of that, aren't you, Inspector Burgess? We were all together in the conservatory the entire time. No one left in order to freshen up or for any reason."

"It could just as easily have been an intruder, Lady Darling," said Burgess, giving her a beady-eyed look as he attempted to regain control of the conversation. He went on with great pomposity, "We police officers are quite adept at looking at all possibilities—"

"It most certainly could not have been an intruder," Irene said patiently. "I confirmed it myself. There was simply no way anyone could have let themselves out of the courtyard, for the gate was locked and the key was hanging by the house. Mark my words, Inspector, it was one of the five men sitting at the dinner table. Now, I will happily answer any of your questions, but at this time, none of them—the five men—leap to mind as the obvious culprit. Although I must admit to a slight prejudice against Mr. Bentley-Bodham. He seems to have a bit of an *air* about him that everything he says and does is far more important than anyone else. *And* he actually suggested I was wrong when I announced that Mr. Tripley was murdered. Not to mention the fact that by all accounts, he is an ar—" she heard a smothered gasp from Rose and redirected herself— "er, a difficult person."

"Oi...I see, my lady." Burgess seemed to struggle to gather his thoughts, which was precisely Irene's intent. She had learned long ago that a verbal torrent of information and options could easily distract an opponent. "Could you tell me what happened, from your perspective, if you please?"

"Of course, if you think it would be helpful. Have a seat, Inspector. This may take some time." She gestured graciously to the hard-backed chair next to hers.

By the time she finished her very, very detailed description of what had happened, along with what she'd noticed and concluded, the Scotland Yard inspector appeared to be thoroughly dazed.

"Is there anything else?" he asked. He'd pulled a notepad from his pocket along with a pencil—presumably to take notes—but had never applied pencil to paper.

"I should like to know about the murder weapon," she said. "The knife—or was it a letter opener? I couldn't tell, and I certainly didn't think it would be quite the thing to pull it from his chest. If it was a letter opener, that might suggest the killer hadn't actually *planned* to do away with Mr. Tripley, and that he used a convenient weapon at hand. The cord around his neck, after all, was from the curtains. They were drawn, of course, but the tie-back was still hanging from its hook."

"It was a letter opener that belonged to Mr. Tripley," replied the inspector, then his eyes bugged wide as if he'd realized he'd spoken. "I am supposed to be asking the questions, Lady Darling."

"But you asked me if there was anything else," she replied, giving him a wide-eyed, innocent stare.

"I meant if there was anything else you wanted to add to your statement," he said, still looking a bit out of sorts.

"Oh, yes, of course. No, I don't think so." She folded her hands in her lap and smiled benignly. "Now, Inspector Burgess, if there *isn't* anything else, I really must ask you to leave. I have a number of things to do this afternoon and you have quite put me off my schedule." The formidable marchioness had appeared.

He rose and was in the process of putting his hat back in place when he froze. "Wait one minute, there, Lady Darling. Blimey! *That's* how I know you." His eyes narrowed suspiciously. "You were there some years ago at the Enfield Ball—the night Lord Milbright fell off a balcony and died."

It took all of Irene's firm motherly skills to get rid of her daughters after the inspector's unnecessary reminder that, yes, Irene had in fact been present when Lord Milbright had fallen to his death in the middle of the Enfield Ball four years ago.

After all, it wasn't a *secret*. She rolled her eyes mentally (because if she actually did it in front of Rose, she'd earn another gentle reprimand from her ever-so-proper daughter) over the silliness of dragging up something that had happened years ago.

Not only had Irene been present when the horrible incident occurred, but she had been in the midst of a most voluble and scandalous altercation with Lady Enfield herself, on the very balcony from which Lord Milbright fell. Their contretemps had been dramatic and loud, and all eyes had been drawn to the two women...until Lord Milbright's tragic tumble from the balcony shocked everyone into stunned silence.

Before she shooed them off to go home, Rose, Violet, and Jane had all pleaded with Irene to reconsider and avoid the Enfield Ball. They'd even offered to eschew the event themselves in a show of solidarity with her—a great sacrifice in particular for Violet, who was known for her exquisite taste in fashionable attire and had, as usual, a most stunning gown prepared for the evening.

"But, Mother, don't you think it would be in poor taste to attend in light of what happened last night?" Rose said earnestly.

"Whyever would it? *I* didn't murder Mr. Tripley last night, and as I am determined to help discover who did, I see no reason to hide myself at home. Doing so," Irene added in a slightly louder and firmer tone meant to subjugate any further arguments, "would only add fuel to the fire. Now, I thank you very much for your unnecessary, and I daresay, unwanted entreaties about my social life, but I must be on my way myself. I have to leave for a—er—a fitting with Monsieur Claude for the event in question." She decided at the last minute not to remind the girls that she'd been about to leave earlier in order to commence with her investigation into the Tripley Murder.

It had been mildly surprising that Priscilla had not found her way downstairs whilst the girls were visiting, but Irene was rather relieved she had not.

Not only did she not want or need a *fourth* young, inexperienced, and presumably well-meaning woman to attempt to convince her not to attend the ball, but she'd also appreciated having her girls to herself without any outsiders putting a damper on their interactions and her request that they help her in the detection process.

The visit had also given Irene the opportunity to reassure herself that, yes, all three of them were happy and healthy...and perhaps at least one of them was in the process of making her a grandmother. Violet loved lemon flavor, and the fact that she'd discarded a biscuit of that flavor was an interesting occurrence.

Not that Irene was *that* eagerly anticipating such a daunting milestone as becoming a grandmother. She'd always felt that grannies were the sort who were frail and rickety or plump and vague, fluttery and hesitant—or any combination thereof—and she certainly was none of those. Grannies were meant to sit at home in the parlor with an ear trumpet, repeating, "Eh, what was that, dearie?" and occasionally dandling a babe on her knee.

But she would face that eventuality—becoming a grand-mother—with as much fortitude and grace as she'd faced every other obligation and development that had come her way.

Having finally ushered her offspring out the door and had Josephs order her carriage, Irene looked at the clock. Drat it all! It was getting rather late to call on the Feverley household, which was where she'd intended to go first since she knew the family well. She fumed for a moment, thought about going anyway, then decided—why not?

She was the bloody Marchioness of Darling. She would be received.

Besides, Irene had a suspicion that today's calling hour might be going long in light of last night's tragedy. There would be ever so much to talk about.

She carefully placed the red hat with the tiny tinkling bells that had so dismayed Violet, pinning it atop her silver-threaded hair. She thought it looked quite fetching—and fun, despite her daughter's comments. Then she considered whether to tuck Beatrice into the small reticule she often took on calls, but decided it was best to leave her home today. The little beast had already had enough excitement—and biscuits.

Besides, invariably when she took Beatrice on a social call, two things happened: first, everyone crowded around and cooed over the sweet darling, which made it difficult to extricate oneself from a conversation or make an exit when one needed to; and two, the greedy little thing always managed to snarf up too many treats far too quickly for her little tummy. Then she vomited everything up in the carriage on the way home.

When Irene alighted from her conveyance in front of the Feverley household, she discovered she had been correct in her prediction that social calling hour had gone long, for there were several carriages parked along the street, with drivers obviously waiting for their tardy passengers.

The butler appeared slightly panicked when he opened the door to yet another visitor, but Irene merely smiled and breezed in. It wasn't necessary to hand him her calling card; he knew who she was, and if he didn't, the coat of arms painted on the carriage door would have told him. She didn't pause and he had to hustle in order to reach the parlor door in time to open it for her.

"Lady Darling," he announced.

A little ripple of murmuring swept the room as every person in the place stood, the women bowing their heads gracefully, then sitting once more. The gentlemen remained standing, each giving a slight bow as well.

As marchionesses did not apologize for arriving late—or ever —Irene merely nodded to the room at large, then, with a warm smile, she went directly to Mrs. Feverley, whom she knew quite well, and took both her hands in a warm greeting. Miss Nanette Feverley, who was sitting next to her mother, rose to offer her seat to Irene.

"I'm so sorry about all of this, Caroline," Irene said, sincerity in her voice and gaze as she sat. "It was such a terrible, unex-pected tragedy to happen last night, and I only wanted to make certain your dear Matthew wasn't suffering any indignities over it all. As I well know, those Scotland Yard inspectors can be quite unpleasant when they have a bone in their teeth."

"Quite," replied Mrs. Feverley, squeezing Irene's hands in acknowledgment. Her smile wavered a little. "You speak from experience, of course. An inspector has come by and he did speak to Matthew. He was quite civil about it all, but one does worry about one's children."

"Quite," Irene replied with great feeling. "But of course Matthew has nothing to worry about at all."

"Certainly not," replied Caroline Feverley. Even so, her attention strayed to her son, who stood at one side of the room, speaking with two other gentlemen.

Irene understood her friend's concern. Matthew Feverley, although extremely civil and pleasant, always seemed to be standing at the outskirts of every event. If a man could be considered a wallflower, he would qualify. He rarely attended balls or fêtes or dinner parties, and despite his mother's prodding, had, to date, shown not the least bit of interest in courting a wife. He was nearly thirty, several years older than Irene's Edward, and past time to marry. In fact, knowing his lack of desire to socialize (something with which she empathized), Irene had been mildly surprised when she learned he was to be in attendance at the Tripleys' last night.

"Do you have any idea how this could have happened? Or why? Poor, dear Trudy," said Caroline. "It's simply ghastly—all of this! I sent over a note, of course, and some flowers, and will call as soon as is proper, but I'm certain it will be quite some time before she's receiving. I cannot imagine what she's going through. To have her husband *murdered* in their own home!"

"It must have been some sort of vagrant or thief who broke in, looking for valuables," she went on with an edge of desperation. "I'm so grateful Matthew wasn't in the wrong place at the wrong time." She shuddered. "What if *he'd* been the one who came upon the thief?"

"Lady Darling, would you care for some tea?" asked the elder Feverley daughter, who had become Mrs. Inkstead a year ago. She was a particular friend of Rose's.

"Oh, no thank you, Mandy, dear," Irene replied, holding up a hand to stay her from pouring. "I shan't stay long—and I know it's getting late." She rose, waving Amanda Inkstead to remain seated when she would have stood as well. "I only just wanted to call and express my sympathies for the difficulty last night, and to give my best to your brother. And I shall do that as I leave. Do take care of yourself, Caroline, and please send for me if there is anything I can do."

Having done her duty, Irene made her way swiftly but without obvious hurry to Mr. Feverley, who'd caught her eye briefly when she sat with his mother.

"Lady Darling, how good of you to call today," he said, executing a neat bow. He wasn't a particularly handsome man, but he was far from homely. His features—chin, cheeks, face— were narrow except for a nose with a round, bulbous tip. He had intelligent eyes of a vibrant blue and a neatly trimmed golden-brown mustache that nicely balanced a head of thick hair. "May I make known to you Mr. Stevenson and Mr. Philpott."

Although she'd never officially met them, Irene knew both of the young men by sight. She greeted them briefly then said in an imperious voice, "Mr. Feverley, I require a moment of your time, if you please."

"Of course, my lady. Gentlemen, please excuse us." There was a glint of understanding in Matthew Feverley's eyes as he took her arm to gently lead her away. "I say, it was very kind of you to come and comfort my mother, Lady Darling."

Irene cast him a sidewise smile. She always appreciated a

sly, subtle wit. He knew very well she was there to speak with him.

"Your dear mother is quite overset by the thought that you might have been the victim of last night's tragedy, accidentally coming upon a thief rummaging for valuables in Mr. Tripley's study. Which as you must know is nonsense. Harold Tripley was killed by someone who knew him—one of the very people who sat at dinner with us last night. Specifically, one of the five men who joined him in the billiard room after dinner."

"And you are certain of that, Lady Darling?"

"I've no doubt in my mind. Which is why I came with the intention of speaking to you. I am working under the assumption that *you* did not wield the small blade that took Harold Tripley's life—but, I assure you, if you did, I will not only be heart-broken for your mother's sake but also quite annoyed with myself for completely misjudging your character. After all, I have known you since you were in leading strings, Matthew Feverley."

He chuckled. "Far be it from me to be the cause of Yyour Esteemed Ladyship's self-recriminations. I assure you, my lady, I did not take Mr. Tripley's life. And, to be frank, I am delighted to have the opportunity to speak with someone about the incident who is of the same mindset as my own."

"Quite. Now, tell me, who left the billiard room other than Mr. Tripley."

"That, my lady, is impossible. You see, everyone left the billiard room at one point. Even myself."

Irene was not happy with this information and she fixed a glare on the young man to prove it. "You're saying *everyone* left the room. What about Harold Tripley? When did he leave? Good Heavens. This is going to be more complicated than I had expected." She frowned, then decided that even Sherlock Holmes had not solved all of his puzzles so quickly. Why, it had taken him several days to work out the villain and his motive in *A Study in Scarlet*.

And of course, Sherlock Holmes was a fictional character after all. One couldn't truly compare oneself to a figment of an imagination, could they?

"Mr. Tripley never came into the billiard room," Mr. Feverley replied. "You see, we were in the corridor just making our way there when he told us to go on and settle in, that there were cigars and whisky and brandy, and that he would be along in a few moments."

"And he never came back," Irene said thoughtfully. "Did he say what was keeping him?"

"No. Only that he had something he needed to attend to; something that couldn't wait any longer. Thought it was odd at the time to have business—suppose I got the impression it was business—that would take him away from a dinner party he was hosting, but what was a chap to say?"

"Quite so." She pursed her lips thoughtfully. "Can you remember the order in which everyone left the room, and whether two or more were gone at the same time? Did each person return to the room? What excuses did they give for leaving?"

Mr. Feverley gave a little laugh. "I say, Lady Darling, you are more insistent—and thorough—than that Inspector Burgess. In point of fact, I have been trying since last night to remember who left and when, and I'm afraid I can't really be certain. I was playing billiards with Bentley-Bodham for a time, and then I had another game with Chessley. Garington opened the doors and stepped onto the balcony terrace to smoke a cigar. Shaw left to freshen up but was back rather quickly, as I recollect, but he went out on the balcony to smoke as well. Chessley...I do remember him leaving, but he did come back a bit later and he took it upon himself to play host and refill our glasses. After our game, Bentley-Bodham went to get a business card or something from out of his coat pocket, for Garington I believe..." He shook his head. "I simply wasn't paying attention. It wasn't as if we were sitting around playing a hand of whist or bridge and you'd notice when a chap was gone."

"That is not terribly helpful," Irene grumbled. "You're certain everyone left and everyone came back? And then what happened? Certainly you were all expecting Mr. Tripley to return."

"Quite so. And when he didn't, and the clock was striking half-nine, we decided he must have gotten caught up in whatever business that called him away and lost track of time. And so we came to the study."

"Where we were all waiting," Irene said. "But Harold Tripley was already dead. And the killer had done the deed then came back and joined you all in the billiard room. You say you never saw Mr. Tripley alive again after he left, but I wonder if any of the others did—besides the killer, I mean to say."

"Please forgive the impertinence of me asking, Lady Darling, but why are you so interested in the details of this terrible event?"

"I was there, of course. And I was the one who noticed that he was dead, after all. Someone intelligent and capable must be responsible for finding the villain who did such a thing. I am the most intelligent and capable person I know—and I have little else to occupy my time—so why shouldn't it be me?"

Chapter Six

Mr. Feverley gave a short laugh. "Why shouldn't it, indeed. I can think of a number of reasons, my lady, but I suspect you'll hear none of them."

"Quite right," Irene replied crisply. "Now, one last question, and then I must be on my way. Can you think of any reason someone would have wanted Mr. Tripley dead?"

"Another thing I have been racking my brain over since last night, and no, I cannot. He seemed a nice enough chap; didn't know him that well but never saw an uncivil word pass his lips."

"That begs another question, now you mention it, Mr. Feverley. Why *were* you at the dinner last night? I know how much you abhor social events, and if you didn't know the Tripleys very well..."

"Oh, it's very simple: my mother insisted. I do believe she actually wrangled the invitation for me. She knew there would be several eligible women present, and she thought I would be more inclined to find my future bride during a quieter, smaller social engagement than something like the Enfield ball." His eyes danced with mischief, but behind that lightheartedness, Irene thought she saw something else. A bleakness, perhaps.

"I can attest that mothers do tend to be creative in their endeavors to marry off their children," was all she said. "Very well, Mr. Feverley. Thank you for your information, as thin and negligible as it was. I must take my leave."

"My lady," he said with a little bow.

"Ah, one more thing," she said, turning back to him.

"Yes?"

"Does Mr. Bentley-Bodham cheat at billiards like he does at cards?"

Mr. Feverley gusted out a short laugh. "Not if his opponent is good enough to run the table in two turns." He winked and Irene smiled back at him, then once more excused herself.

She escaped from the parlor without being stopped by anyone else—a small miracle, really, considering the fact that everyone in the room must have known she had not only been present at the Tripley dinner party, but that she'd been the one to notice Harold Tripley was dead.

Barth had, as instructed, remained parked as close to the front of the Feverley home as possible. A footman dashed out to direct him forward. Moments later, with the help of her own tiger, Benny, who rode on the back of the vehicle, Irene climbed in and was ensconced in the carriage with nothing but her thoughts.

She wanted to speak to the other four gentlemen who were suspects, but it was definitely after social call time and she couldn't very well hunt them down at their clubs. (She actually considered doing so for far longer than she should have done, but in the end decided the uproar of a woman—even a marchioness...or perhaps *especially* a marchioness—breaching the sanctuary of a men's club like Brooks's would only make matters worse.)

Instead, she reluctantly settled on her second choice, which was a return to Monsieur Claude's. Despite what she'd told her daughters, the gown she was wearing to the Enfield ball was already hanging in her dressing room. However, she did have other reasons to speak with her modiste. Even if he was busy or had appointments—which was extremely unlikely at this late time of day—he would be glad to see her.

When she arrived on Bond Street, there was a large, sleek, black brougham pulled up in front of Monsieur Claude's. Irene couldn't help but notice that it boasted no coat of arms or identifying factors. It was far too expensive and elegant to be any sort of for-hire conveyance.

She eyed it curiously as Benny helped her down from the carriage, then turned her attention to more important things, such as murder.

Despite the CLOSED sign in the window, she rang the bell at Monsieur Claude's door because she saw his figure inside. He was always delighted to see her, even without an appointment (which she did not have). Although she couldn't hear anything through the glass, she saw him whirl around, jolt with surprise when he recognized her, and then whirl back, facing into the depths of the shop.

One of Irene's eyebrows rose and she felt that strange prickling on the top of her scalp. She stood at the door, contemplating her next move. A marchioness did not ring twice, nor did she stand there, waiting, like a maidservant, to be admitted.

Luckily, before she had to make a decision, Monsieur Claude hurried to the door and eased it open. "Lady Darling, what an unexpected delight," he said, hardly imbuing any bit of sincerity in his tone.

"I should like to come in, Claude," she said crisply. "And I do not think it would do either of us any good for me to continue standing here on the street."

"But of course, my dear lady!" he cried and jumped back, dangling measuring tapes fluttering about his person. The door swung wide and Irene strolled in. The small train of her skirt had barely crossed the threshold when the door slammed closed behind her.

The only person she saw inside other than Monsieur Claude was a comely young woman of perhaps twenty, quite fragile in appearance. She bore a lovely, milk-white complexion, delicate features, and silvery blond hair. Her eyes were pale blue and fringed with blonde lashes that all but disappeared. The appearance of fragility didn't come from the suggestion of illness or poor health, but from the moonlight hair, fair skin, and slight build that made her seem ethereal. Her clothing indicated that she came from wealth: the fabric was excellent and expensive, the cut and fit and style were modern...and yet there was something about her that seemed...not quite as she appeared.

Irene stood expectantly, waiting for Monsieur Claude to make introductions. He was quite obviously utterly discombobulated, for his broad mustache fluttered and shivered, and his long, slender fingers twisted around themselves. A few dots of perspiration had appeared at the edge of his thinning hairline.

Irene lifted a brow at him and cleared her throat gently.

Monsieur Claude jumped as if he'd been poked by an andiron. "L-lady Darling, may I present M-miss...um...M-miss..."

"Adina Trewlove," said the young woman when he didn't appear to be able to emit the syllables. The young woman dropped into a proper curtsy, rising gracefully.

Irene inclined her head in acknowledgement even as questions darted through her mind. Her body might not be as agile and coordinated as it once was, but her mind was as facile as ever.

Why on earth was Monsieur Claude acting so strangely about this young woman—who, by all indications, seemed to be here without a chaperone or maid? Hmm.

The fact that Irene wasn't familiar with the young woman's name caused another niggle of interest. She, of course, knew of everyone in the London peerage by their family pedigree and surname. Not because Irene cared all that much about status—unless she could use it to her advantage in accomplishing things like solving a murder or marrying off a daughter (a woman must use any and all tools available to her because she was at a disadvantage simply being female)—but because she simply needed to know.

"Miss Trewlove," she said. "I must congratulate you on making an excellent choice in modiste. I presume that is why you're here?" She gestured to the bolts of fabric lying on the table—taffetas and silks, satins and light wool, all in colors that would suit Miss Trewlove perfectly.

"Yes, my lady." She gave her nerves away with a quick dart of her eyes toward the depths of the back room. "Monsieur Claude has been very kind."

"You are in excellent hands with the monsieur." Irene turned her attention to the gentleman in question. A few more dots of perspiration had appeared on his forehead, but his mustache had settled into place. "Monsieur, if I am interrupting...."

She let the statement dangle unfinished, for everyone in the room knew that the Marchioness of Darling didn't give a hoot about interrupting, and even if she *was* interrupting, she *wasn't*.

"Ah, no, no, no, madame, my lady," gushed Monsieur Claude. "Miss Trewlove and I, we were just finishing her appointment."

"That's your very elegant brougham out front, then?" Irene asked. She suddenly felt as if she'd stumbled upon another mystery—this one far more benign than murder, but still one that intrigued her.

"Yes, my lady," replied Miss Trewlove with another little curtsy. "Well, I mean to say, it's not *mine*, but—"

Monsieur Claude erupted in a fit of coughing, and to Irene's surprise, he fixed a desperate, pleading gaze upon her that clearly requested she not ask any further questions.

Of course that meant Irene wanted nothing more than to ask further questions, but she stifled that urge. For the moment.

"Perhaps I shall simply wander into the back room and look over some of the special fabrics I know you keep back there, monsieur, whilst you are finishing Miss Trewlove's appointment."

Monsieur Claude looked as if he were about to faint. "In the back room? M-my lady, I—it would be...I mean to say—"

She allowed him to fumble for a few more seconds, then, taking pity on the man—who really was a good friend, and who'd just confirmed her suspicions that someone was, in fact, hiding in the back room—said: "Good Heavens, I've just noticed the time! It seems I cannot stay after all, Monsieur Claude. I do hope you'll forgive me...I can't imagine where my brain has gone off. That does happen when one is of such an advanced age as I, you know. I've another engagement at this very moment and I shall be late." She gave him a pointed look that said, *I shall be collecting on this favor very soon, and you know very well my age is not that advanced*, then swept toward the front door.

"Oh, yes, yes, of course, my lady," he stammered, rushing to the door to open it for her. "*Merci, merci*, madame," he said in a low huff as she continued on her way past him.

She cast him another meaningful look, and heard the door rattle closed behind.

Instead of moving to her own carriage, where Benny and Barth waited patiently, she approached the sleek black brougham.

"Hello, good sir," she said, the tiny bells on her hat tinkling quietly as she looked up at the driver.

He sat in his place high above the horses he managed, whip safely tucked away, a cap on his head. The man wore no recognizable livery; instead, his uniform was a well-cut coat and trousers of black with black braid trim.

"What a fine carriage this is. I don't believe I've ever seen such an elegant and comfortable conveyance."

"Aye, 'tis, ma'am," replied the driver, tipping his hat slightly. "I never drove anything nicer meself."

"Quite," she said, ignoring his incorrect address. "Whose conveyance is this? I should very much like to speak with the person with the taste" —not to mention the funds— "to acquire such a vehicle. I'm after a new one myself, you see."

"Aye, ma'am, why that'd be Mister—"

Just then, the door of Monsieur Claude's shop opened. Miss Trewlove trotted out, and she was accompanied by a figure that could only be a male person. He was tall and quick and rather large, enveloped in a swirling black cloak with a high collar that obscured all but the hint of a sharp-bridged nose, and a top hat that rode unfashionably low over his face, shielding his eyes. With his gloved hand, he held a mahogany cane topped with a heavy metal knob.

He swirled past Irene, gesturing for Miss Trewlove to climb into the carriage. He followed the young woman inside so quickly Irene could hardly attest to the fact that he'd been there.

The door closed smartly after the two, and the carriage immediately lurched off into the street. Hardly before she realized it, Irene was standing on the sidewalk alone, blinking in astonishment. Fortunately, it was so late in the day that it was unlikely anyone she knew would be visiting Bond Street at this hour.

"Madame! Lady Darling!"

She turned at the hissed sound from behind. Monsieur Claude stood in the half-open door of his shop, beckoning wildly to her.

She leveled a look at him that suggested he had a great amount of explaining to do, then said to Benny and Barth, who were watching with all the alertness of excellent servants, "Did you speak to the driver of that brougham?"

"No, my lady," they chorused.

She resisted the urge to grimace with frustration. The one instance when she would have wanted her servants to while away their time gossiping whilst waiting for her, and they didn't have the temerity to do so. "Very well, then. I shall be another bit of while."

She turned and marched to the open door of Monsieur Claude's and swept inside without pause, nearly running the poor man down. She privately lamented that she had given up carrying a walking stick after the Enfield Ball incident; they made such a peremptory, arresting noise when she thumped it on the floor—as well as being excellent for expressing irritation or displeasure.

"Oh, Lady Darling, please, please forgive me," Monsieur Claude implored. His mustache drooped, matching his hangdog expression.

"Who was that?" she asked without preamble.

"M-Miss T-Trewlove—"

"*That man,*" she snapped. "Who was the man hiding in your back room when I came in here?"

"Ah, Lady Darling, please, please, I beg of you, don't make me tell you. Madame, you must know I adore you above all of my clients. It is your patronage that has made my establishment the success that it is. You know there is no other woman who has my heart besides you" —she scoffed loudly and in a very unladylike manner— "but I cannot, I *cannot,* speak about it."

She gave him a good look. He was earnest and truthful, and perhaps even petrified.

She relented a trifle. "I am more concerned about whether that young woman is safe with that man. She climbed into the carriage with him—*alone*. At least as far as I could tell. There might have been a maid inside, but if there had been, why on earth wasn't she in here with her mistress? *Well?*"

Monsieur Claude gulped audibly, his Adam's apple plunging then rising just as quickly. "Miss Trewlove was w-with her u-uncle, my lady."

Irene sniffed, eyeing him carefully. "And who is her uncle?"

"He is very gentle with her, my lady. And—what is the word?—*deferent*, *oui*, that is it—to her as well. She has nothing to fear from him, I am confident, and in fact, she gave no such indication that she was." He said these words in a rush, clearly fully aware that he was avoiding her question. "If anything, it seemed as if she was—er—making the decisions."

"You do realize that your reticence only spurs me on to discover just who this man is, don't you, monsieur?"

"*D'accord*," he replied sadly.

She eyed him for another moment, then turned her attention to the real reason she'd come. "Did you hear about Harold Tripley?"

"Oh, yes, my lady, I did," he replied, relief coloring his voice at the change of subject. His grand mustache, which had been drooping with nerves, straightened, along with his shoulders. "You were there, I understand?"

"Quite. It was a horrifying moment, to be sure, when he was discovered with a *blade* sticking out of his chest! And of course, I was surrounded by a gaggle of squawking geese and shrieking fools during it all. Why, if I hadn't been there, the entire scene would have been trampled and any clue that might have been left behind, destroyed. Although it is Inspector Burgess who's on the case," she added meaningfully, "so I'm doubtful he'll appreciate the care I took."

Monsieur Claude's brows lifted and his mustache twitched. "I see your concern, madame."

"Quite right." Irene realized she was still standing and lowered herself into a nearby chair. "For that reason—and others—I've decided to inquire after the killer myself."

Monsieur Claude's eyes widened in surprise, then a little glint of interest lit them as he smiled broadly. "But madame, that is most *wonderful!* What an *excellent* idea. I can think of no one better to detect and investigate a murder than the woman who inspired Mr. Holmes's nemesis."

Irene smiled. "You are the first person to react in such a manner—although, to be fair, you are likely the only person in the world—aside from myself and Mr. Conan Doyle, of course—who is aware that yours truly was the, ah...inspiration for that character."

She gave a little huff of irritation. "Every other person I've spoken to about my intentions has acted as if I've announced I'm about to take a balloon ride to the moon or ride astride through Regents Park or something equally absurd. Although I suppose *you* might simply be flattering me in order to keep me distracted from asking you any difficult questions, hmm, Claude?"

"Not at all, madame, not at *all*," he replied with great earnestness.

"Very well, then. I shall expect your assistance in the matter," she went on.

"You shall have it, of course, madame. Unreservedly."

"*Très bien*," she replied. "Now, I have four—well, five—suspects," Irene said, and enumerated them all: Mr. Matthew Feverley, Mr. Chessley, Lord Garington, Mr. Bentley-Bodham, and Mr. Harry Shaw.

Because Monsieur Claude, for all of his flattery and fripperies and fussing, was a very intelligent man, he did not need to be led through the process. He immediately understood that she was asking him to gather any pertinent information from any of the clients who came into his shop and gossiped—a prospect which happened constantly due to the fact that Tatiana and Monique spoke only French in the presence of the customers, which led them to believe, falsely, that the seamstresses didn't speak English.

As Irene was well aware, people—particularly of the aristocracy, who were always surrounded by servants and the like—had little regard for what they said and did in the presence of those in service or trade. Monsieur Claude and his assistants likely overheard far more gossip than even Irene imagined, for women tended to chitter-chatter and exchange confidences when they got together, especially while in the process of shopping.

"You see," Irene said after describing in detail what had happened last evening, "I don't yet have any idea why someone would want to do away with Harold Tripley. He seems—seemed, rather—boring and straight-laced; risk-averse and very conservative in action and belief. But *someone* had a reason to kill him. And it's my hope that *someone else* knows what that reason is—they know something about him, or about his relationship with one of those gentlemen at the dinner.

"I'm quite certain the killer decided *during the dinner party* to murder him—it was not premeditated or planned. He used the letter opener that was on Harold Tripley's desk. So something had to have happened at Tripley House to cause the villain to decide it was worth taking the chance of being discovered."

"*Bien,*" said monsieur, nodding. "Of course, the men, they do not often step over my threshold into this domain—"

"But it is the women who gossip," Irene reminded him. "Besides, I have Josephs and Vella on the job as well. The servants all talk, and they know everyone in service because everyone in service is always looking to get a job in one of the Darling households." She grinned wickedly.

"But of course they are," replied Monsieur Claude. Then the dancing light in his eyes faded a little. "But, madame, as much as I find your intentions laudable, I must implore you to be careful as well. Killers do not appreciate being unmasked."

Unconcerned, Irene flapped a hand. "No one will give me a second thought, dear Claude. To all of London society—or most of it anyway—I'm either a doddering old woman or a strange and off-putting harpy. But rest assured, I shall be very careful as I go about my business. I have no intention of being the villain's next victim."

She chuckled as she rose from her chair. "Now, Monsieur Claude, I shall be on my way, leaving you with these last words which I have so often longed to say: *the game is afoot!*"

Chapter Seven

Vella had been Irene Whitney's friend long before she married Ronald Josephs and Irene became the Marchioness of Darling.

In fact, they met nearly forty years ago when one of Captain Whitney's ships had docked at the wharf in Istanbul.

Back then, Irene had dressed in clothing that suited a life at sea—loose trousers, a fluttering tunic, and sturdy, soft-soled shoes excellent for climbing ropes to the crow's nest. If not for the two long braids Irene wore pinned in a knot at the back of her head, Vella might have mistaken the brown-tanned girl for a young sailor boy when they nearly collided on the busy street near the wharf.

That moment—a random event of inattention—changed both of their lives.

Vella had been unwillingly betrothed to a man chosen by her tyrant father, and she was looking for a way to escape that future. Passage on a ship—whether by legitimate means or by guile—had seemed to her the safest way to put a great distance between herself and her intended groom. She sneaked out of the house to loiter around the docks whenever possible, looking for a way to put that half-formed, impossible plan into action.

Encountering Irene Whitney, daughter of the incomprehensibly successful sea captain and shipping magnate Theodore Whitney, turned out to be the best stroke of luck Vella could have asked for.

This was true for Irene as well, as she'd told her friend countless times over the years. The two young girls—aged twelve and thirteen—were immediately intrigued by the other. Confidences were shared, plots were developed, and two days after meeting Irene, Vella sailed away from Istanbul on the *Sea Empress*, commencing a different life with her new friend, who was delighted to have another female on the ship.

Despite their fast and deep friendship, Vella never imagined she would spend the next thirty-some years as the confidante and companion of the girl who would become the formidable and notorious Lady Darling...but she never regretted a moment of it.

"You are simply the only person in the world I can trust implicitly," Irene told her when she'd had to come to live permanently in London, after many years traveling the world with her father. "And my greatest hope is that you can say the same for me."

Vella could, and did, and that was why she was currently alighting from a hansom cab at the side door of the Tripley household. She possessed an ulterior motive along with the towel-swathed apple cake she carried.

Vella rang the bell at the servants' entrance. As she waited for someone to answer, she peeked through a tangle of climbing rose canes laden with fragrant, creamy white blooms, peering into the walled garden behind the house. It was just as Irene had described: closed off with only the small gate, locked, leading to the very mews in which Vella now stood. She peeked a little more and located the hook on the wall of the house, where the key to the gate should have been hanging...but was not.

The door opened.

"Oh, Mrs. Josephs!" One of the kitchen maids recognized her, and it took Vella a moment to remember her name.

"Susie," she said. "I'm so very sorry about Mr. Tripley. I don't mean to intrude, but I was hoping to speak to Mrs. Cane-field, to offer my condolences." Vella gestured with the towel-covered dish.

She well knew that downstairs folk often grieved just as much as their employers did when someone died or became sick or injured, but more often than not, those emotions were required to be set aside in order that they continue serving the family of the house.

"I've brought an apple cake," said Vella. "I'm certain everyone would rather not be thinking about cooking right now, and there must be something to offer the guests, or for the staff to enjoy."

"Oh, come in, Mrs. Josephs," said Susie, fighting back tears. "Only, it's just awful, it is, what's happened. I just can't stop crying, I can't. Poor Mr. Tripley!"

"I know," said Vella, putting an arm around the girl and hugging her close while balancing the cake in her other hand. "It's just about the worst thing that *can* happen, isn't it?"

"It really is!" Susie burst into full-blown sobs. "Only, now we're all just *scared to death* that we're going to be murdered in our beds! Even way upstairs in the attic can't keep a mad killer away, can it?"

"There, there, *canim*," said Vella, maneuvering the girl and herself into the back hall. She pushed the door closed behind them with her boot. "I don't think anyone would take it upon themselves to climb four flights of narrow stairs just to do away with a person who's never done a thing to harm them, would they?"

Susie gave a choked laugh that ended on a sob. "No, I don't think so, Mrs. Josephs. Mrs. Canefield is in the kitchen with Mrs. Newton. They've been busy making do for all the visitors, they have, and only now they can finally sit down."

"I suspected as much," Vella said kindly. "Do you want to take this apple cake to the servants' dining room, then? It would be very nice with a bit of tea, and all of the downstairs people have to eat too, don't they?"

Susie sniffled and looked at the towel wrappings with interest. "Yes, Mrs. Josephs, and it smells very good."

Vella relinquished the cake to the maid and continued to the kitchen to find the housekeeper, whom she knew fairly well.

"Anne," said Vella when she arrived at the doorway and saw her friend sitting at the small worktable with Mrs. Newton, the cook.

"Oh, Vella!" Mrs. Canefield, the Tripleys' housekeeper, rose from her chair. "I'm so glad you've come. How nice of you."

"I'm so terribly sorry about Mr. Tripley," said Vella, embracing the other woman. "I know it was rather awkward last night, with Lady Darling being here, but I simply had to come and express my condolences. I've given Susie an apple cake from Mrs. Mittens at the dowager house, and I told her to put it in the downstairs dining room."

"That's so very kind of you, Vella," replied Mrs. Canefield. She was a tall, angular woman with a head of thick, dark hair and an efficient if retiring manner. Her pointy nose was tipped red but her eyes were dry. Still, she crumpled a lacy handkerchief in her fist. "It's been a day, hasn't it, Mrs. Newton?"

"Don't know *why* the master had to go'n get himself killt like that," said the cook, wiping her streaming eyes and nose with a large handkerchief. "He never hurt nobody. Never bothered no one."

"Who could have done such a terrible thing?" asked Vella, sitting in the chair Mrs. Canefield pulled out for her.

"And *here*, right in the house while we were all just sitting ducks!" cried Mrs. Newton, wringing her hands with the hand-kerchief. Her nose was bright red and shiny. "Why, he could have come right here in the kitchen and slaughtered us all like hogs!"

"It had to be someone—oh, someone who just came in. Sneaked in through one of the doors or windows. A thief or a vagrant," said Mrs. Canefield. But Vella knew by looking at her expression that even the housekeeper didn't believe that.

"Lady Darling is quite certain it was one of the gentlemen at dinner last night," Vella said.

"Lady Darling? Why—why how would she know? Why does she think such a thing?" replied Mrs. Canefield cautiously. "How could that be?"

Vella briefly explained all of the details Irene had given her and Ronald over several draughts of whisky—and, in her husband's case, a cigar—last night. They'd discussed theories and gone over deductions until well into the morning hours. "I noticed the key for the mews gate is missing," she said. "Doesn't it usually hang on the outside wall by the back door?"

"O' course it's gone!" cried Mrs. Newton, who, it seemed, was unable to express any words without them being forcefully ejaculated. "We can't be having *murderers* just letting them-selves inna the house, can we now?"

Mrs. Canefield exchanged looks with Vella. "Mrs. Tripley insisted the key be taken down and put away so no one could get it," was all she said. "The poor thing. She's overcome and confused—and I'm certain she didn't really mean what she said to Lady Darling last night. She was very out of sorts."

"Not at all," replied Vella with a wave of her hand. "Lady Darling doesn't think a thing of it. She'll call as soon as she's certain Mrs. Tripley is feeling up to receiving. But that's why she's so determined to find out who did such a horrible thing. But who? Who would have it in for Mr. Tripley?" She looked at Mrs. Canefield, holding her gaze meaningfully. "Someone must have some idea."

The downstairs folk were never supposed to gossip about anything that went on inside the house where they worked. The family's privacy was of utmost importance, and an excellent, responsible servant knew that maintaining the privacy of what went on behind the walls and doors of their employer's home was a requirement for keeping their job.

However.

Every downstairs person knew things, saw things, heard things...whether they wanted to or not. It wasn't necessary to listen at keyholes or to linger outside a closed door to know what was going on behind it. The upstairs people simply forgot or ignored that their servants were around, and they did and said all manner of things with no regard for privacy.

Servants knew everything.

But getting loyal ones to talk about it was another matter.

Still. Vella was, by all outward appearances, a servant herself—albeit a high-ranking one—and it was far more common for gossip to pass between those in service than, for example, with a member of Scotland Yard. After all, how else would a person know whether they wanted to work in a certain household or not? They talked among themselves, the servants did.

"Why, I have no idea who would have wanted to hurt Mr. Tripley. He was very enthusiastic about the dinner party last night, and he was puffed up like a pigeon to show off the portrait of the mistress," said Mrs. Canefield with a sad little smile. "It's still swathed with the curtain. No one had the heart to uncover it."

"Had Mr. Tripley been acting different at all lately? Anxious? Nervy?"

"No...not at all. As I said, he was very proud of Mrs. Tripley's portrait, and he seemed in good spirits yesterday." Mrs. Canefield glanced at Mrs. Newton, who'd been gawping intently between them during their conversation. "Mrs. Newton, I do believe there is a roast that should be going in the oven. And the sausage pies?"

The cook started a little as attention turned abruptly to her. "Oh, quite right, of course, Mrs. Canefield," she said, lumbering to her feet. She was, as many cooks were due to their occupation, a large, sturdy woman. "Where has that dratted Susie gone off to now, anyway?" She scowled, looking around the small kitchen as if the maid would materialize.

Mrs. Canefield rose as well. "Thank you so much for coming by, Vella. It was very kind of you to bring over the cake. I do hope Lady Darling will call soon. I should hate for the two women to be at odds." She didn't mention the fact that Lady Enfield and Lady Darling had been at odds when the scandalous event occurred four years ago at the ball, but of course the comparison was at the forefront of both their minds.

"Of course," Vella replied, hiding the frustration that she hadn't been able to get any information at all.

"I'll see you out myself," said the housekeeper. "Susie, Mrs. Newton is looking for you," she said when they encountered the sniffling maid in the back hall.

"Yes, ma'am, I'm sorry, I only—"

"Never mind, Susie." Mrs. Canefield waved the girl on toward the kitchen, then murmured to Vella, "As you can imagine, everyone is out of sorts and no one can cease sobbing." She shook her head grimly as they reached the outside door. "And the police inspector was here, asking everyone questions...the maids were all terrified. I had to sit in with each of them during their interviews."

Vella stepped outside. She beckoned for her friend to follow, giving her a pleading but firm look.

Mrs. Canefield sighed, then, looking around to see that they were alone, ducked her head and stepped over the threshold into the mews. "This is all just so very horrifying," she said, twisting her handkerchief. It was as if she knew Vella was going to pin her down, asking more questions.

But she *had* come outside...

"Lady Darling wants to help. You know she's quite capable of anything she puts her mind to," Vella said, closing the door behind them.

"She is rather terrifying, I must say," Mrs. Canefield replied with a weak smile. "But I should rather face her than that Scotland Yard man. Burgess is his name."

"Indeed. I assure you, anything you tell me will be kept in the strictest confidence, and it might help. Surely you want to find out who did that to Mr. Tripley? If nothing else, it would calm the household," Vella reminded her. It was a housekeeper's sole role to have the household run smoothly, and one couldn't pull that off if one had maids startling at the slightest sound or sobbing constantly in the corner.

Mrs. Canefield nodded, pressing her lips together.

"Did Mr. Tripley have any unexpected messages or letters or visitors over the last few days or a week? Was there anything that seemed to have upset him? Anything that seemed strange at all?"

Mrs. Canefield shook her head. "The inspector asked the same questions. And I told him no. The master was just as always: said hello if he saw one of us in the hallway, but didn't ever stop to talk or ask how the day was, or anything. Couldn't remember the staff's names ever, either—every one of them is Betty or James, no matter how long they've been here. But..." She sighed, looking up to the heavens as if to ask for guidance.

Vella clamped her lips shut, suppressing the urge to push further, and waited as her friend struggled with the decision of whether to go on and divulge something that could be considered gossip but that could also be important in bringing justice to Mr. Tripley's killer. But the fact that she had stepped outside with Vella suggested she was wavering.

Mrs. Canefield straightened her shoulders as if in resolve. "I did hear Mr. Tripley on the telephone," she said slowly. "He didn't sound very pleased."

"What did he sound like? When was this? Can you remember anything he said?" Vella couldn't keep the questions from tumbling out even though she was aware her eagerness could spook the woman into silence.

"I...well, I certainly wasn't listening," she said firmly, looking out into the garden. "And I most certainly didn't tell any of this to the inspector." She glanced at Vella meaningfully.

"Of course not. But one can't help overhearing when a person's voice gets loud or agitated, now, can they?" Vella said in an encouraging tone.

"Right." Mrs. Canefield hesitated, then, after a long moment, went on. "It's just that the master did seem agitated in a way. Very serious like. And I heard him say something like, 'I'm not waiting any longer. You've had your chance to make it right.' Then the other person said something, and Mr. Tripley got very firm, almost angry, and he said, 'It's too late, I tell you. First thing tomorrow, I'll be speaking to him'—and then I didn't hear anything more. Millie dropped the dirty mop bucket from the top of the main stairs and it fell down with such a clatter—

and a terrible mess," Mrs. Canefield said grimly. "We were getting ready for the dinner party, and then we had that to deal with."

"I can only imagine," said Vella sympathetically. "Gritty, dirty water everywhere with guests arriving soon—and, I venture to say, a maid crying about it too, hm?"

Mrs. Canefield gave a little laugh. "How well you know, Vella. Yes, poor Millie was fairly useless for thirty minutes after, and the footmen had to carry out the wet rug. It was positively *drenched*."

"Do you have any idea who Mr. Tripley was speaking to on the telephone during that exchange?" Vella asked. "Who answered the telephone when it rang?"

"I did," replied Mrs. Canefield. "That's why I was...er...in the vicinity, of course."

"Of course," replied Vella. This was very good information, but she kept the excitement from her voice. "Did the caller identify themselves?"

"No. They only asked for Mr. Tripley. But it was a man, of course," replied Mrs. Canefield.

"Of course," replied Vella. There was simply no reason a woman would be telephoning to a gentleman like Mr. Tripley. "What about his voice? Did he have an accent? What did it sound like?"

"It was a gentleman, I'm quite certain," Mrs. Canefield replied. "He sounded...you know what I mean to say...posh."

Vella nodded. "Did you recognize his voice? Could it have been one of the dinner guests from last night?"

Mrs. Canefield shook her head. "I couldn't say, Vella. I really couldn't. It was so very fast, and why should I pay attention? He said, 'Mr. Tripley if you please,' and I said, 'May tell him who it is?' and he said—and I remember this now—'Never mind who, you tell Tripley there is an important telephone call.'" She spread her hands. "He sounded annoyed and impatient."

"When you have a quiet moment, perhaps try to remember what he sounded like, and perhaps...well, if you hear that voice again, will you send word to me?" Vella gave her an imploring look.

"I—I will," replied Mrs. Canefield, but Vella wasn't confident she'd comply.

"Thank you. Now, when you were sitting in with the maids and their interviews with the police inspector, did any of them say anything important?" she asked, uncertain how much longer she'd be able to keep the other woman talking.

"You see, Lady Darling is certain one of the gentlemen had to have left the billiard room, and that was when Mr. Tripley was murdered. And so if anyone noticed one of the guests somewhere not in the billiard room between dinner and the time Mr. Tripley was found...well, it would be very helpful."

"Oh. Of course." Mrs. Canefield bit her lip nervously. "I can't quite remember. But I could ask," she added quickly, surprising Vella. "I mean to say, I could ask the maids if they saw anyone. And the footman too."

"Yes. And what about Mr. Smayle?" said Vella, referring to the butler. "Could you ask him as well?"

"Oh dear...I don't know, Vella. He's so..." She flapped her hands nervously.

"He's a butler." She gave a wry, sympathetic laugh. "I do understand—after all, I am married to one."

Mrs. Canefield smiled. "Quite. I...I don't know, Vella. I just don't know. I don't feel right, poking around and all—"

"But Mr. Tripley was murdered, here in this very house. Don't you want the killer to be caught—and soon?"

"Oh, I do. Yes. We all do." Mrs. Canefield sighed. "Yes, I suppose I could ask Mr. Smayle—but only because he does hold

Lady Darling in high esteem. Why, he has never let us forget that it was her ladyship who recommended him for the position. It wasn't long after Lord Darling passed on, and she still took the time to write him a recommendation."

"Lady Darling is a good person." Vella used this opportunity and pushed a little more. "She's trying to do right by Mr. Tripley —and Mrs. Tripley. Imagine how much better your mistress will feel once the culprit is behind bars. Perhaps I could speak to Mr. Smayle whilst I'm here."

"Oh. Oh...dear, I don't quite think..." Mrs. Canefield trailed off and heaved a sigh. "This is all so...so...*upsetting* and *disruptive*. No one seems to be able to concentrate on anything..." She sighed again. "I suppose I could speak to him, and...will you wait here, Vella?"

"Of course I will," she replied.

Vella waited, pacing about the mews, wondering whether Mr. Smayle would come out to speak to her after all—and if he did, would he even have anything important to tell her? She did have to get back to the dowager house to run her own household.

A number of minutes later—so many Vella had begun to despair that anyone would return—the door opened. To her surprise, both Mr. Smayle and Mrs. Canefield came out, and a teenaged girl dressed in a parlormaid's uniform and cap accompanied them.

"Mr. Smayle," she said. "Thank you very much for agreeing to speak to me."

"I find it very irregular, but then, murder is irregular." He delivered these lines with great pompousness as he looked out at her from beneath incredibly bushy black eyebrows. He wasn't quite sneering, but it was close. After all, Vella was only a housekeeper.

"Indeed, it is." Vella glanced curiously at Mrs. Canefield,

who was standing there quietly but with an expectant expression. "Thank you for arranging this." Vella lifted a brow in the direction of the maid, who was standing at attention as if she were a soldier being dressed down. "And who is this?"

"I'm Charlotte," replied the maid in a quiet voice.

Vella waited but nothing more was forthcoming. Mr. Smayle cleared his throat, and Mrs. Canefield murmured, "Go on, dear. Tell Mrs. Josephs what you found. This might be helpful to Lady Darling."

"Only, it was under the desk, m'um," said Charlotte, clasping her hands in front of her. Vella was uncertain what it was about herself that made the young woman so nervous; she certainly wasn't intimidating like Irene. "I found it after the— after the..." She looked at her boss and swallowed hard, then managed to go on, "after they took M-Mr. T-Tripley away. Th-this morning, it was, m'um. I was cleaning up, I was, with the carpet sweeper, there in the s-study..." She shuddered violently and seemed unable to continue.

"They took Mr. Tripley away last night, of course," Vella said, hoping to soothe the nervous girl with a practical recitation of the events, "and presumably the Scotland Yard investigator looked round the room. But you came in to clean this morning, and you found something under the desk?"

"Y-yes, m'um."

"What did you find?" Vella prompted after another hesitation.

"The carpet sweeper...it made a clinking noise, it did." Charlotte looked at Mrs. Canefield, and the housekeeper nodded in permission. The girl slid a hand into her apron pocket, then withdrew it. She opened her fist to reveal a cufflink from a man's shirt.

Vella felt a little prickle rush down her spine as Charlotte tipped the piece into her palm. The cufflink was faced with mother-of-pearl and had a tiny ruby set in the center—a rather fancy piece, to be sure. "Could this be from the killer?" she mused quietly. "Coming off during the struggle?"

"It's not from Mr. Tripley's shirt," said Mr. Smayle. "He doesn't have a set like this. I spoke with Willem, the valet, to be certain."

The prickle came back. "One must assume that this wasn't on the floor before the dinner party."

"No, m'um," said Charlotte earnestly with a glance at Mrs. Canefield, who looked on like a proud parent. "Only, I cleant the room meself, I did, and I do a good job of it, I do. It wasn't there before."

Mrs. Canefield nodded in agreement. "Charlotte is correct. She would never have missed the cufflink under the desk."

The maid straightened a little and her cheeks flushed pink with pleasure at being so publicly lauded.

"But the Scotland Yard investigator missed it," murmured Vella, still looking down at the glinting ruby. "How handy for us." She looked at Charlotte, then Mrs. Canefield and Mr. Smayle. "May I take this to Lady Darling?"

"Of course," replied Mr. Smayle. "If the inspector didn't see it, then he has no right to it."

Vella agreed wholeheartedly, and assumed Irene would as well. "Thank you. Is there anything else that might be important?"

"No. But I will question all of the maids, and Mr. Smayle has agreed to speak with the footmen to see whether anyone noticed anyone roaming the halls when they shouldn't have been." Mrs. Canefield seemed more confident in her desire to help, a fact which Vella attributed to the complicity of Mr. Smayle.

"Thank you. Of course, you can always send word to me at the dowager house," Vella said.

"Mrs. Josephs." The butler spoke just as she was about to turn away. She turned back and waited. "If you would...well, I suppose, express my gratitude—and that of the staff here—to Lady Darling for her...erm...interest in the situation."

"I certainly shall. And I am just as certain she will be quite grateful to all of you for the information you've provided. Thank you," Vella said. She couldn't wait to get back to the dowager house and show Irene.

Priscilla was in the sitting room with a book when Josephs came to the door. She had ventured down from her bedchamber only after she heard the visiting voices from below cease and the noise of Lady Darling's carriage going off.

"Miss Bedwith, a Mr. Bafferty has called. Will you see him?" he asked. "He asked first for Lady Darling, and when I told him she was out, he asked to see you."

Priscilla's stomach dropped. Hugh was here? But it was so late in the day! She had been certain it was safe to emerge from her bedchamber, for surely no one would call after four, and now here she was—trapped.

She hesitated, then curiosity—and, if one were honest, the desire to speak to someone (and whether she liked to admit it or not, Hugh was a reasonable and intelligent person) about Lady Darling's mad intentions—had her nodding. "Yes, thank you. Shall I receive him in here or in the parlor?" she asked, still uncertain about some of the practices at the dowager house.

"Whichever you prefer, miss, but, if I may say, this room is far less formal and a bit...er...cozier." He smiled and Priscilla barely refrained from smiling back.

One didn't make friends with servants. Even butlers. One was polite and civil, of course, but one didn't share jokes or private moments with them. But Josephs was so very personable and kind. Not at all remote and snobbish like most butlers.

"This will do, then," she replied a bit haughtily in order to remind herself that she was of the upper class.

"Shall I have Matilda bring tea? Mrs. Josephs is still out."

Once again, Priscilla wavered. Ordering tea suggested that she was being hospitable, but she had no intention of being hospitable to Hugh. Mr. Bafferty. Still, she was feeling a bit peckish, and tea and biscuits sounded quite lovely. She'd been just about to ring for a little tea, anyhow. "Yes. Just a small service for—for the two of us."

Josephs nodded and withdrew, leaving Priscilla a moment to stand and go to the small mirror above the side table to check her hair. She pinched her cheeks and lightly bit her lips to bring some color into her face.

"Priscilla."

She turned. Hugh—Mr. Bafferty; she must remember that—stood in the doorway. Her heart gave a little strange thump. She ignored it, knowing that emotion could only be from irritation that he'd found his way here—and calling so late in the day! It was fortunate Lady Darling wasn't here to witness this breech of etiquette.

"Miss Bedwith," she corrected him coolly. She was still standing, but at least she'd already stepped away from the mirror so it wasn't obvious she'd been primping. Even so, it was only expected that one should make certain oneself was presentable when a person called, no matter who it was.

"Yes, of course. My apologies, Miss Bedwith." He strode into the room, coming to an abrupt halt at a proper distance. His eyes seemed unable to cease tracing over her figure as he stood in front of her. "I'm terribly sorry for calling so late, but I—I'd only just heard, and I...I had to come. I had to see for myself that you were all right."

He did have the most soulful brown eyes. Rather like a friendly dog, Priscilla thought, even as her heart thudded harder when his gaze caught hers.

"I presume you are speaking of the incident at the Tripley home last night," she said, trying her best to sound like Lady Darling at her most imperious. "Of course I am quite all right. Never better."

She wasn't about to admit to him—or anyone—that she'd had nightmares during the night over her dinner partner (either Mr. Shaw or Mr. Chessley; she hadn't seen his face) suddenly turning to her with a steak knife and slicing her throat. She'd bled out on the table during the main course, and no one had even noticed until Lady Darling peered at her from behind a pair of oversized pince-nez and exclaimed, "My dear Priscilla, are you quite all right?" whilst Mr. Timms dipped and banked around in the air above them, squawking about intruders and pickles.

"Thank Heavens," said Mr. Bafferty. He stood rigidly, giving Priscilla the sense that he was somehow holding himself in restraint.

Just then, Matilda, one of the parlormaids, came in with a tray. This gave Priscilla not only an excuse to sit (her knees were embarrassingly weak) but also a distraction.

After the maid withdrew, leaving the door properly wide open, Priscilla managed to pour tea for both of them without sloshing any onto the table or saucers.

Mr. Bafferty had chosen his seat a proper distance from hers —on the chair next to the divan where she sat. The low table was between them.

"Was it quite terrible last night, Miss Bedwith?" he asked once they'd each settled with their tea and a small plate of lemon biscuits.

"It certainly wasn't a pleasant experience," she replied

tartly. "But I didn't fall completely to pieces, even though I'd never seen a person who'd been m-murdered before." What had started out as cool, firm words softened into a little tremble near the end.

It had, actually, been quite ghastly. But there was no need to dwell on it. It was past, and Priscilla need never think of it again.

"Do you want to tell me about it, Pr—Miss Bedwith? I'm certain it's been on your mind, and perhaps..." His voice trailed off and he gave her an imploring look from steady dark eyes. "It's just that it seems sometimes, when one talks about a terrible thing that happened, it can help a person to feel better."

Priscilla had the impression he wasn't asking out of bald curiosity, the way people liked to gawk and gawp and gossip about tragedies that happened to people other than themselves. She sensed he wanted to hear about *her* experience, for some reason.

And for some reason, she realized she wanted...needed...to talk about it. Lady Darling had been absolutely no help in that regard, leaving Priscilla to her nightmares and memories and fears without a second thought as Her Ladyship decided to gallivant off and inquire after a murderer.

"It was after dinner," she said, lifting her teacup from its saucer. Her hand was steady and she sipped the sugary tea before continuing. "The men had gone for their cigars and billiards and we were supposed to meet at half nine at the study, where Mr. Tripley was meant to unveil a painting of Mrs. Tripley. Lady Darling insisted I attend, although I have no real interest in art."

"Lady Darling is, I'm quite certain, merely seeing to the task that has been asked of her," Mr. Bafferty said quietly, holding her gaze with his. "Making certain you are seen about in Society, introducing you to important people, and showing you off to all of the eligible bachelors in London. Of course she would do nothing less."

Priscilla hastily took another sip of tea. She didn't know quite what to say. His eyes were very steady on her. She looked away, her cheeks warm.

She would *not* think about that night, under the moonlight, with the stars above and rose scent on the breeze…and his lips on hers.

"After dinner, what happened?" he prompted.

"We couldn't get into the study and Mr. Tripley was nowhere to be found. The footman and some of the gentlemen broke down the door, and—and Lady Darling saw him. Mr. Tripley. H-he was on the floor, dead, lying behind his desk. Th-there was a little knife sticking out of his chest."

"Good Lord," murmured Mr. Bafferty, his gaze remaining steady on her. "How terrible and frightening. What did you do?"

"Some of the other ladies screamed and acted as if they were going to faint," Priscilla told him. "But Lady Darling told me to get a cool cloth for Mrs. Tripley, and of course I did so. I—I didn't get a very close look at the—the man on the floor" —she couldn't bring herself to say "body"— "and I sat with Mrs. Tripley for a bit."

He smiled at her. "Of course you did. You're made of quite stern stuff, Miss Bedwith, as I well know. It's not every young woman who will jump into a freezing pond to rescue a kitten— or who has the presence of mind to offer comfort to a woman who's just lost her husband in a most horrible way."

To her shock, Priscilla felt a surge of heat rush up from behind her bodice, over her chest and throat to her cheeks. "That's very kind of you, Mr. Bafferty."

"I'm not being kind, Miss Bedwith," he replied firmly. "I am stating a fact." He set his teacup gently into its saucer. "I—"

A knock on the sitting room door—which was still open, of course—had both Priscilla and her guest jolting in surprise.

"Miss Bedwith," said Josephs, standing in the doorway. "There is another visitor here for you."

"Another...visitor?" she replied, confused. Who on earth— "For me? Who is it?"

"It's a Mr. Harry Shaw," replied the butler.

Chapter Eight

When Irene arrived home, she discovered Priscilla Bedwith in the sitting room, staring into space. To her surprise, Beatrice was curled up in the girl's lap, snoring.

The table in front of Priscilla was cluttered with the remains of tea, and Irene could see evidence at least two others (aside from, presumably, Beatrice) had partaken besides her charge. But she already knew that, for Josephs had murmured to Irene the names of the callers. This information had brought the curve of a smile to her lips.

"It seems you had a successful day, pet," Irene said, coming into the room.

Lord, she was tired. It had been a long day with many people, and the evening still loomed ahead of her. At fifty, Irene didn't quite have the energy to bounce back after a late night, especially one filled with whisky. Perhaps she could snatch the time for a quick nap before she had to get ready to go out.

Priscilla jolted, obviously pulled from whatever thoughts had taken her away. Beatrice snapped awake and saw that her mistress had arrived. She launched herself from Priscilla's lap and bounded toward Irene, who scooped her up.

"Yes, my lady," Priscilla said, standing. She brushed at her skirt as if to remove dog hairs, but Beatrice wasn't rude enough to shed. "It was...well, I was surprised to have such late callers." A little rosy blush stained her cheeks.

She really was an attractive thing, even with the dark circles beneath her eyes. And she was well-behaved and charming. It shouldn't be very difficult to marry her off—as long as the girl wasn't too stubborn about it all.

"Well, that's precisely what we're hoping for isn't it, pet? Callers." Irene waved her back into a seat and took one of her own as Beatrice gave her a delicate swipe of a kiss on the side of her jaw. "The Duke of Wessley notwithstanding," she added before the chit could open her mouth to argue. "There is an argument to be made that when a woman is found to be desirable by one man, it tends to make her more desirable to others."

Priscilla closed her mouth and nodded.

Irene had asked Josephs to have tea brought for her, and was mildly surprised when Matilda came in with the tray instead of Vella. "Thank you, Matilda. Where is Mrs. Josephs?"

"Why, she's not back yet, my lady," Matilda explained as she set the tray on the table in front of the sofa.

"That must mean she is making some progress. Excellent. Please send her to me the minute she returns. Beatrice, *no*. That's not for you. I suspect you've already had your share today, anyhow. Now," she said, turning her attention to Priscilla. "I do hope you aren't going to beg off on going to the theatre tonight." She lifted an imperious brow to suggest that it would not be the best idea.

"I...well, of course not," replied the girl bracingly. "I shouldn't want anyone to think I've hidden away after that terrible experience last night."

"Quite right," replied Irene, pleased that the chit was showing some gumption. She gave Beatrice a quelling look when the beast inched her little brown nose closer to the table. "*No*, Beatrice. Your tea is in the kitchen with Mrs. Darnley. Now, the carriage will be waiting by half eight. It's half five now, so that is plenty of time." For a nap, too, Irene thought hopefully. "If you will, Priscilla, tell me about the visits from Mr. Shaw and Mr. Bafferty."

"Oh. Well, there is quite nothing to tell, really, my lady. They both called in order to determine whether I was feeling all right after the incident last night. And they both came rather late. After four," she added with a confused look.

"I see." Irene had her suspicions as to why that was the case —namely, to ensure that other callers had left and thus the girl's attention wouldn't be divided. "And what did you tell them?"

"I told them both that I was suffering from no ill-effects," Priscilla replied a bit tartly.

"Very good. I can see that—although I suspect the dark circles beneath your eyes are an indicator of a difficult night of sleep. Which is to be expected, of course. One doesn't encounter a dead body, murdered, in a study, every day. Now, since Mr. Shaw is, in fact, a suspect in the Tripley Murder, I should like you to encourage him."

Priscilla blinked, then her eyes went perfectly round. "You wish me to encourage a possible murderer to—to *marry* me?"

"Not to marry you—that is unless we determine that he is quite innocent, for I do believe he could be a possible match— but to court you." When Priscilla gaped and gasped like a fish who'd been thrown onto a ship's deck, Irene went on, "Well, how else will we learn about him and whether he had reason to do away with Mr. Tripley?"

"W-we, my lady?"

"Never fear. I shall not leave you in any danger with the

man, should he in fact be unmasked as the villain. Of course you would always be properly chaperoned, so there would be no danger to you, anyhow, would there? You're certainly not foolish enough to slip off into a dark garden with an unmarried man or to meet up with one unchaperoned at the park."

"No, of course not," replied Priscilla. The rosy flush that had been in her cheeks at the mention of her gentlemen callers had disappeared.

"Excellent. Now, relate to me everything he said. Precisely everything. There could be a clue hidden in even the most inane of comments." Irene leaned forward, watching her intently, her desire for tea and biscuits momentarily forgotten.

"Um, well, he asked how I was, and I introduced him to Mr. Bafferty. And we talked about how terrible it was for Mr. Tripley, and I reminded him how terrible it was also for Mrs. Tripley, and he agreed. And he asked if I had slept all right, and then he asked where you were, my lady." She shrugged. "There was little else."

"Did he mention Mr. Tripley or anything about his relationship with him? Business, social, familial?"

"Not that I remember. Only that they saw each other at the horse races or the club sometimes. And then he and Mr. Bafferty began talking about that." Her lips moved into an irritated pout.

Irene hid a smile. "Ah, yes. I've heard Mr. Shaw has an interest in the horses. It is an interesting path to investigate. Perhaps someone is in great debt due to poor betting, although how that could relate to murder I shall have to consider. Thank you, Priscilla, you've been very helpful. Oh, and Mr. Bafferty? How was your visit with him? I understand he was here first."

"He came so late to call that I'm glad you weren't here, Lady Darling. It was rather presumptuous of him, I dare say. He said he'd only just heard about what happened, and he wanted to know whether I was all right. As if I would have been confined to my bed with the vapors," she added with some spirit. "He knows me far better than that. After all, he was the one who helped me out of the pond after I went in after a kitten."

She stopped suddenly and lifted her tea to sip. "He seems to find it necessary to remind me of that incident nearly every time we are together. That or when we found a nest of newborn bunnies and I chased the dogs away from them."

"And rightly so," Irene said, still smothering her smile. "Chasing dogs away from tiny, vulnerable bunnies." The poor girl had no idea how much Mr. Bafferty was in love with her. And, Irene suspected, how much the girl loved the man in return. She only wondered why Priscilla was so set against having the man.

At least there had been no question, no pussyfooting around when Irene met Edward. They'd seen each other, and it was as if a lightning bolt had struck each of them simultaneously. They'd fallen in love right then, and nothing—not the judgment of Society, his interfering mother (God rest her soul), the difficulties in getting permission to wed, nor the scandal when they did so—could keep them apart.

Irene sighed internally, looking down at her empty tea cup. How she missed him. And how she also missed being held, stroked, cuddled, kissed, loved...

She might be fifty, but she certainly wasn't *dead*.

Giving herself a mental shake, Irene looked up to find Priscilla eyeing her. "I believe I'm more tired than I realized, and the play will go very late. It is one of the last performances at which Mr. Stoker will be in attendance, and I expect there will be some gathering after. I shall have a little nap and then we will leave at half-eight, sharp."

❧

"Lady Darling, earlier did you say Mr. Stoker?" asked Priscilla as the carriage lurched away from the curb in front of the dowager house. "The man who wrote 'Dracula'? I didn't know he was an actor."

"He isn't. He's the manager of the Lyceum Theatre, and a close friend of Mr. Irving, who owns the theatre and who is, of course, starring in a revival of 'The Merchant of Venice' tonight. Incidentally, Henry Irving's Shylock is quite a departure from other interpretations. I do hope you enjoy it," replied Irene, adjusting her multitude of skirts so that they wouldn't wrinkle. Why *must* women be required to wear so many layers of clothing? "Mr. Stoker will soon be leaving his post at the theatre, I believe to spend more time on his writing and also some other pursuits. Did you read 'Dracula'?" she asked.

"No, I...I thought it would be too frightening," Priscilla confessed. "I prefer the stories of Miss Austen and the Misses Bronte."

"Ah, yes, I see. It's a shame you haven't read the book about these Un-Dead, as Mr. Stoker calls them. The character of Count Dracula was quite inspired by Mr. Irving, and you might have found it interesting to know that whilst watching him onstage tonight. Incidentally, Mr. Stoker is also quite good friends with Mr. Conan Doyle. I noticed you were reading one of his stories in the sitting room today," she added with a smile. "I hope you were enjoying it."

"Yes. It's very clever. I was reading 'A Scandal in Bohemia,'" Priscilla replied.

"Ah." Irene smiled. "One of my favorites."

"It's rather interesting that the only person to outsmart Mr. Holmes—at least in all of the stories I've read so far—is a member of the fairer and weaker sex," said Priscilla, with a surprising amount of perception and a bit of saltiness in her voice.

"Quite," replied Irene, still with the small smile.

Priscilla looked at her closely in the dim light of the carriage, but refrained from speaking again on that topic.

"You look quite well tonight, Priscilla," said Irene. "Monsieur Claude was correct about the buttercup yellow for you. It suits you very well. It makes your eyes look more blue."

"Thank you, my lady. You also look quite beautiful." The sentiment "for your age" had been prudently left off her comment.

They rode in silence the rest of the way to the theatre. Priscilla was, presumably, occupied with thoughts about snaring the Duke of Wessley (Irene had refrained from mentioning that he would very likely be there tonight, and that his box was adjacent to theirs) into marriage, whilst Irene considered her approach should she encounter any of her suspects at the theatre tonight—which she was quite determined that she would.

Vella had returned from her visit to the Tripley home during Irene's much-needed nap, but she'd related all of her findings as she and Cissy were helping Irene dress for the evening. Vella told her about the telephone call Mrs. Canefield had overheard, which was quite intriguing to Irene. But the mother-of-pearl and ruby cufflink was obviously the biggest topic of conversation.

"It must have been dropped by the killer—for no one else went into the vicinity of the desk once I discovered Mr. Tripley," Irene had said as she examined the little stud Vella gave her. "It must have come loose during the struggle and bounced down and beneath the desk, and of course Inspector Burgess didn't think to look very closely around the area. What a shame for him." She caught Vella's eyes in the mirror and grinned. "The next thing we must do is find out to whom it belongs."

"I've already begun to put out the word," Vella replied.

"That's what kept me gone so long. I stopped at the little park near the market, where the maids and governesses like to sit on their days off to feed the ducks—"

"And, I daresay, have the opportunity to speak with a handsome or charming footman or laborer on his evening out," said Irene with a smile.

"Exactly." Vella smiled back. "I showed the cufflink to everyone I spoke to and said it was important we found the owner of it, and to send word here if they had any information."

"Brilliant. Do you think the maids will care to follow through?"

"I think most young maids would take any opportunity to have an excuse to speak to a valet," said Vella. "Especially a young and handsome one. And," she added, meeting Irene's eyes in the mirror with ones that danced with mischief, "since there is a reward involved—"

"A *reward?*" Irene looked at her in shock, then burst into laughter. That was a mistake, as the sudden movement of her head caused the pin Cissy was sliding into her coiffure to jab her in the scalp. Irene winced, but as it was her own fault, she said nothing but, "That was excellent thinking, Vella. How much will I be in for, for this reward?"

"Half pound," replied her friend, her mischievous smile growing wider.

"Good Heavens! Are you trying to drive me into the poor house?" Irene said, laughing—but this time, she kept her head from moving.

Irene was smiling to herself over the memory as the carriage lurched (sigh) to a halt in front of the Lyceum Theatre.

Being Lady Darling, Irene would not be waiting in the long line of people that led to the pit entrance. Instead, she and Priscilla were helped down from the carriage by a footman beneath the portico. The ornate stonework of the theatre's facade was the result of a redesign in 1882, but there was already talk of doing another one.

Walking up the steps and between two of the Greek-style columns, the pair crossed the colonnade and entered the building, with Irene watching the milling crowd with a hawk-like eye for any sign of her suspects.

"I've never sat in a box at the theatre before," Priscilla said in a hushed voice as they settled into their seats a few moments later.

"We're so close you'll be able to see whether Mr. Irving has sprouted any chin hair after shaving," Irene said jovially.

Their private seating room was on the middle level of box seats, closest to the stage: a prime location, where one could see and be seen...unless the curtains were drawn. At the moment, the curtains were open wide and Irene and Priscilla took their seats in the front row.

Each theatre box was of a size comfortable enough to boast three rows of four comfortable, cushioned seats each, with each row being slightly elevated above the one in front of it. There was also sufficient space for visitors to gather in the area behind the seats and to the side during the intervals, or even during the performance if there was gossip or visiting to be conducted. In short, the little chamber was very much like a tiny sitting room that could be swathed in curtains if privacy was desired. A single door led out into the gallery, and a footman waited beyond for any service necessary.

Irene settled into place and slipped out of the lacy wrap she'd pulled over her shoulders and low décolletage and looked around.

The theatre was filling with people. A dull roar from conversation filled the space as people greeted each other and gossiped, at times calling across the space. The stalls, on the floor, were the venue of the lowest-class members of the audience, and the ones who'd been waiting in line to enter through the pit. These seats consisted of rows of hard, backless benches fixed to the floor so that they couldn't be moved should altercations or protests about the show erupt.

Other seats for the more well-off and aristocratic viewers ringed the auditorium at three levels of balcony, protected by a sort of proscenium. There were five private boxes on each side of the stage, one on the first level and two at each of the others. Dark red curtains for each one matched the ones on stage, as well as the decorative painting on the walls of the theatre.

Irene unabashedly pulled out her opera glasses and began to scan the auditorium, hoping to catch sight of some of her suspects. There were five acts, which suggested at least two intervals (Act Five was very short)—a perfect opportunity for viewers to visit other boxes or to summon audience members to their private box. As the Dowager Marchioness of Darling, Irene did not deign to make calls on other attendees; people would come to her box to speak to her. She expected there would be a large number of interested parties who'd want to know about her experience at the Tripleys'.

"Goodness, my lady, isn't that rather...erm...obvious," said Priscilla, obviously referring to her use of the opera glasses. Nonetheless, the girl was peering greedily into the neighboring boxes (no doubt hoping to catch sight of the Duke of Wessley) and at the upper rows of seats where the gentry would sit, but without the assistance of binoculars.

"Quite so," Irene replied, unconcerned. "It's what one does at the theatre. You'll note I'm not the only one with opera glasses, pet."

Indeed she wasn't, and indeed, it turned out the Duke of Wessley was in attendance.

"Yes, that is the Wessley box directly next to ours," Irene said when Priscilla turned to her with wide eyes as the space in question began to fill with people, including the young man who held himself like a prince, though he was merely a duke. "And yes, I shall make certain you are introduced. Now do sit down and cease gawking in that direction."

Priscilla sat promptly, a red spot high on each cheek due either to the reprimand or the proximity of her quarry.

The private boxes were such that one could easily converse with those in the front row of the adjacent one if the curtains were open. Irene, who'd been required to actively and vigorously employ her fan due to a sudden rush of heat that had overtaken her, was sitting in the seat closest to the Wessleys.

Once the flash of heat subsided and she'd dabbed with a handkerchief at the perspiration that had gathered on her forehead, upper lip, and throat, she turned to greet the duchess—the mother of the eligible duke—who also sat in the front row.

"Apparently there was some to-do at a dinner party last night, was there?" said the duchess, flapping her own fan. She had a long, slender nose with a hump in its bridge and a little bit of a hook at the end—an appendage which she tended to lift, flare, and sniff when displeased. Her son had been bestowed with an identical proboscis, which he employed in much the same manner.

"Yes, indeed," replied Irene. "It was a terrible thing, to be sure."

"Quite. To be *murdered* in one's own home. Absolutely *ghastly*." The duchess shuddered, and her attention slid beyond Irene to Priscilla. "Is that the girl I've been hearing about?"

Irene felt Priscilla snap to attention next to her. "Yes. May I make known to you, Duchess Wessley, my ward, Miss Priscilla Bedwith."

Priscilla didn't need to be nudged to stand; she was already on her feet. "Good evening, Your Grace," she said with a curtsy.

"It's a pleasure to meet you. Are you and your son looking forward to the play tonight?"

The duchess, who could smell a desperate debutant a mile away, snapped her fan closed and gave Priscilla a once-over with cool eyes. "I expect so, Miss Bedwith."

The only reason the duchess hadn't completely frozen out Priscilla for her temerity in attempting to launch a conversation was due to the fact that she was Irene's ward. Irene and the Duchess of Wessley weren't particularly close friends, but they were more than cordial. They respected each other, for their respective ranks placed them at the highest levels of Society.

"I've never seen 'The Merchant of Venice,'" Priscilla went on in a painfully obvious attempt to charm the woman she hoped would be her mother-in-law. "I do—"

"That is a particularly lovely tiara, Duchess. Sapphires are one of my favorite gems." Irene had to intervene before the girl made a total cake of herself. If she could have done without it being noticed, she would have yanked the chit back into her seat. One of a lower rank did not natter on at duchesses—or marchionesses, for that matter—without being invited into a conversation.

"Sapphires are a favorite of mine as well, Lady Darling. This piece belonged to the previous duchess and it's only the second time I've worn it. I must say, I am quite astonished by the beauty of your gown. Monsieur Claude, I assume?" The duchess gave Irene a small smile that could only be interpreted as a thank you for the intervention. She wasn't an unkind woman, but neither was she one who abided small talk with those she barely knew, especially when they were of lower rank and were not candidates for her son's hand.

"Of course," Irene said, grateful the awkward moment had passed. Just then, the duke came into view behind his mother. "Ah, Your Grace. How fine you look this evening."

"Lady Darling, what a pleasure to see you," said the duke with a little bow. He'd grown a full, brown mustache and mutton chops since she'd seen him last, and Irene couldn't help but wish he'd finished the job and cultivated a beard as well, for he had a weak chin that would have been better served by being obscured. "What pleasant happenstance has brought you from the country back to London?" He could be supercilious and haughty at times, but the young man could also be charming when he was of a mind to be.

Irene felt Priscilla fairly quivering next to her, and in light of the duke's question, she had the perfect opportunity to make the introduction her ward had been hoping for. "Your Grace, may I present Miss Priscilla Bedwith, whom I have the honor of sponsoring in her first season."

"Your Grace," said the girl, offering a perfect curtsy.

"Pleasure to meet you, then, Miss Bedwith, and how kind of you to be Lady Darling's excuse to return to London," he replied with a quick grin. Then, before Priscilla could respond, he turned away to greet the two lovely women—both young and unmarried—who'd entered the Wessley box with their chaperones.

Priscilla sank back into her seat.

Irene could almost hear the girl deflating as her hopefulness was punctured by the arrival in the Wessley box of Lady Pengelley and Miss Wentworth, both far more beautiful, wealthy, and of higher rank than herself. Irene could only imagine that Priscilla had hoped for that rare and elusive event upon her first meeting of the duke: love at first sight.

Since Irene had been the recipient of such a rare and elusive event herself, she couldn't blame the girl—after all, her marriage was a perfect example of that to which Priscilla Bedwith aspired: a wealthy and powerful peer falling in love with and marrying a woman all of Society would deem an unsuitable match. The difference was, Irene had not been searching for love, or grasping at the prospect of wedding a wealthy, aristocrat. It had simply just happened.

Before Irene could attempt to soothe the girl's disappointment, she caught sight of a familiar figure on the other side of the stage. Even without the assistance of her opera glasses, she recognized Lord Garington settling into a seat in the box that belonged to the Earl of Chumley.

Excellent. At least one of her suspects was present—ah, there was *another*! Mr. Chessley was making his way between two rows in the middle balcony, obviously looking for his seat. He was accompanied by two other men; one of whom she recognized as Mr. Feverley. Three of her five suspects were here tonight, just as she'd hoped. Excellent!

Now she had to devise a way to induce them to call on her during one of the intervals. But she had the entire first act to figure that out, and she settled back into her seat as the illumination from electric lights was lowered then raised, then lowered and raised again, as a signal that the performance was about to begin.

It was Henry Irving who'd introduced the idea of darkening the theatrical auditorium during performances. Prior to his taking over the Lyceum Theatre, the lamps in the house had always remained lit throughout the show—which had, of course, contributed to conversation and distraction from the audience during the performance. This intriguing development of darkening the house lights had only been instituted within the last twenty years, and Irene still found it quite thrilling when the lights went dark and the stage lit up.

Just as the electric bulbs dimmed for the last time, Irene noticed the first sign of movement in the uppermost box on the other side of the stage from them, next to the Earl of Chumley.

A young woman was settling into a seat in the front row,

alone. Behind her was the figure of a tall, sturdy man. He wore a top hat pulled low over his brow. He sat behind her and far off to the side, staying in the shadows as the pretty girl—who appeared just as ethereal and fragile as she'd done earlier today —folded her hands in her lap. She looked eagerly toward the stage as the curtains swept open and a swath of light spilled into the darkened auditorium.

How very interesting that Miss Adina Trewlove was here, with, presumably, her uncle.

Chapter Nine

During the first act, Irene spent far more time than she should have done looking toward the box across the way, where Adina Trewlove sat all by herself in the front row. Irene unapologetically employed her opera glasses to peer into the depths of the box, attempting to catch a glimpse of the girl's companion. The man stubbornly remained shrouded in shadows. It was almost as if he knew someone was trying to get a good look at him, drat it!

The only way to find out who he was and why he was determined to remain hidden from view was to speak with Miss Trewlove. Easy enough to do during the interval, except that Lady Darling did not call on others in their boxes. She waited for visitors to come to her.

She decided she would send word via one of the footmen, inviting Miss Trewlove to call on the Darling box. It was the proper thing to do; Miss Trewlove wouldn't presume to come to her otherwise. Irene could use wanting to introduce Miss Bedwith as an excuse. The girl wouldn't come alone; her chaperone would be required to accompany her, and therefore, the problem would be solved.

Despite arriving at this practical decision, Irene still found herself attempting to see into the girl's box, hoping that her companion—whoever he was—would move enough for her to make out some more details of his features.

Due to this distraction, by the time the act ended, Irene had barely given any thought as to how she might attract each of her suspects to visit during the interval. Now the house lights had gone up and the murmur of conversation—which had never completely subsided, even during the performance—became louder and more prominent. After all, viewing the performance was merely second-fiddle to the social aspect of attending the theatre: seeing and being seen, and gossiping. Even in the dark.

Irene noted that Miss Trewlove had risen and moved toward the back of her box, out of sight. She rang for the footman to come in so that she could send the message to the young woman.

Then, with a start of annoyance, Irene remembered that, even more pressing than the mystery of Adina Trewlove was the murder investigation. A dutiful glance at the box next to Miss Trewlove confirmed that Lord Garington was still in the presence of Lord Chumley. Perhaps she would send word for Garington to call as well, since the footman was going in that direction.

"What do we do now, my lady?" asked Priscilla, glancing hopefully at the duke's box. "Shall we pay a call on the Duchess of Wessley?"

"We wait, pet," replied Irene. "Those to whom we wish to speak will come to us." She'd previously instructed the footman outside her box to allow any and all visitors tonight.

Priscilla didn't try very hard—or perhaps not at all—to mask the sigh of frustration and disappointment. But instead of sitting in her seat, she rose and moved toward the side of the box closest to the duke's. She positioned herself at the edge of the box's opening, likely imagining being noticed as she stood there, trying to appear pensive and pretty.

Irene also rose, a bit more slowly due to the fact that her blasted hip had gone tight during the performance. She really ought to start doing those movements called *yoga* that Vella had taught her. Vella, who was only a year younger, was very rarely pained by these sorts of aches and pains and she claimed that was part of the reason. The other reason, or so she said, was that she rarely ate meat, fowl, or cheese.

The door to the box opened and the footman came in with a little wheeled tray. Irene always had sherry and whisky served in her box, and most of the time, no one could tell that she sipped the latter instead of the more lady-like sherry.

She had a small glass poured for herself, gave the messages for Miss Trewlove and Lord Garington to the footman, and waited for the onslaught.

There was plenty of room to stand and chat with people at the rear of the box, and, sure enough, callers were already streaming in…including Matthew Feverley and Mr. Chessley.

"Good evening, Mr. Feverley," said Irene, greeting him warmly. "How nice to see you again. And Mr. Chessley. How fine of you to call this evening."

"We, er—well, thought it would be the thing to visit after last night," said Mr. Chessley. He was a slender man—other than the paunch that strained his waistcoat. He was in his thirties and possessed a skimpy mustache that hung, neatly trimmed, over his upper lip. He also possessed forty thousand pounds a year, which made him a reasonably eligible bachelor. Mr. Chessley moved with a slight hesitation, almost a limp, and when Irene noticed that, she was reminded of her daughter's comment about a carriage accident.

"Quite so," replied Irene smoothly. "It was rather a horrifying and terrible event, wasn't it? Did you happen to misplace a cufflink last night, Mr. Chessley?"

"A cufflink?" He reached automatically to touch one of the fastenings on his current shirt. "No, I don't believe I did. Have to ask my valet to be certain though. Heh."

"Of course. Who on earth would have wanted to do such a thing to Harold Tripley, do you think, Mr. Chessley? Kill him in his own study?"

He looked taken aback at her forthright question. Women weren't supposed to *do* such things: speak plainly, or be curious, or—in Irene's case—be nosily blunt. "Why, I'm sure I don't know. Why would I know?"

"It had to be someone who left the billiard room," she said, watching him closely. "I understand you did. Leave the billiard room, I mean to say. Did you see Mr. Tripley?"

"Why, I—I—why what are you suggesting, Lady Darling?" he asked, his face having gone very pale, then flushed red above his wispy mustache.

"Only that if you left the billiard room, you might have seen someone else...someone coming in or out of Mr. Tripley's study, perhaps?" She gave him an encouraging smile.

"Oh, quite right. Quite right. Yes, indeed, that could be. Well, now, as a matter of fact, now you mention it, I did happen to see Garington in the hall."

"You were on your way to...where was it, Mr. Chessley, when you saw Lord Garington?" Irene kept her tone easy and the warm smile on her face.

"Why, I...well, I was coming back from, er...well, I was returning to the billiard room and passed him in the hall, now you mention it."

"Which hall was that?" asked Irene. "The Tripley home is so very large and it can be quite confusing, even just trying to find the water closet. One time I actually stepped into the butler's pantry by accident!" The dithering old lady mien slipped into place effortlessly as she fluttered a hand over the front of her bosom.

"Oh, well, it was by the study and the parlor, there on the first floor." Mr. Chessley looked a bit like a trapped rat.

"You passed Lord Garington in the hallway near the study?" The manufactured dithering evaporated. "Could he have been coming out of the study? Or was he going inside?"

"Don't know. Only just saw him in the hallway." The trapped rat was looking for a way out of the figurative corner, but Mr. Feverley had helpfully positioned himself so that Mr. Chessley had no easy escape without running him down.

"That's quite helpful, Mr. Chessley," Irene said with a placid smile. "One needs to pin down the whereabouts of all the suspects in order to determine who might have done the deed, you see."

Mr. Chessley's mustache twitched. "Suspects? Deed? What nonsense is this?"

"Why, it's quite elementary, my dear Mr. Chessley," she said, unable to keep from quoting her literary inspiration. "One of the five of you had to have done away with Mr. Tripley, and I've decided to look into the matter myself."

"What do you mean one of the five of us?"

"It wasn't a vagrant or thief who broke into the house, Mr. Chessley. It was someone who knew their way round the place —and, more importantly, someone who had a reason to silence Harold Tripley. Do you have any idea if any of your fellow gentlemen had any problems with Mr. Tripley? Any business dealings gone bad, perhaps? Any *secrets*?" she added, thinking of the telephone conversation that had been overheard by the housekeeper.

Someone knew that Mr. Tripley had planned to divulge a secret the following day. Surely it wasn't a coincidence that he'd died before he had the opportunity to do so. If only she could find out who'd telephoned him!

"Well, n-no, of course not," replied Mr. Chessley, blinking rapidly. "I-I can't think of anything like that."

"Was it you, Mr. Chessley?"

"Me?" He reeled backward as if he'd been struck.

"Did you do away with Harold Tripley? Was he threatening to expose some dirty deed of yours?" She was watching him very closely.

"M-me?"

"Yes, Mr. Chessley, you. Did you kill Harold Tripley?"

"Of *course* I didn't do such a thing. What sort of mad question is that? Why—why—I do think you've gone round the bend *mad*, Lady Darling. Excuse me, my lady." Chessley spun and pushed unsteadily past Mr. Feverley, his stride hitching a little.

"Well," said Mr. Feverley, his eyes lit with humor. "You certainly upset him."

"I did. But I believe he was acting more offended than guilty," replied Irene, unaccountably annoyed.

"And he did mention seeing Lord Garington near the study," mused Mr. Feverley, looking into the small crowd that had filtered into the box. People were waiting their turns to visit with Irene. She spotted a number of people she wouldn't normally be adverse to speaking with, but she was in the midst of a murder investigation. Still, she supposed she would have to be sociable, drat it all.

There was, so far, no sign of Miss Trewlove.

"He said he'd seen Lord Garington, which means," she said, giving Mr. Feverley an arch look, "that Mr. Chessley was *also* by the study."

"Indeed." Mr. Feverley's brows lifted. "That is quite true, isn't it?"

Irene humphed quietly at him, then turned away to greet a

woman standing there. "Why, Mrs. Putnam, how lovely to see you," she said. "And Miss Putnam. How lovely you look tonight!"

"Lady Darling, you look positively delightful, as usual," said Mrs. Putnam, taking her gloved hands in greeting.

"Thank you, Lady Darling," said the woman's daughter with a little curtsy.

"Terrible about Harold Tripley," said Mrs. Putnam, who shifted aside as another of her friends—Mrs. Yarrow—approached.

"Simply *ghastly*, I'm sure," said Mrs. Yarrow, taking Irene's hand in greeting and kissing the air above her cheek. "You seem to have come through it quite courageously, Lady Darling."

"It *was* quite horrible," Irene said, even as she scanned the cluster of visitors in hopes that Lord Garington might have made an appearance. And what about Mr. Bentley-Bodham or Mr. Shaw? She hadn't seen them here tonight at all.

Her diligence was rewarded, for just then, she caught sight of Harry Shaw slinking around behind everyone, along the perimeter of the box. He was making his way to the front, where Priscilla was still posed hopefully near the duke's box.

Irene was drawn back into conversation with her visitors, however—for everyone was determined to find out what Lady Darling had to say about being witness to another untimely, unexpected death. She would have to leave the interrogation of Mr. Shaw in the questionable hands of Priscilla Bedwith.

"Miss Bedwith. May I say how terribly lovely you look this evening," said Mr. Shaw.

Priscilla bit her tongue from replying that he'd already said so, therefore he didn't need permission. And who wanted to be "terribly" lovely anyway? It seemed a sort of back-handed compliment, if you asked her. "Thank you, Mr. Shaw. Are you enjoying the performance?"

He shrugged. "Ah, well, Shakespeare ain't quite my thing, you know. But attending the theatre is a handy excuse to be able to speak with certain young ladies." His gaze left no doubt that he was speaking specifically of her. His hair and mutton chops shined with whatever pomade he'd generously applied to them, giving him an overall damp appearance. When he spoke, a strong waft of spirits emanated from his breath. She stepped back a little. "What an unexpected pleasure to be in your presence twice in one day, Miss Bedwith."

"That's very kind of you," Priscilla said, trying not to be too obvious that she was looking into the duke's box whilst still posing artlessly in hopes of catching his eye. The duke was standing there, actually facing in her direction, but he seemed to be distracted by the young woman and man with whom he was speaking. Then something Lady Darling said suddenly dropped into her brain, and Priscilla straightened up.

There is an argument to be made that when a woman is found to be desirable by one man, it tends to make her more desirable to others.

She smiled up at Mr. Shaw and angled herself just so, partially facing the duke's box. She laughed charmingly, rather a bit too loudly if one were honest—but that was the intent—pressing her hand modestly to her bosom as if Mr. Shaw had just spoken some great compliment to her.

"You are too kind, Mr. Shaw," she said, looking up at him from beneath fluttering lashes.

Even as she did so, her heart gave a thump and a little flutter, for *the duke had looked over!* She tore her eyes away and smiled coquettishly at her companion. "It is quite an unexpected pleasure to have seen you earlier today as well."

"Right, then," he replied, his eyes fastening...not on hers, not on her lips, but lower....

Much lower.

Beneath where her hand fluttered just above the swell of her breasts....

Priscilla felt a rush of heat and surprise, and it took every bit of control not to step back, for his expression had gone rather... predatory.

And it made her uncomfortable, the overt avidness of it...as if he could see beneath her gown. Her skin prickled, and not in a pleasant manner. He hadn't given her this uncomfortable feeling at the dinner party, nor when he called earlier today.

But when she looked over and saw that the Duke of Wessley was still angled in her direction, and that his attention had stayed on her, she remained still. Her pulse throbbed wildly in her throat, for she knew the duke was looking at her.

At *her*.

At last.

"Miss Bedwith," said Mr. Shaw. His voice had gone low and rough, and he stepped so close that the hem of her skirt, thrust forward by layers of crinoline, brushed his shoes. The smell of spirits was exceedingly strong. "I wonder if perhaps you might take a turn with me through the gallery. Perhaps I could fetch you a cup of lemonade. And there is a lovely place to stand outside and see the moonlight."

"Oh." That was not at all what Priscilla had been hoping for, nor wanting. "I—"

"Miss Bedwith!"

She looked up, for the voice—a shockingly familiar one— had come from a direction in front of her.

From the duke's box.

But it wasn't the Duke of Wessley who'd spoken her name with some earnest surprise and pleasure. It was the man to

147

whom the duke been speaking a moment earlier, whose back had been to her. She hadn't really noticed him until now.

It was Hugh Bafferty.

What on *earth* was he doing in the duke's box?

Priscilla stepped forward as if in a trance, her eyes darting from her childhood friend to the duke and back again.

"Mr. Bafferty," she managed to say. She barely stopped herself from continuing with, *but what are you doing here?*

"It's a shame there's no way to get from one box to the other, eh, old chap?" The duke was saying with a grin from beneath his mustache.

Both of the men, as well as the young woman who'd been speaking with them, had moved to the edge of the box closest to Priscilla in order to facilitate an easier conversation.

"I suppose a person could launch themselves right over the railing if they wanted to badly enough," said the woman, who was very beautiful. She looked at both of her companions and smiled. A charming little beauty mark danced next to the corner of her mouth, and all at once, Priscilla realized she disliked her immensely.

"Right you are, Lady Pengelley," said Mr. Bafferty gallantly, smiling down at her. "But I don't suppose I ought to try just at the moment. I believe the interval is about to end and the play will begin again. I must return to my seat before the lights go dark."

"Not at all. Stay and sit with us, Hugh," said the duke warmly. "There's plenty of room, and I have more questions about this scheme of yours about investing in motorized farming vehicles. I say, what did you call 'em, again?"

"Tractors," replied Mr. Bafferty with a smile. "I've been doing my research and the idea seems to be catching hold. It's early days to get in on such an investment."

"Oh, do stay, Mr. Bafferty. His Grace simply doesn't appreciate the finer points of Shakespeare. If you sit with him in the back and discuss all of that business nonsense, he won't be talking to *me* during the performance, so I'll be able to enjoy it." Lady Pengelley smirked up at the duke, who—as Priscilla watched—seemed to melt right in front of her under the young woman's gaze.

Priscilla struggled for something to say—something witty, something interesting, something relevant—that would yank Wessley's attention from the flirtatious young woman to her, but nothing formed at the tip of her tongue.

"Ah, right, then, I say, Wessley—I meant to ask you about your new stud. Is he racing this weekend?"

She'd utterly forgotten about Mr. Shaw until he spoke now, coming to stand with her right at the edge of the box. He positioned himself such that she felt a little crowded there, almost trapped...and she stiffened when she felt his hand rest lightly on her arm. As if he were staking his claim.

Mr. Bafferty's attention shifted, lowering to that place where Mr. Shaw touched her. Priscilla edged aside so that his hand fell away. She looked up and suddenly found her gaze trapped by Hugh's.

Warmth rushed up from her throat into her face, heating it terribly. Surely anyone could see the flush in her cheeks. Her lips parted; she couldn't look away from that strong, compelling gaze...she felt that she needed to say something...but no words came out.

Just then, the lights began to lower and then brighten in warning. Hugh—Mr. Bafferty—looked away, turning to Lady Pengelley.

Priscilla stepped back, putting even more distance between herself and Mr. Shaw.

"The interval is over," she said to him, unable to keep the

gratitude from coloring her voice. "Thank you for calling, Mr. Shaw."

"Are you quite certain you don't want to take a turn about the gallery anyhow?" he asked, giving her a hot, heavy smile.

"Oh, Mr. Shaw. There you are! How kind of you to call." Suddenly, Lady Darling was there and Priscilla was saved from having to respond to an invitation that felt...not quite right. In fact, it made her stomach hurt a bit, thinking of walking in the gallery with Mr. Shaw. She didn't understand the change. He'd been much less...insistent...last night.

"Lady Darling." Mr. Shaw gave a little bow as the lights dimmed once more. They were about to go dark permanently, but that didn't seem to matter to Lady Darling.

"How kind of you to call today...twice," Lady Darling said. Priscilla noted, with a bit of envy, the way the older woman skewered the man with her gaze. She seemed to see more than was obvious. "Presumably you were concerned over last night's events, Mr. Shaw, and meant to ascertain that I had come through them without difficulty?"

"Of course. Quite a tragic affair," Mr. Shaw replied.

"Indeed. It was. Poor Mr. Tripley," said Lady Darling as the lights went out for the final time.

The footlights on the stage popped alive as the curtains swept apart to reveal Act Two. The murmurs of the crowd quieted, but didn't go completely silent.

"Mr. Shaw, there's no need for you to attempt to find your way in the dark. Please, do sit with us for this act," Lady Darling insisted.

Priscilla would have preferred that not to happen, but she was certainly in no position to contradict her sponsor. Instead, she settled into the seat closest to the duke's box, her ears trained, not toward the stage, but to hear any bit of what might be happening in the seats next to her.

She found herself listening not for murmurs from the duchess or even the duke, but from Mr. Bafferty—although she couldn't fathom why she should care what he said or to whom he should speak. She noted that Lady Pengelley was, in fact, sitting in the front row next to the duchess, and that the gentlemen had moved toward the rear of the box. They were out of earshot, but they were also away from Lady Pengelley of the dainty dimple and smirking smile.

"Mr. Shaw," said Lady Darling as she settled in her chair with a rustle of petticoats. Priscilla heard the shifting and creak of another seat as the gentleman lowered himself into a chair nearby. "Do tell me...what do you think happened last night? Who could have done such a terrible thing?"

"Oh...well...I'm certain *I* don't know," said Mr. Shaw.

Somehow, he had come to be sitting on the other side of Lady Darling from Priscilla. As that realization settled over her, Priscilla felt a rush of relief that suggested she wasn't at all interested in being courted by Mr. Shaw, no matter how wealthy he might be. The raw heat in his eyes when he looked down at her had left her with a slightly unsteady feeling in her belly. She did not want to take a turn under the moonlight with him.

"I understand you left the billiard room during the cigars and whisky, Mr. Shaw," Lady Darling said. "Did you see any of the other gentlemen when you were gone?"

"Suppose I might have done," replied Mr. Shaw. "Had to—uh—get something from my coat, you see."

"Of course. Did you happen to see anyone else whilst you were getting that item?"

"It was...er...well, I mean to say...Garington was there. Saw Feverley as well, you know. I say, why are you asking all of these questions?"

She looked at him in the dim light. "Because it's quite obvious that one of those five gentlemen did away with Mr.

Tripley—I do include you in that number of course, Mr. Shaw—and I'm trying to determine who it was."

"You think one of *us* did it?" Mr. Shaw's voice ticked higher than it should have done but was still not very loud. "That's preposterous!"

"It's nothing of the sort. Surely *you* must have an idea about who had a reason to do away with Harold Tripley." Her voice dropped conspiratorially, coaxingly. "A man like you notices things."

Mr. Shaw's chair creaked again. "Of course I do. Notice things. Have to, you see. That's how I pick the winners at the track you know. Rather good at it, if I say."

"Quite so," she replied approvingly. "Have you noticed anything about any of the other gentlemen last night? Something that might suggest a less than cordial relationship with Mr. Tripley? Or something else that seemed odd?"

"Can't say that I—well, now, wait just a moment," he said. "There was a conversation I overheard between Tripley and Lord Garington before dinner. Sounded rather heated, if you ask me."

"Mmmm." She made an encouraging sound and waited.

"Couldn't really hear what they were saying, but it didn't end well. And I can tell you, Garington wasn't pleased when he came away."

"Did you hear anything of what was being said?"

"Only the impression that Tripley was determined not to do whatever it was the chap wanted." It was dark, but she could tell that he shrugged, for when he did, the smell of whisky wafted stronger toward her nose.

Irene hmmed to herself; more quietly this time. She had so many things on which to think...lost cufflinks, gentlemen leaving the billiard room at different times, mysterious telephone calls, unhappy conversations...And then there was the fact that Miss Trewlove had not come to call during the interval.

Surely the girl would come during the second one. Who would be so bold as to decline an invitation from the Dowager Marchioness of Darling?

Miss Trewlove did not come to call during the second and final interval, and neither did Lord Garington, for that matter.

Irene couldn't help but wonder whether the footman had actually delivered the messages to their boxes, but by then it was too late to correct the problem. The lights were lowering once more.

Mr. Shaw had taken his leave from them, but not until after he'd attempted once more to coax Priscilla to accompany him on a walk through the gallery. Irene was pleased the girl had declined. She showed no interest in the man, who definitely leered at her generous bosom whenever he had the opportunity. Men were so very simple sometimes, and over-imbibing in spirits—as he had clearly done—often tended to embolden them.

Unfortunately, the girl's disinterest would likely put a damper on his courting Priscilla—and therefore give Irene less opportunity to investigate him as a suspect. Not that she could blame Priscilla; she didn't particularly care for Mr. Shaw herself. And a man who came to the theatre already well into his cups was not a very good prospect. She wondered if he'd overindulged because he was feeling guilty about murdering someone.

That was an interesting thought.

The lights went dark.

Act Four was beginning, and Act Five would be brief and so the performance would soon be over.

Irene grumbled to herself and employed her opera glasses once more, spying into the boxes across the way. She told herself it was to confirm that Lord Garington was still in the Earl of Chumley's box. He was there—she could make out his thick shock of red hair even in the dim lights—sitting in the front row.

She grimaced and slid her attention to the box next to it. Miss Trewlove was still there, with her shadowy chaperone lurking in the background. Irene tried and failed not to be irked that the young woman had not responded to what amounted to a summons to the Darling box. What on earth was the girl thinking?

Such thoughts, along with those of murder, occupied her through the rest of the performance. When the curtain fell for the final time, Irene surged to her feet with relief and a sharp pain in her hip.

She'd decided that she and Priscilla would exit the theatre in a roundabout fashion, walking the long way about and past the Chumley box. Perhaps she could kill two birds with one stone, so to speak, and see both Miss Trewlove *and* Lord Garington by going in that direction.

But that was a plan bound to be foiled, for no sooner had she and her companion gathered up their wraps and the small wristlet bags they carried, than the door to their box opened and more visitors made their way in.

Irene fumed a little, but, after all, she had told the footman to allow any and all visitors tonight. She simply hadn't specified that he should *cease* allowing visitors once the performance was over.

It was more than twenty minutes before Irene managed to extricate herself from the last wave of friends, acquaintances, and curiosity-seekers. The delay in this case was that there was no escape from the box: there was one entrance, and people packed in between it and Irene, and it was difficult to try and subtly maneuver in that direction. She would have had to bowl them over to get out, and even though Irene disliked societal constraints and small talk, she was never outright rude.

She'd finally made it through the throng of guests and was nearly to the exit when she realized Priscilla was nowhere in sight.

Now how had the dratted girl slipped past her, and where on *earth* had she gone?

Irene marched out of the box, her gait a little off due to having been seated for so long. She pushed her way through the remaining stragglers who, thankfully, were more interested in what sort of view one got from the private box than visiting.

The gallery was nearly empty. Most of the audience members had made their way out of the theatre. Footmen, ushers, and other staff were beginning to close things down for the night.

Becoming quite annoyed, Irene turned and found herself outside the entrance to the Duke of Wessley's box, whose door stood open. She looked inside, and there was Priscilla.

The determined little chit had somehow gotten herself invited into the duke's inner sanctum. Irene couldn't quite hide a satisfied smile—after all, she'd have done the same thing if she were in Priscilla's shoes.

She only hoped the girl hadn't made too much of a nuisance of herself with the duchess...but if she had, the set-down might help to steer her away from an unattainable target.

Irene was just about to step inside to greet the duchess and rescue Priscilla when someone screamed.

It came from inside *her* box—Irene's box!

She spun as quickly as her heavy, frothy, swinging skirts allowed, and darted—well, tried to dart; it was more like a stumble-step—back into the little chamber.

The stragglers were gathered at the front, gawking out at

something in the auditorium. One of them—Miss Vining—had a pair of opera glasses to her face, and she was gaping and gasping and saying variations of, "Good Heavens. Oh, good Heavens...I simply can't..."

"What is it?" Irene snapped. She snatched the opera glasses from the wide-eyed chit and slapped them to her eyes.

It was immediately evident what had caused Miss Vining's hysterics.

A man was slumped over the front of the Earl of Chumley's box, having fallen through a gap in the closed curtains.

His shock of red hair identified him as Viscount Garington.

The blood on his shirt identified him as dead.

Chapter Ten

I rene was out of the theatre box and hurrying along the gallery before anyone could stop her, heedless of the shocked looks, horrified gasps, and shouts that came her way.

It was no simple feat for a fifty-year-old, high-ranking gentlelady to run in evening attire. The soles of her slippers were thin and smooth, and they slipped and slid on the marble floor. Irene was corseted tighter tonight than she liked to be thanks to Monsieur Claude's latest fabric confection, so it was impossible to draw in deep breaths. Her cumbersome skirts and crinolines rustled, dipped, and swayed around her legs and ankles, the weight and momentum of them working against her desire for speed. Her breasts bounced alarmingly behind the low décolletage, threatening to pop free from their confines due to such unexpected and unusual activity.

However, although her mode of transport couldn't be termed "running," she reached the Chumley box relatively quickly, though not completely unscathed: out of breath, her coiffure and its jeweled pins loose and sagging on top of her head...and she was *perspiring*. At least her breasts hadn't escaped. She was going to have to speak to Monsieur Claude about the impracticality of female clothing when it came to these sorts of activities. Perhaps he could devise some more practical wear.

Others had arrived before her, drawn by the hullabaloo, but she pushed her way past them, trying to catch her breath whilst doing her best to ignore the stitch in her side. Someone had pulled the curtains wide, which allowed more light into the box from the auditorium.

"Lady Darling! Good Lord! I say—"

"Mr. Bentley-Bodham," she said, somehow managing to do so without giving away that she was terribly out of breath. "What on earth are you doing here?" She hadn't known that the fifth and final of her suspects was at the theatre tonight. He was the only one she hadn't seen before now...

And yet Mr. Bentley-Bodham was here, at the side of one of the other suspects—in fact, the one who, until just this moment, had become Irene's favored, prime suspect.

And now Lord Garington was dead, drat it all.

As Irene's question had been rhetorical, she didn't pay any mind to the stammered, outraged, nonsensical response of Mr. Bentley-Bodham (which went something along the lines of who was she to ask and what was she doing here and how dare she... something). Instead, she pushed her way through to approach the scene, where a pair of gentlemen seemed to have taken charge of the situation.

One glance confirmed what Irene had seen through the opera glasses: Lord Garington was dead. It appeared he had had his throat cut, and he'd been left to die in the front row of the Earl of Chumley's box, bleeding all over the railing.

The killer had obviously closed the curtains before doing

the deed, but when his victim slumped forward, he'd fallen partway through the gap.

"From behind," she murmured, ignoring the others as she stepped closer, her gaze avidly tracing over the scene. "It had to be, for the blood spray is only—"

"Blast it, wo—er, my lady, what do you think you're doing?"

A man she didn't know had moved into her peripheral vision and was clearly attempting to place himself between her and the dead man. His voice was peremptory and annoyed without containing the shock and consternation that had colored that of Mr. Bentley-Bodham.

The stranger was tall and possessed an imposing figure (which did not daunt Irene in the least) that was further accentuated by a tall top hat and a coat that billowed about him like a matador's cloak. He was no young man, either (had he been, it might have explained his impertinence), and nor was he anyone she recognized from the *ton*.

He had eyes so dark they were almost black, and, most interesting of all, he was bald of the head with only a very trim, very short mustache and patch of beard over his chin. The unfashionable lack of hair on his head revealed a smooth, well-shaped skull and ruggedly-molded face that was neither handsome nor homely. There were deep grooves on either side of his mouth, bracketing the narrow beard, that were not the least bit like dimples, and crinkles at the corners of his eyes that surely couldn't be from smiling. His thick, dark brows frowned into the point of a vee over his nose, expressing displeasure.

Irene froze him with her most, haughty, marchioness-like stare and replied, "If you would remove yourself from my way forward. Sir."

He did not move.

Instead, he stood there, like an implacable statue, glowering —actually *glowering* down at her.

The only man who'd ever been permitted to glower at her (at least, without severe consequences) was Edward. Young Edward had attempted it once, to his great regret.

"My lady, I must insist that you remain back—"

"If you don't move out of my way," she said crisply, "I shall make the forthcoming moments exceedingly uncomfortable for you, sir. I assure you, I possess a high, ringing voice that carries into the farthest corners of a room, and I have no hesitation in using—"

"Lady Darling! Good Heavens!"

She turned at the sound of Matthew Feverley's voice. Her heart was pounding wildly from fury as well as indignation. Who on earth did this man think he was?

"Mr. Feverley. Thank Heavens you've arrived. Ah, and I see Mr. Bafferty and Mr. Stoker as well. Excellent. Gentlemen," she said in a carrying voice that was meant to command attention, "we have a murder on our hands—"

"*Our* hands?" muttered the Wall of Man who stood in front of her.

She ignored him. "And it is my belief that this murder is directly related to the death of Harold Tripley last night. Inspector Burgess of Scotland Yard must be notified at once."

Mr. Stoker, as—at least for now—the manager of the theatre, took the reins of the situation. Whilst he spoke to the two men who'd been standing near Lord Garington—including the imperturbable one who'd blockaded Irene—she slipped around behind them to get a better look at Lord Garington.

Joseph Bell would be very pleased with her and the attention to detail she was giving this scene. Now, what could she learn and surmise from these close observations?

She immediately realized her initial assessment was correct: the spray of blood from the cut to Garington's neck had shot forward and slightly to the left. The person who'd sliced the viscount's throat had to have done it from behind, for they would have blocked most of the blood had they been in front of him or next to him.

Irene felt more than a little nauseated and lightheaded when she realized just how much blood there was, and how far and wide it had spread: over the railing, down the front of it, onto the seat next to the viscount, and surely on the insides of the curtains. Good Heavens! It might even have splattered on someone below once the dead man slumped forward! Who would have thought the man would have had so much blood in him? Irene shivered as a paraphrase of Lady Macbeth's words reverberated in her mind.

That made her wonder whether the killer had escaped without getting any blood on himself. Surely if it had sprayed that far and that generously, there'd been some on the killer's sleeve or glove. And, of course, he had to have done something with the knife...

Eyes narrowing in thought, Irene turned away from Lord Garington's body and found herself nearly hem to boot with the Wall of Man.

His expression was no longer stonelike and forbidding. Instead, she thought she detected something like abashment.

"Lady Darling," he began. He glanced aside then back again. His gloved hands flexed open and then closed at his sides. He gritted his teeth, then went on, "I did not realize it was you who...uh... My niece informs me that you...are..." He stopped and growled under his breath, then tried once more. "My niece informed me that I should have been a bit more...understated... in my approach with you."

"Your niece?" Irene lifted one brow, giving him another of her looks designed to freeze a person in their tracks. But as she asked the question, she realized she already knew the answer.

She turned in the direction he'd just glanced and discovered

Adina Trewlove standing there. The girl looked as pale and fragile as ever, but there was a surprisingly determined gleam in her light blue eyes.

"Miss Trewlove. This is your uncle?" Irene said. She resisted the extremely strong urge to add, "The one who hid from me at Monsieur Claude's earlier today?"

Instead she gave a regal nod. "Perhaps you might introduce us properly, Miss Trewlove. After all, this is the second time we have crossed paths today, isn't it?" She flickered a sidewise glance at the man. At this little dig, he stiffened and the bit of deference he'd shown evaporated into a sneer.

Miss Trewlove didn't seem to notice. "Oh, yes, of course, my lady, pardon me." She gave a little curtsy. "Lady Darling, may I present my uncle and guardian, Mr. Finley Marshall."

"Your guardian," Irene said thoughtfully. She'd never heard the name Finley Marshall in her life. He couldn't be part of the peerage, so who the devil was he? And why was he driving a sleek, expensive brougham? And why on earth was he hiding from people—her—at Monsieur Claude's?

There was a definite pause, then he said, "A pleasure to meet you, my lady."

"I expect so," she replied, lifting her nose a trifle. "Now, if you will excuse me, I have a murder to investigate. A second one."

As she swept past him, she easily identified a footman, who stood at the side of the box near the door to the gallery. He appeared very ill-at-ease, but he was precisely the person she needed.

Whilst everyone else was standing about nattering on over how terrible this situation was and how horrible that it should happen at the theatre, who could have imagined, and on and on, she was going to speak to someone who actually *knew* something: a servant.

At that moment, she noticed Priscilla standing next to Mr. Bafferty just outside the chamber's door and realized with a start that she'd not only abandoned her charge as she ran off to see to Lord Garington, but she'd nearly forgotten about the girl until just now. That was quite unlike her.

Well, Irene could berate herself about that momentary lapse later. For now, as she'd pointed out, she had a murder to investigate.

"Young man, I am Lady Darling," she said, approaching the footman.

The footman straightened up sharply, his prominent Adam's apple bobbing wildly. "Milady. How can I help you?" He bowed.

"What is your name, young man?"

"Bobby, milady," he said with another bow.

"Quite so. Now, Bobby—you needn't bow again—I should like you to answer some questions for me. Are you the footman for this box?"

"Yes, milady." He moved, then remembered himself and remained upright.

"And this box belongs to the Earl of Chumley, is that correct?"

"Yes, milady."

"Tonight, Lord Garington—that's the man who has, er, met an untimely demise—was a guest of the earl's, is that correct?" When the footman nodded, she went on. "Were there any others in the box tonight besides the earl and Lord Garington?"

"Yes, milady. There was three ladies and two other men tonight. I was told not to be allowing any other visitors during the innervals, milady, and so's I didn't."

"Are any of the men who were in the box with the earl and Lord Garington here in this room right now? Take your time looking round before you answer," she added sharply.

He seemed to comply, for there was a satisfactory pause before he responded. "No, milady. I don't recognize none of them. Except, er, Mr. Stoker, of course, but 'e's the manager."

Irene pursed her lips thoughtfully, ignoring the double negative in favor of the intended sentiment. Mr. Bentley-Bodham, Mr. Feverley, and, she noticed with a tick of surprise, Mr. Chessley, were all in the room at the moment.

That left Mr. Shaw who was absent.... Was that important?

"Tell me what happened. Who discovered that Lord Garington was dead?"

"Well, you see, milady, I thought everyone, they'd come out o' the box, you see, and I was going to get me broom to sweep up like always and then I hears some lady screaming and carryin' on from out'n the theatre, so I come into the box with me broom to see if I could see what's what, and there 'e was...just...there." His throat convulsed and the Adam's apple danced. His skin took on a slick, greenish cast.

"Deep breath, Bobby. Take a deep breath," Irene said sharply.

He did, audibly, and exhaled in a rush of foul-scented breath.

Irene recovered and went on with her questions. "Am I to understand that Lord Chumley and the other members of his party had already left the box? You didn't notice that Lord Garington hadn't come out?"

"No, milady, I didn't notice. Everyone, they all come out in a swarm, you see, most times, and then there was no one and I thought they was all gone. I went to get me broom—"

"Where was that?" Irene asked so sharply he jumped.

"I-in the closet, there," he said, pointing to a narrow, unassuming door across the gallery from the two boxes—the one where Lord Chumley had been, and the one adjacent to it...

...Where Mr. Finley Marshall and Miss Trewlove had been ensconced.

Irene hmmed thoughtfully again. "Did you see anyone going in or out of Lord Chumley's box *or* the one next to it, with Mr. Marshall and Miss Trewlove, whilst you were retrieving your broom?"

"No, milady," he replied, looking at her a little strangely. "No one walked into the boxes or out of'm."

"But you had to turn your back to the boxes for a moment in order to retrieve your broom, didn't you? To go into the closet? Even if it was only for a moment."

"Oy, right, milady, but it was only then."

"Indeed. But that was certainly a long enough instant where someone might have slipped inside the box whilst your back was turned."

His eyes widened and now his face went pale. Irene hurried to assure him. "Not to worry, Bobby, it's not your fault. You were only doing your job, weren't you?"

"Yes, milady! Yes, I was—I was getting me broom so's —"

"Quite so. Now, did you see when Mr. Marshall and Miss Trewlove left their box? Was it before or after Lord Chumley and his companions?"

"I...well, I can't remember that, milady. It was all very busy and Stevens, the footman there, was attendin' to that one, you see, and I wasn't paying it any mind."

"And where is Stevens now?"

"He's in there cleaning it all up, sweepin' and all the stuff I should be doin', milady." He looked around the Chumley box, misery in his face. "I can't go 'ome till I do."

"I'm certain Mr. Stoker will allow you leave. In fact, he should insist upon it and I will tell him so. After all, this is a crime scene and it *shouldn't* be cleaned up until it's been closely examined," she said. "That could take quite some time."

Bobby perked up a little at this. "Truly, milady?"

"Of course. I shall speak to Mr. Stoker forthwith. But I should like to have a word with Stevens first." Her lifted brow was a silent command that Bobby should conduct her to his friend.

They found Stevens working industriously in the box where Mr. Marshall and Miss Trewlove had been seated. Irene had to give the boy credit for getting his work done whilst all sorts of other exciting activity—such as murder—was going on around him.

"I should like to know whether anyone came into this box to visit Mr. Marshall or Miss Trewlove tonight," she said without preamble.

"No, my lady," Stevens replied after a quick glance at Bobby, who'd nodded encouragingly at him. "It was only the two of them all night, my lady. No one even knocked. Only, a message came for them, but that was it."

Irene frowned. Apparently, her invitation to call at the Darling box had been delivered. "When did they leave the box? The last time, I mean to say, after the performance had ended?"

"It was at the very end, my lady, right away, when the curtain fell. It seemed the lady...well, it seemed she wanted to freshen herself," said Stevens a little bashfully.

Irene nodded. That made quite good sense. Miss Trewlove had waited until the performance was over to visit the ladies' resting room so that she wouldn't miss any of the play.

"They came back, they did," said Stevens, surprising her. "Oi, Oi thought they'd gone on home, you see, my lady, but they came back."

"They came back to the box?"

"Not to the box, but they come along the gallery here. Oi— well, my lady, Oi ain't one to listen in on things—"

"Quite so," she said in an encouraging tone, and nodded for him to continue.

"It seemed...well, it seemed they might have been disagreeing 'bout aught," said Stevens. "My lady."

"Disagreeing?"

He shrugged. "Oi only thought it looked as if, my lady."

Irene bristled. "What did he do to her? Was he forcing her along? Did she appear to be frightened?" She was going to have to speak to Miss Trewlove alone and find out precisely what her uncle—and Irene had been around long enough to know that the term "uncle" could mean something not at all like a relation —had been doing.

"It weren't that, my lady. It were she—the lady, Oi mean— she were pulling him along, and he weren't having none of it. He wanted to leave, and she—why, it seemed she didn't want to go."

"Are you quite certain of this?"

"Yes, my lady. Because they stopped right here, and she said, 'Oi'll go by myself then, and won't that make a stir.'"

"Indeed." That was not at all what Irene had expected to hear. "It seemed she was the one who was insistent, and not him?"

"Yes, my lady. Oi mean, it's what Oi thought Oi 'eard." Stevens shrugged.

"Very well. Thank you for that information. Did you see anyone go in or out of the box after Mr. Marshall and Miss Trewlove left it?"

"No, my lady, but Oi went down for a problem down the way." He gestured toward one end of the gallery. "One o' the maids, she dropped a tray and Oi went on to 'elp her for a moment, Oi did." From the pink coloring his cheeks, Irene surmised that Stevens had been waiting for such an opportunity to offer help to this particular maid. And, knowing maids as she did, Irene suspected the girl had made certain she required assistance.

"And you were helping this maid for about how long, Stevens?"

He wanted to shuffle his feet—Irene knew the signs quite well—but he held himself in check. "Dunno. Wasn't long, my lady."

She highly doubted that. "So it is possible that someone came into or out of the box when you were gone. When did this incident occur? How long after the people left the box?"

This time he gave in and shuffled a little. "Oi don't know, my lady, Oi really don't."

Irene suppressed a sigh, then said, "Very well. Thank you for your assistance. You may commence—get on with," she amended when he looked confused, "your cleaning. But wait just one moment," she said suddenly. For she noticed the edge of the curtain at the front of the box was askew. It was the edge of the curtain on the side next to the Earl of Chumley's box.

She darted forward, that telltale prickling at the top of her head telling her she was on the right road.

Yes, the curtain was definitely askew in such a way that suggested someone had moved just that edge of it...perhaps someone who'd managed to climb from the box next to it into this one.

She looked around, peering particularly closely at the railing and the disarranged curtain. Surely if the killer came this way, he'd left some trace of blood. She wished she had a lantern or some other light to shine onto the shadowy floor.

"Have you cleaned up in this area yet, Stevens?" she asked, and then gasped when her attention fell on something.

"No, my lady, I ain't got there yet. Just really got started, I did, when everyone started screaming and shouting."

She would have pounced on the item lying on the floor near

the corner of the box, but her corset and layers of skirts restricted that sort of movement. Instead, she had to crouch to get within proximity of the item which...appeared to be....

Yes! A pair of gloves.

Her fingers closed around the fabric and she pulled to her feet on creaky knees.

It was, indeed, a pair of men's gloves...and one of them was wet with blood.

Chapter Eleven

I rene gave a satisfied smile, which faded a little when she realized that not only did these gloves appear too small to have been worn by Mr. Finley Marshall, but also that he had been wearing gloves earlier during his reluctant apology. She'd seen him flexing those big hands at his sides.

Clearly, he wasn't the murderer.

Not that she'd really entertained the thought that he *was*... but perhaps a little part of her wanted him to be since he'd been so rude to her earlier and it would serve him right if she unmasked him as a true villain.

She examined her find, thinking of Dr. Bell as she did so. These were fine evening gloves of soft brown leather. That was helpful, she decided, even though she found no identifying tag or label inside. A gentleman who wore brown gloves for an evening out did not wear a black coat. Unless, she supposed, his neckcloth or waistcoat had brown paisley or checks in it, drat it. She would have to ask a good valet to be certain; Irene was barely interested in female fashion—she certainly didn't pay close attention to what men wore.

But now... Whoever had cut Lord Garington's throat was

without gloves. And was probably wearing some sort of clothing with brown in it. She smiled as she turned to make her way out of the box.

Her suspects were likely still standing around—or, in Mr. Bentley-Bodham's case, getting in the way, for he always seemed to want to be in charge—and she was going to take a very close look at the attire of each of them.

"What is it, my lady?" asked Stevens, still holding his broom.

She'd met him at the door of the box and she was about to respond when something else caught her eye and she stopped abruptly. She'd spied a hardly noticeable glint in the corner, just behind where the door opened.

Two steps brought her closer and Irene snatched in her breath when she saw the metallic shine of a knife. Either the killer didn't care that it would be found by the footman during his tasks, or he wasn't aware that someone would be cleaning up so soon.

"Stevens, if you could retrieve that knife for me. The one on the floor, there, covered in blood." Irene had had enough bending and crouching for the evening.

"A *wot*?" The footman was so startled he forgot the proper address.

Irene ignored his mistake and said clearly and a trifle slower, "The murder weapon, Stevens. There on the floor. If you will, please."

But by the time she'd finished speaking, he'd already seen and retrieved the knife. He held it gingerly by its hilt, gawking at the dark stains on it. "Gor," he muttered.

"Quite so," she agreed, eyeing the weapon. It was an unexceptional hand knife; the sort anyone might carry about for cutting ropes or whittling wood, or whatever it was men did with knives besides slicing one another's throats. "Now, I suppose we ought to wrap that in something so it doesn't—"

"I say, Lady Darling, what on earth are you—good *Lord*!" Mr. Feverley had appeared just outside the box entrance, and it seemed he'd noticed the knife Stevens was bandying about.

"I've located the murder weapon," Irene said with modest satisfaction. "As well as the killer's gloves." Even as she said this, she looked at Mr. Feverley's hands.

They were properly gloved. In black.

She felt a slight easing of tension; it really would be a terrible inconvenience and difficulty if the son of her friend Mrs. Feverley turned out to be the culprit. But she also couldn't help but notice that his waistcoat was made from a fabric of tiny blue and brown checks. Still. He wore gloves.

"Stevens, do wrap that knife in something, if you please. Has Inspector Burgess or anyone from Scotland Yard arrived?" Irene asked Matthew Feverley as they made their way out into the gallery. "I have a number of things to tell him, including how the killer managed to get in and out of Lord Chumley's box."

She didn't wait for Mr. Feverley's response; she was already out in the walkway with the intention of finding out for herself.

She saw Mr. Chessley standing to the side, talking with Mr. Bentley-Bodham and the Duke of Wessley. Priscilla and Mr. Bafferty, along with Lady Pengelley, stood nearby, and Mr. Shaw hovered between the two groups, seemingly undecided as to which conversation he wished to join. He also seemed to be weaving on his feet a bit.

Irene wanted to find out which of her suspects was gloveless, but she couldn't see anyone's hands except that of Mr. Shaw. He was gloved.

Another small knot of ladies and gentlemen clustered even further down the way, clearly uninterested in vacating the theatre when so much excitement was happening. Miss Trewlove watched, standing by herself, from across the passage.

This led Irene to wonder where Mr. Finley Marshall had disappeared to.

One glance into Lord Chumley's box answered that question. The Wall of Man was still in there with Mr. Stoker and, thankfully, Inspector Burgess. The latter was occupied with the matter of the body, which had been removed from its position slumped over the railing. Two other men in workman's clothes were in the process of preparing it to be taken to the morgue. A stretcher rested against the row of seats.

Irene gestured sharply at Stevens, then sailed into the box with him on her heels. "Gentlemen, I'd like to inform you that I've procured the murder weapon as well as the gloves worn by the killer. I've also determined how he came in and out of the box in order to do his villainous deed."

The three men looked at her. Bram Stoker, an Irishman with thick dark hair and an affable personality, appeared only slightly taken aback by her announcement. "And how did this come about, Lady Darling?" he asked in a mild voice.

His lack of surprise was likely due to the fact that he knew her fairly well, for they'd met through Arthur Conan Doyle. The two men were not only friends but distant relatives. She suspected Mr. Stoker was one of the few people who knew why Arthur had named Sherlock Holmes's *the* Woman as he had done.

She explained about the knife and gloves, and concluded with, "Therefore the killer must be missing his gloves. I have a suspicion as to whom it is" —one of four, anyhow— "but I have not ascertained whether he is gloveless at the moment. I shall do that in short order, for he is standing about out there."

"And you're saying the bloke who did the killing's gone about without gloves? Are you quite certain of that, Lady

Darling?" the Wall of Man said in a tone that had Irene's hackles lifting.

"Quite certain. Here are *his* gloves." She produced them with a flick of her wrist, and the ruined pair flopped over her hand. "If I have his gloves, then clearly he does not."

"Unless he took them from someone else," said Mr. Marshall.

"From someone else? A man doesn't simply borrow dress gloves from another gentleman at the theatre," she replied flatly.

"Unless the bloke's gone and killed him first." Mr. Marshall lifted one thick, dark brow.

Irene closed her mouth, her eyes narrowing. "Do you mean to say that Lord Garington is missing his gloves?"

"That is precisely what I mean to say," replied Mr. Marshall.

Drat. So it didn't matter in the least whether she poked around to find out whether Mr. Shaw or Mr. Chessley or Mr. Bentley-Bodham had gloves.

"Well," she said bracingly, recovering herself. "At least we know one thing about the killer. Actually, I know quite a number of things about him, but the characteristic I was referring to is that he must be quick on his feet to realize he must switch gloves during such a stressful situation."

"The bloke's blooming mad is what he is," Mr. Marshall said. "Going off and cutting a man's throat in the middle of the theatre? What's wrong with doing it in a nice, dark alley?"

Irene nearly forgot herself and laughed. She covered it up with a scoff-like cough and turned her attention to Inspector Burgess and Mr. Stoker. "I must also point out that our killer—"

"*Our?*"

She ignored the Wall and pushed on, "—must be somewhat athletic of ability in order to climb from one box to the other."

"I'll stick with mad," muttered Mr. Marshall.

Colleen Gleason

"You say you know who it is, Lady Darling?" Inspector Burgess fixed her with a surprisingly benign gaze.

"I've—well, I've quite narrowed it down," she said stoutly. "It's one of four—most likely three—gentlemen."

"And who are they?" Inspector Burgess pressed.

"I should think *you* would already know," she replied. "It has to be one of the gentlemen who attended Mr. Tripley's dinner party, of course. But perhaps you hadn't got quite that far in your deductions," she added fairly. "Still, it's rather elementary, Inspector."

The detective harrumphed but declined to say anything further other than, "Your opinion is duly noted, Lady Darling."

Opinion? Irene snapped her mouth closed, but she expected the fury in her eyes had not been as easily suppressed as a verbal response.

"Then I am certain you have everything well in hand and an arrest will be forthcoming. Good evening, Inspector," she said in the clipped voice she'd been required to employ when Edward had made the same sort of nonsensical statements. That tone usually sent the maids and footmen dodging into another room.

She gave the inspector one last narrow look, avoided glancing at Mr. Marshall, and nodded to Bram Stoker. "Good evening."

She swept from the room, out into the gallery where the small crowd still lingered. "Miss Bedwith, shall we take our leave." It was purposely not posed as a question, or even a suggestion, but as a command. "Mr. Bafferty. Mr. Feverley. Mr. Shaw. Mr. Chessley. Mr. Bentley-Bodham. Good evening." She nodded to each of them in turn, but her temper was high enough that she was in no mood to make any further small talk.

Yes, one of those four men had just murdered Lord Garington, but there was nothing *she* could do about it at the moment.

She was going to go home, put up her feet, and have a glass of whisky.

At least Vella and Josephs were interested in her theories.

≈

"This has just arrived for you, my lady," said Josephs, offering Irene an envelope.

It was after eleven the next morning, and thankfully, Irene had not ended up having a glass of whisky last night when she returned from the theatre. She'd been hit with a wave of sudden and complete exhaustion in the carriage during the ride home, and when she heard Big Ben strike half-two, she understood why. It was a late night, even for a lady of Society.

She'd made her way upstairs and, with the help of Cissy, undressed and stumbled into bed.

Now, as she breakfasted in the dining room on tea, toast points, and a single boiled egg, she took the envelope from Josephs. It was closed with a wax seal—something that rarely happened since gummed envelopes had become widely available—and when she recognized the crest, her heart gave a little lurch.

"Thank you," she said, dismissing her butler.

Josephs glanced at her in surprise and curiosity—she hardly ever actually dismissed him—but exited the room without comme

Her hands were steady as she broke the seal and withdrew the paper inside. Though the message was brief, its contents were surprising.

My dearest Irene: I have just returned to London and I should very much like to see you, and Ellen as well. Would you call today at one? I've also asked Ellen to come. Gratefully, Lottie

Irene closed the note and slipped it back into its envelope. Lady Charlotte Milbright had left London shortly after her husband's tragic death at the Enfield Ball and had been out of contact these last four years, living on the Continent with her sister. They had once been the closest of bosom friends, the three of them: Lottie, Irene, and Ellen Enfield.

Irene drew in a deep breath and expelled it, slow and long. She supposed she shouldn't be surprised that Lottie had contacted her upon her return. But she was also a little afraid she knew why Lottie wanted her to call.

It was at times like these—very rare occasions—that Irene acknowledged how handy a telephone would be. She'd ring over to Ellen Enfield and hear what she thought about it all.

But that wasn't an option.

Irene didn't consider, even for a moment, not going. Instead, she rang for her lady's maid, Cissy and Josephs; the former to assist her to dress for a social call, and the latter to send for a carriage. For a number of reasons, she didn't want to use one of the ones emblazoned with the Darling crest.

Ellen would answer the summons as well, she had no doubt.

Almost two hours later, when she alighted from a leased carriage at the Milbright home, Irene noticed that the house still had the shrouded appearance of one in mourning during the owner's absence. Lady Milbright had obviously not intended to announce her return to London.

Feeling a little uneasy, even whilst telling herself she had no reason to be, Irene adjusted the heavy veil she'd draped over her hat to swath her face then lifted the door knocker.

Just as she let it fall, she heard the sounds of another carriage stopping on the street behind her. Ellen, of course.

She didn't glance over her shoulder. The door in front of her opened and she stepped inside.

"Lady Milbright is waiting for you in the sitting room," said the butler.

He was new in the position since the tragedy; and, in fact, Irene had never seen him before—but even so, he obviously either knew her identity, or had been instructed to show in any visitors.

Irene hesitated then started down the hall. She didn't need to be shown the way to the sitting room. She'd visited far too many times to count...had sat there and enjoyed tea and conversation, laughter and confidences. There, on the terrace, in the garden behind, in cafes or parks.

But the last time she'd been here, Lottie Milbright had received her in her bedchamber. She'd been unable to leave her bed, due to a terrible accident when she'd fallen down the stairs. It was a miracle she'd survived with only bruises, a sprained wrist, and a badly broken leg. The bump on her head had not, as the doctor had feared, turned into something deadly. Regardless, Lottie had been so ill and bedridden she hadn't even been able to attend her husband's funeral, which occurred only a week later.

It was not the first time Lottie Milbright had met with an unfortunate accident. She was, as she'd said laughingly, so utterly clumsy.

Irene gritted her teeth at the memory, then, ignoring the squirrelly feeling in her belly, she squared her shoulders with resolve. As she entered the sitting room, she could hear the sounds of Ellen being greeted and received at the front door, and knew that she would be right on her heels.

"Lottie!" Irene said, sweeping into the room as she lifted the veil up and off her face, settling it over the top of her hat. She gaped when she caught sight of her old friend. "Why, you look absolutely wonderful!"

This last was an unplanned and wholly surprised—and

truthful—exclamation. Indeed, Irene had never seen her friend look so well: her face was no longer drawn and pale, her eyes sparkled, her carriage was upright and confident.

Lottie had been an incredible beauty when she was younger, and those perfect features had aged well. She almost seemed to have re-bloomed during her time away. Her blond hair was still light but had gone from a rich golden color to become more pale and silver. She was only a few years younger than Irene, and she and Lord Milbright had never had children. That was possibly the reason her figure had remained slender and trim through the years, although Irene thought there were other reasons that might have contributed to that as well. Lottie had always been the quiet member of the trio; more thoughtful than the opinionated and bold Irene, and more of a follower than the regal and elegant Ellen Enfield.

Lottie wasn't wearing black—or even gray—for mourning. Her frock was an understated, soft blue with black rickrack trim and no other embellishments, but it was decidedly not a mourning gown. It had been four years since she had been widowed, but many women—including the queen—wore black or dark gray for far longer. Irene still mourned Edward nine years later—but that was in her heart, and, in her opinion, ought to be private. She saw no reason to dress like a drab, colorless person, so she wholly supported her friend's choice of attire.

"Dear, *dear* Irene, thank you so much for coming." Lottie rose and before Irene could hesitate, she came to her and took both of her hands in hers. She limped from her injury, but nonetheless, moved easily. "I've missed you so very much, and I'm so sorry I haven't written." Before she could continue, they heard the sound of footsteps and the rustle of skirt.

Irene and Lottie both turned to see Ellen Enfield. Irene gave a little chuckle when she saw that the other woman had worn a veil and was folding it away from her face. They always had thought alike.

"Oh, Ellen! Thank you so much for coming," cried Lottie. Before Irene could react, Lottie had pulled both of her visitors into a great embrace. "Oh, how I've missed you both!"

The three women embraced for a long moment, and Irene felt herself vibrating gently with emotion. These two were her oldest friends and she'd missed them more than she'd allowed herself to admit. She was not the only one trembling, and she found herself blinking rapidly. At last, Lottie released them. As they separated and stepped back, Irene and Ellen exchanged uncomfortable, wary looks.

Lottie looked from one to the other and her eyes—also glittering with unshed tears—widened as she took in their expressions. "Is it true? You haven't seen each other since...since..."

Irene looked at Ellen, whose image wavered due to her watery vision.

"No," they said together. Ellen reached out and took Irene's hand, giving it a good, heartfelt squeeze. Irene squeezed back and more tears dampened her eyes.

"But...I thought for certain you'd..." Lottie appeared shocked and discomfited. "I..." She'd stepped back and now she stared at them. "*For four years?*"

Irene and Ellen exchanged looks, then nodded in tandem.

"Good Heavens," breathed Lottie. "I...oh, Heavens, was I wrong to ask you both here? I just assumed...I thought... That explains the veils, doesn't it!" She shook her head, passing a hand over her forehead, and took on—for the first time—the same startled, doe-like look she'd used to wear often.

Before.

"Not at all," said Ellen, flapping a hand.

Ellen Enfield's annual ball had always been notorious for being one of the highlights of the season because the woman herself was the epitome of elegance and propriety and *everyone* wanted to attend her gathering. With her sharp, patrician features, thin, arching brows, and high forehead, Ellen often gave off a haughty impression even though in private she could be as relaxed and earthy, even silly at times, as Irene.

She and Irene were almost the same age, and although Ellen and her husband, the very wealthy but untitled Mr. Ralph Enfield (his brother was a viscount), had had two children, the Enfields were not the least bit the love match that Irene and Edward had been. They were amicable with each other, but rarely interacted unless required to do so.

"Right, then. Shall we sit?" Lottie said. Her color had come back and she seemed more at ease.

"You look *incredibly* well, Lottie," said Ellen. "Paris—or wherever you've been—seems to have agreed with you."

"Vienna," replied Lottie with a smile. "I've been in Vienna. And thank you. I fear I was rather a mess the last time I saw you. Either of you...and then..."

"And then your husband died tragically, and you had many other things to worry over," said Irene. "We completely under-stand, Lottie. I'm so grateful that your sister was able to take you away from...all of it."

"It's just that I never...I never really understood what happened that night," Lottie went on. A little furrow appeared between her brows. "Of course, I wasn't able to attend your ball, Ellen, and—"

"Due to a *terrible, violent* fall down the stairs," said Ellen in a tone that had Irene glancing at her with a worried look.

"I can only wonder whether, if I'd *been* there, things might have been different," Lottie went on as if she hadn't heard.

"You were lucky to be alive, let alone worrying about attending a *ball*," Ellen said.

The cracked door to the sitting room opened all the way,

and the housekeeper—also new, Irene noted with interest—wheeled in a two-tiered tray with tea service.

"Thank you, Betty. That will be all. Please close the door when you leave," Lottie said. "I'll ring if I need anything else."

They were silent as Lottie served tea. It wasn't a strained silence, but it was a pregnant one, an expectant one. The three women had once known each other so well that a momentary pause in conversation would have been unusual, but also unremarkable and certainly not uncomfortable.

Lottie remembered how each of her visitors took their tea; also not a surprise.

Irene picked up her cup but had no desire to drink. She glanced at Ellen and found her old friend looking at her with the same questioning expression she knew was in her own gaze.

Lottie picked up her own cup, eyed it, then set it down. She looked at Irene and then Ellen and said, "I need you to tell me what really happened that night."

Chapter Twelve

I rene glanced at Ellen. Her friend looked as stricken as she knew she did. Ellen drew in a breath and nodded, and Irene knew that was her cue to do the talking.

"Ellen and I were up on the small balcony overlooking the ballroom. We had had a disagreement earlier," Irene said carefully, "and neither of us were prepared to let it go, I suppose."

"Irene was being terribly stubborn about it all—"

"And Ellen wasn't listening to a *thing* I said."

They'd spoken these same lines many times over the last few years and so the words came naturally; easily.

"And when Irene came up to the balcony to confront me again, she was still quite angry. And I was too," Ellen admitted ruefully. "Our altercation became heated—"

"Sadly, I suppose no one fights as hard or as thoroughly as good friends can," Irene commented. "Rather like sisters."

"Indeed. And, well, I was so angry—I really was," Ellen said, and Irene knew it was the truth; they both had been so angry—which was why they'd done what they'd done, "that I pushed her."

"Everyone was watching from below but we didn't even

realize it. We were so heated," Irene explained. "She pushed me, and I bumped into Lord Milbright—he was standing right behind me. I think—I think he was trying to get to the stairs to go down, to...er...distance himself from the...er...scene."

"I pushed Irene so hard she stumbled back and bumped into Milbright," Ellen said. "And he...he...must have... I think he tripped over her walking stick—"

"And then he fell against the railing," Irene said. "And it...it didn't hold. The railing gave way."

"He fell. Right there, in the ballroom. Right in front of everyone." Ellen's voice was very calm and controlled.

Silence fell.

The image of Lord Milbright, crumpled on the floor, blood seeping from his ears, neck at a terrible angle, had never left Irene's memory or nightmares. She didn't look at Ellen, for she suspected the same image was burned into the mind of her friend as well.

Lottie stared into her teacup as the silence stretched.

Suddenly, she looked up. "I don't believe you."

Irene's stomach lurched. "What do you mean? Everyone was there. Everyone saw what happened. It was an awful, scandalous scene that ended in a tragedy."

Ellen scoffed at the word "tragedy," but said nothing more.

"There are too many things wrong with what you said," Lottie explained. "No one goes up on that smaller balcony during the ball, Ellen. You've always had it closed off. And what was Lord Milbright doing up there anyway? He wasn't the sort to—well, I don't understand any of it. And Reenie...a walking stick? You? Whatever for?"

"I'd strained my ankle," Irene explained quickly.

Lottie shook her head and went on. "And the two of you? Pushing each other? Shouting in public? Why, what on *earth* could have caused the two of you so much anger and anguish that you would do such an appalling thing?"

"Why I...well, I don't even remember what we were—"

"Nonsense!" Lottie cut off Ellen. "You expect me to believe you don't remember what you were arguing about when a man died?"

"Lottie, darling," Irene said, avoiding looking at Ellen. "We've just tried to put it all behind us. It was a tragic accident. And you've certainly come through the...er...the situation well enough," she added quietly. "I've never seen you look so well, Lottie—not since you were..."

"Not since before I married Milbright, you mean."

"He was a *devil*," Ellen burst out. "That man was evil and a devil and he *hurt* you, Lottie. I know he did. *We* knew it. All the time. It's lucky he didn't kill you."

"He would have eventually," Irene said. She knew they were skirting too close to dangerous topics, but it had to be said. "He would eventually have killed you. That last fall down the stairs..." She shuddered, and reached over to clasp Lottie's hand. "We know he pushed you, dear. We know he did it."

"It wasn't a tragedy," said Ellen flatly, though her voice was tinged with withheld sobs, "that that man died. It was a *blessing*."

There was silence again. This time it was filled with the sounds of suppressed sobs and unsteady breathing. Irene couldn't bear to look at either of her companions.

"H-how did you know?" said Lottie at last. "That he... that he..."

"That he *hurt* you? That he beat you? That all your illnesses and injuries weren't from your own clumsiness, but from his violence?" Irene said. "It wasn't terribly difficult to tell, Lottie. You hid it well, you made excellent excuses, you stayed home when you were really bruised up and hurt, but...we knew you. We knew you and—"

"And we knew *him*. I could see it in his eyes," Ellen said. "One time he...he gave me a look like he wanted to kill me when I said something he didn't like. And you only had to see the condition of his horses to know. The way they shied, the way their eyes rolled when he came near them."

It was almost a relief to have it all out in the open, Irene thought.

Lottie was sobbing now, tears streaming down her face, her cheeks red, her breath coming in deep gulps. "I thought... I didn't think... I thought I hid it so well. Everyone liked Lord Milbright. He was s-so affable and amiable."

Wasn't it so telling, Irene thought, that Lottie continued to refer to her husband in such a formal, distant manner—even now?

"No he wasn't," snapped Ellen. "He had a look in his eye. I'm not sorry he's gone, Lottie. I'm not the least bit sorry. He can't hurt you anymore."

"I..." Lottie couldn't speak. She just looked at Ellen and then Irene and then all at once, her eyes widened. Her flushed cheeks went dead white and a hand slapped to her bosom as she gasped. She opened her mouth to speak.

"And we needn't talk about it ever again," Irene said quickly and firmly.

"Indeed. It's over and done with," Ellen said in the same no-nonsense voice.

Lottie looked at each of them in turn and her eyelids fluttered. She drew in a shuddering breath. "Right. Right, then." A sad little smile wavered over her lips.

Irene felt the tension ease from her shoulders. She hadn't realized how tightly she'd been holding herself. She smiled at

Lottie. "It's really so very good to see you. Are you planning to stay in London?"

"I...I'm not certain," Lottie replied. "You see...there is one other thing I haven't told you quite yet."

"What is that?" said Ellen. She sounded easier now, too, and her smile was more relaxed.

"I've gotten married again." Lottie's cheeks flushed, but this time it was from pleasure, not pain or sorrow. "He's...he's very different from Lord Milbright."

"I'm quite certain he is," replied Irene, patting her hand. "You look very happy, Lottie...and perhaps even in love?"

"Oh, yes," Lottie replied, her flush growing deeper. "Bertrand is wonderful. So kind and caring. I...I've never felt this way before. I never imagined I would...at my age, and after..."

"It's a wonderful feeling, being in love," Irene said warmly. "I'm very happy for you."

"As am I," said Ellen, "even though I can't say I've ever been madly in love as it appears you are, Lottie." Her smile was filled with genuine affection and perhaps a bit of sadness over the absence of romantic love in her own life. "I do hope we get to meet this Bertrand soon."

"Of course," replied Lottie, her cheeks still rosy. If she'd looked pretty and happy earlier, now she seemed to glow with delight and beauty. "He's at the Savoy because I didn't want... well, I thought it best if I came here alone first, you see. I've all new servants, and...well, I wanted to speak to both of you straight-away. Before anyone knew I was returned. To tell you, and to—"

"Yes, of course," Irene said, interrupting before Lottie could wind the conversation back to topics best avoided.

"And now, the two of you...I do hope you'll be friends again," Lottie said.

We never stopped, Irene thought. She looked at Ellen, who was looking at her as well, a quiet smile curving her lips. Irene's eyes stung and she looked away, blinking rapidly.

"Of course," Ellen murmured, and Irene echoed the sentiment.

Irene was fifty years old and she'd lived through many difficulties, delights, and events in her life. But there was one thing she'd come to understand: there was nothing like a close female friend; a person who understood you, who accepted your moods and faults and foibles, who shared fun and sorrow, secrets and confidences.

One with whom, even if you hadn't spoken in years, it was as if you'd never parted when you finally did once again.

Irene felt unaccountably weepy—almost like she had when she was expecting—as she climbed into a hired carriage to take her home.

She'd left Lottie knowing that her friend was happier than she'd ever been, and she looked forward to meeting her new husband, who was one Mr. Bertrand Villaneuve. The man had made a small fortune by exporting French limestone into Vienna during the expansion of that city over the last decade, so it seemed clear he hadn't married Lottie for the Milbright money.

Ellen had also sent for a carriage, but Irene's arrived first. They said their farewells in the sitting room with Lottie.

"You're attending tomorrow night, Irene?" Ellen said. She was referring to the ball.

"I received your invitation. Of course I'll be there," Irene replied.

Ellen nodded, but there was a flicker of relief in her dark eyes. "It's long past time."

"Quite so." Irene squeezed Ellen's hand, then excused herself to get into the carriage.

She realized, as she settled into the seat and closed her damp eyes, that she hadn't given Harold Tripley's murder one thought during the last several hours. She wasn't certain whether that was a good thing.

It was a shame she hadn't been able to tell Ellen about her investigation. She suspected Ellen would have latched onto the idea of detecting a murder like a kitten climbing a curtain.

And if Irene had told her about the Wall of Man, Ellen would have leaped on that intrigue like Beatrice on a scrap of beef roast.

Irene's fond smile faded as a little pang of sadness plucked at her, and she pushed it away. There was no reason to be forlorn. She had a good life, a comfortable one, filled with love—from both people and animals—and soon, God willing, she'd be back in the country and away from the hustle and bustle of societal expectations and too many layers of crinolines.

Irene gave herself a little shake from her doldrums and considered what she ought to do next. She needed to focus her thoughts and her attention on the deaths of Harold Tripley and Viscount Garington.

The biggest question was: why had someone killed the viscount? As with the murder of Harold Tripley, the killer was taking a great risk by doing the deed in such a public setting. Therefore, she reasoned as the carriage rolled along, the killer must have been desperate to silence Lord Garington...which then meant that the viscount must have known or seen something that would threaten to expose the murderer.

And whatever it was that he knew or saw could very well have occurred at the theatre last night, which was why the killer had taken such a risk. Good Heavens—what a risk it was! Anyone could have walked into the theatre box and seen him.

The killer had to have gotten some blood on him; Irene was certain of it. On his gloves, of course—and they'd been discarded —but also on the cuff of his shirt or the sleeve of his jacket.

Whichever of the four suspects had done it had been standing there in the gallery, speaking to others. Maybe someone had noticed a few drops of blood on a sleeve or cuff.

But there *was* someone who would notice for certain: the killer's valet.

Irene settled back in her seat with a satisfied smile. It certainly came in handy, when one was detecting, to have servants who were friends with other servants.

When she arrived back at the dowager house, Irene ordered a tray with tea. She hadn't eaten or drunk anything at Lottie's house due to her upheaval of emotions, and now that things had gone well and she was returned home, she was famished.

While she waited for the tea tray, Irene settled in the little sitting room and gathered her loved ones round: Beatrice next to her lap, prepared to snuffle up any crumbs that might tumble her way; Mr. Timms sitting on his favorite perch next to her chair and within eyesight of the dish of nuts; and Watson sprawled on her feet, snoring whilst chasing rabbits in his dreams.

Irene couldn't have asked for a more comfortable, more delightful scene...except to have Edward sitting in his chair, looking up and over at her whilst smoking a pipe. He'd had a way of gazing at her that made her heart swell and her entire self feel as if she'd been wrapped in a blanket warmed by the fire. As if she was the most important thing in the world to him.

"My goodness, I have no idea why I'm feeling so morose," Irene said aloud, blinking rapidly. "Why, I've turned into quite the waterpot today." Beatrice's head popped up from where she'd been tucked next to her, napping soundly. Irene stroked the soft fluffy head until the wee beast sank back into sleep, having ascertained there was no food in the proximity.

Mr. Timms tilted his head and looked at her with bright eyes so intelligent she knew he was contemplating a sober reply. "Thank you, Darling," he said, tilting his head affectionately. "I think so too, Darling."

This caused her to laugh, and she opened the little dish to offer him a treat. Of course, the rattle of the lid had Beatrice popping up again, and Irene couldn't resist those soulful eyes. She offered the tiny poodle a little bit of nut as well.

Then the door opened and Vella wheeled in a tray.

Irene was very happy to see her friend. She had much to chat at her about.

"Sit with me, Vella," she said. "I know you well enough to know that the household is running just fine on its own—and in fact, it runs so fine that you're hardly needed at all. Ring for another teacup and plate, won't you?"

Vella didn't need extra encouragement. She sat and grinned. "I don't need to ring." She produced a second teacup and saucer. "I was certain you'd have things to tell me, and I have information for you."

"Excellent," said Irene, pouring tea for both of them. "Do I need to pony up a reward?"

"Indeed you do." Vella's thick, dark brows danced comically.

"And so you discovered to whom the missing cufflink belonged?" Irene passed the teacup across the little table, then turned her attention to the stacks of tiny, crustless sandwiches piled on the tray.

Beatrice had gone on high alert as soon as the essence of chicken salad crossed the threshold, and now she sat next to Irene, fairly quivering with excitement and hope. Unlike with her mistress's daughters, Beatrice knew better than to attempt to help herself to anything in front of Irene. She had to wait until it was offered.

And it was. A tiny corner of bread, a little sliver of chicken... even a delicate wedge of cucumber...all were given to her, and she ate them neatly and with gusto.

"I did. It seems the cufflink belongs to Mr. Matthew Feverley," said Vella, reaching for a sandwich of strawberry and mint leaves and a spread of whipped white cheese.

Irene's cup rattled on its saucer. "Mr. Feverley? Are you *quite* certain?" Her heart and stomach plummeted. Oh dear. She had not expected—had not *wanted* it to be Matthew Feverley! Why, he'd been so kind and intelligent, and had even seemed to share her sense of adventure over this whole debacle.

"I'm quite certain. The ladies' maid at Horling House is being courted by Mr. Feverley's valet, and I spoke to her because our own Cora is her close friend. The valet told her the ruby and mother-of-pearl cufflink had gone missing after the night of the dinner party. You don't appear pleased to have identified the culprit," said Vella, frowning.

"It's only...well, I didn't think it would be him, that's all," Irene said. She'd picked up and then put down a plate of sandwiches, leaving them untouched.

"I don't believe one is allowed to choose who the killer is when one is investigating a murder," Vella said wryly.

"No, of course not. And of course I can't—and won't—ignore unpleasant and unwanted facts when they are dropped in my lap...even if it does cost me a dratted ha'penny to find them out," Irene said with a little scoff. "But I must say I had very nearly stricken him from my list as a suspect."

"He was present both times," Vella reminded her.

"And he was wearing a brown and blue checked waistcoat last night," Irene said. Nonetheless, she was still dissatisfied.

"What does that matter?" Vella asked, frowning. "The waistcoat?"

"Oh, yes, of course," Irene replied. "I haven't told you about Lord Garington's unexpected demise. He was my favorite suspect," she said sadly. "I mean to say, he was my favorite in the sense that I thought he was the most likely to have done it. And now he's ended up dead and so I have to start all over again."

She described the events at the theatre, ending with, "And so it is very possible that Mr. Feverley was wearing brown gloves." She sighed. "Which is another point against him. I suppose I shall have to speak to the young man about it all. I can't even fathom a reason he would want to kill Harold Tripley. He just doesn't seem the type. But how else would his cufflink be found beneath the desk by the body?"

Then a thought struck her. "Ah, but Mr. Feverley was standing near the desk like a sentry, to keep the others away whilst I investigated. Perhaps he could have dropped it then," she said, recognizing the relief that traversed her.

"He was standing near the desk?" Vella asked. "The maid said the cufflink was well under it, so I suppose..."

With a pang of disappointment, Irene sighed and shook her head grimly. "No, that can't be how it happened. I'm certain he never went round the back. He stood in the front—I kept an eye on him and the others, even when I was investigating the terrace. Mr. Feverley was in front of the desk, and so he couldn't have dropped his cufflink *under* the desk from there."

Vella didn't seem to sympathize with Irene's disappointment. Instead, she asked, "Why would Mr. Feverley kill Lord Garington too?"

Irene tilted her head. "I suppose he killed Garington because the man had seen or heard something that connected him to the murder. Mr. Chessley told me that he'd witnessed Harold Tripley and Lord Garington in a rather adversarial conversation on the night of the dinner party, and that the viscount was quite unhappy at the end of the conversation. It was that information which caused me to suspect Garington more strongly—he'd exhibited signs of anger and discord with Harold Tripley. But now Garington is dead, and whatever they were arguing about either had nothing to do with Harold Tripley's murder—"

"Or had everything to do with it," finished Vella.

"Precisely. Devil take it!" Irene said, knowing that Vella wasn't scandalized when she cursed. "This is becoming exceedingly confusing, investigating a murder."

"It certainly is much more difficult than reading the solutions in a Sherlock Holmes story," said Vella with great sympathy and perhaps a bit of irony.

Irene cast her a sidewise look through narrowed eyes. "I'm not giving up," she told her firmly. "I shall speak to Mr. Feverley and demand he tell me why he did such terrible things. I only wish I didn't have to disappoint his mother and sister. And my dear Rose, too, for she has been quite friendly with the family for many years." She sighed. This was, she supposed, the cross one must bear for wanting to find justice and expose criminals. Once in a while, the criminal was a nice, amiable, charming person—other than his murderous tendencies, of course.

"What a risk he took, cutting a man's throat in the middle of a crowded theatre," Vella mused. "And then climbed or jumped into the next box to escape!"

Irene nodded. "Quite. I can't seem to get beyond that fact. To do such a thing...why, a person must be half mad to take such a chance!"

"Or be very desperate," said Vella. "People do very strange things, very unbelievable things, when they are desperate. Like stow away on a merchant ship." She grinned, her eyes dancing.

"Quite so, but you didn't truly stow away. I hid you until it was too late for Papa to bring you back," Irene said with a smile. Then she heaved a sigh. "I suppose I should send word to Mr. Feverley that he is to present himself to me soonest."

"Or you could simply give the information to Inspector Burgess and allow him to handle it," Vella said far too reasonably.

That was the thing with having long-time friends who knew you very well: they said what they thought, even if they disagreed with you—or, worse, if they made excellent sense.

Irene gave her a little glare. "I should think not. I could hand him the culprit on a silver platter and the inspector would likely drop it and let him go free. No. I shall see this through myself, no matter how difficult it might be." She rose to write the message, momentarily forgetting her abandoned plate of sandwiches.

Beatrice pounced and Irene spun at the sound of the clatter as Mr. Timms took flight, squawking, "Intruder! Intruder!"

"Drat it, Bea!" Irene navigated around Watson, who'd lumbered to his feet at the excitement, flinging drool everywhere, and snatched up the little dog. Beatrice's mouth was full of chicken sandwich, and she had her jaws clamped stubbornly closed as Irene glared down at her, trying not to laugh. "You conniving little beast!"

Vella was laughing as she picked up the plate and moved it to a safer location. "You always warn the girls not to turn their backs on their food."

Irene put the little dog back down, and Beatrice bolted under the chair to finish her spoils in peace. Watson stood panting expectantly as Mr. Timms swooped and glided across and around the room, crying, "Give it back! Give it back!"

Irene heaved a sigh, then burst out laughing. "The three of you are quite a handful," she said, and dutifully doled out treats to the parrot and the shaggy dog. At least they hadn't *stolen* them. "Now, what *was* I doing?"

"Writing a message to Mr. Feverley, I expect," said Vella.

"Right." Irene's exasperated humor faded as she returned to the unpleasant task.

Just as she finished the note, Priscilla appeared at the door. Vella rose to her feet, earning a surprised glance from the girl (a housekeeper sitting in the presence of her mistress? *Quelle horreur!*).

"Lady Darling, is everything all right? I heard a bit of a to-do."

"Yes, yes, it was just Beatrice being a greedy little thing," Irene replied. "You look quite lovely, pet. Are you expecting visitors? A gentleman caller, perhaps?"

Priscilla blushed. "Not really, my lady. Only...Mr. Bafferty suggested he and the duke might call today. I told him of course we would receive them."

Irene smothered a smirk. Oh, that Hugh Bafferty was a sly one, wasn't he? "Then I suppose you ought to sit in the parlor and wait for them...I mean to say, should they call. And what about Mr. Shaw?"

Priscilla blanched. "Oh. Well, I suppose he might pay a call, but...quite honestly, Lady Darling, I have no desire to encourage him. Especially if he is a murderer."

"Well, my dear, you may rest easy over that at least. I don't believe he is a murderer. We've identified the culprit and it isn't Mr. Shaw."

"Oh. Well, even so, I don't wish to encourage him," Priscilla said with a firmness of which Irene approved.

A woman ought to know whether she would entertain marriage to a particular man or not.

"Quite so. I don't blame you one bit, my dear. He's rather... shiny, isn't he? With all that pomade? And a bit...well, he was very in his cups last night and couldn't seem to keep his eyes at a proper height, now could he? Ogling one's bosoms all the time."

Priscilla gasped out a surprised laugh. "Lady Darling! It's not proper to say such a thing!"

"It's not proper to leer at a woman's bosom, is it? And I take exception to the idea that it isn't proper to speak about gentlemen who make the hairs on the back of one's neck stand on end, or one's middle curdle like bad milk. I think that if women spoke more about such things and helped each other with them, there would be far less tragedy in the world."

Her smile faded as she thought of Lottie Milbright. Perhaps her friend's life would have been different if ladies *had* spoken more honestly amongst each other instead of looking only at the contents of a man's pocket, and if their guardians had been more sensitive to their feelings instead of simply trying to marry a girl off to the highest bidder.

"Yes, my lady. I never thought about it that way." Priscilla seemed both admiring and taken aback. "I suppose I shall go to the parlor in case they do come to call. The duke and Mr. Bafferty, I mean to say." She started out, then paused at the doorway. "Do you know Lady Pengelley well, Lady Darling?"

"She's a lovely young woman," replied Irene. "Delightful. Very amiable and not at all full of herself as some of these young, wealthy girls are. She's got a rather wicked sense of humor. As I understand it, she came out last year and declined three offers of marriage."

"I see," replied Priscilla. She didn't look very pleased at all.

"She's a very good match for the duke," Irene said blithely. "I believe his mother is quite taken with her as well."

Priscilla's expression did not do the girl justice, but Irene didn't comment. Her ward was going to have to learn about reality soon enough. It was one thing to be firm and confident. It was another to have impossible, unattainable plans—and to be angry at the world when they didn't come to pass.

"Please excuse me, Lady Darling," said Priscilla.

Irene gave her credit for retaining her manners, and merely nodded her permission. She rang for Josephs or a footman to have the message to Mr. Feverley delivered.

And then she had nothing to do but wait and stew over it.

∼

But Matthew Feverley didn't come. Nor did he send word.

Irene ate supper with Priscilla, still so caught up in her own thoughts that she neglected to ask how it had gone when Mr. Bafferty and the duke had called.

Yes, the two had called...along with Lady Pengelley.

Irene had declined to attend the little gathering in the parlor, for she could predict precisely how it would go. She sent her excuses, citing the "ghastly incident" at the theatre last night, and contented herself with mulling over what she would say to Matthew Feverley when he arrived.

But he didn't arrive.

Did he realize he'd been found out? Had he run off to the Continent to preserve his freedom? Or had he simply not yet received the message?

"What time shall we leave tomorrow night?" asked Priscilla, jolting Irene from her contemplations.

"Tomorrow—oh, yes, of course. For the Enfield Ball. The carriage will be ready to leave at half-nine. I intend to be within, and you will as well, I presume."

"Of course, my lady."

Now Irene perceived a sort of sullenness from her ward and attributed it to the presence of Lady Pengelley earlier today. She sighed internally and hoped that Priscilla would abandon her dream of marrying the duke and open her eyes to an eminently suitable suitor who seemed quite determined to win her hand.

It was quite clear that Mrs. Bedwith was pleased enough with the idea of a match between Mr. Bafferty and Priscilla—else, she would never have directed him to them in London. And, Irene had been making discreet inquiries about Hugh Bafferty, and absolutely nothing worrisome had come to light.

Irene and Priscilla finished dinner, and, since they were staying in tonight, Irene was planning to repair to her bedchamber and have a good long soak in a warm tub of water scented with rose oil. It was an experience she'd first been introduced to in Istanbul when she was twelve, and, despite the scarcity of bathing tubs in London, she had had a bathing room installed in each of her homes so she could indulge in such a luxury whenever possible.

She'd ordered the water to be heated and was just about to climb the stairs to the second floor when someone rapped at the front door.

Ah. Matthew Feverley, at last.

Irene bid Josephs to bring him to the sitting room. She'd decided on that location in lieu of the parlor, the latter of which was larger and more formal. This conversation, she knew, would best be held in a small and more private setting. She was determined to encourage him to confess, and to explain *why* he'd done such terrible things.

Irene had no fear for her own safety. Perhaps she should have done, but she simply could not believe Mr. Feverley—despite doing what she suspected him of doing—would cause her any harm. Especially in her own sitting room.

"My lady."

Josephs stood in the doorway of the parlor.

"Yes? Bring him in, please."

"He is not here. There is only this message for you, my lady."

Surprised and disappointed, she rose and met him halfway across the room. She took the folded paper, opened it, and read:

We must speak.

It was signed with an ornate, flourishing J. Or was it an F?

She frowned, squinting at it closely. Drat it, where were her spectacles when she needed them?

J or F?

It must be F, for Feverley, of course. J made no sense at all.

"And what does this mean? Of course we need to speak," she groused. "I do loathe it when people can't come right out and say what they mean. It's extremely inefficient. A waste of time."

"Er...Madam, there is a carriage waiting without."

"A carriage?" Irene considered, then understood. Mr. Feverley wished to speak with her anonymously and in the privacy of his carriage. As someone who'd done precisely the same thing earlier today—arriving at Lottie Milbright's swathed in a veil and in a hired hack—Irene comprehended his reasoning.

But she was also not foolish enough to climb into a dark carriage with a murderer. Receiving him in her sitting room was one thing—there were servants about, fully aware that she was expecting a visitation from a killer, and she was in her own home. But climbing into a carriage was not at all a prudent thing to do...

Unless she was prepared.

"Josephs, I'm going out."

"Going...out? Now? Alone?" He gaped at her. "Sh-shall I call for the carriage to be brought round?"

"No. I'll be leaving with Matthew Feverley, in his carriage. If I have not returned by midnight, send word to his mother and call for Inspector Burgess. Vella will explain. But for now..."

She turned from the desk, holding the tiny, pearl-handled pistol she'd retrieved from one of the secret drawers in the back. Not long before he died, Edward had given it to her after one of their friends had been robbed whilst walking to their carriage from the theatre one night.

"It's a little thing, but it's quite deadly," he'd told her. "I'll feel better knowing you have some protection from these brazen thieves and brigands! I insist you have it on your person at all times, my love. Do promise me that."

Irene had cooed over it, thanked him, and taken the pistol— and barely managed to keep from patting him affectionately on his balding head. She hadn't committed one way or the other to have it with her at all times—for of course she wasn't about to do any such thing. Firearms were far too bulky and complicated to be toting all about in one's reticule. Not to mention dangerous.

Instead, she stowed it away to be forgotten until five months ago, when she'd moved here to the dowager house. Since then, she'd taken it out exactly four times to test it (she'd gotten out of practice with handling a firearm) and always returned it to its safe place, in the very back of the drawer.

Now she was pleased with herself that she'd kept it oiled and ready, and tucked away. She'd never expected to use it, but times changed.

Josephs was gawking at her, likely trying to find the words to stop her, but she paid him no mind. Of course he was going to assume she was being foolish, but then again, butler or no, he was a man and she was a woman; men always seemed to think that women were incapable of clear thinking and preparation.

"But my lady...."

"Be still, Josephs. You have my direction. I shall return anon."

She swept past him and the footman, George, and across the pentagonal foyer. Josephs had to leap in front of her in order to reach the door in time to open it for her to pass through.

The spring night air was balmy and still but for the rattle of a carriage passing by and a dog barking in the distance. Big Ben struck half-ten, his dull, metallic toll rolling over the city like a heavy blanket. There was no chance of spotting any glitter of stars here in London; everything was clouded over and shrouded with fog. Even the moon, which was full tonight, barely made an impression through the heavy mist, which roiled and seethed like an angry ocean.

The carriage—unmarked, no surprise—waited in front of her house, the driver standing next to the door, ready to help her inside. The walkway was brief—a mere six steps from door to street—which gave Irene little time to reconsider her decision (not that she would do), or to work up a staid, firm countenance for the confrontation she was about to have with Matthew Feverley.

The driver handed her into the carriage and she sat down.

The door closed and she realized it was *not* Mr. Feverley in the carriage.

Chapter Thirteen

"Who the devil are you?" Irene exclaimed as the carriage lurched into motion. Her heart made the same sort of jolt as she realized she was riding off in a vehicle with a man she didn't know.

A small lantern bobbed from the wall near Irene's head, which had the effect of casting her in its illumination, but only throwing shadows and a bit of meager light toward the man who sat across from her.

But her lap was hidden in the dark. She stealthily closed her fingers around the pistol inside her reticule, prepared to employ it at the earliest sign of villainy...for the man sitting across from her looked like the most villainous person she'd ever encountered.

What little she could see of his face was covered not only by a heavy mustache and thick beard that just brushed the top of his shirt, but a black patch over his left eye. He was a large person, taking up a good portion of the seat across from her—granted, this wasn't a roomy, luxurious brougham, but he sprawled there, taking up most of a seat for two. A bowler hat was perched on his head, covering most of the dark brows that peeked out from beneath its crown. Dark hair winged up from beneath its brim.

From what she could tell, he wore the mean clothing of a laborer; there was no suggestion of a neckcloth or gloves, although his shirt did seem to fit properly. Even in the low light, it didn't look grimy or stained.

The scent of woodsmoke and something else...perhaps sawdust?...hovered in the small space. Beneath that was a tangy sort of smell, like cedar...which seemed rather incongruous for a man who appeared as scruffy and disreputable as he did.

His single visible eye glittered from the shadows as his mustache curved. "They call me One-Eyed Jack."

So it had been a J on the message, not an F. Drat it! If she'd realized this, Irene might have been better prepared for this unexpected event.

"And you wished to speak with me?" she replied haughtily, gripping the butt of her pistol tighter. She wished she wasn't sitting so near the lantern where he could clearly see her face and any emotion that might be in it.

"I hear yer lookin' f'the bloke wot done away wi' Harold Tripley." He spoke coarsely, in a low, gruff voice as he remained tucked in the shadowy corner. One arm was thrown casually across the top of the seat.

"Your information is correct. And the one who also cut the throat of Lord Garington, of course, as it is quite obviously the same person." Her pulse was beginning to slow a trifle, for the man hadn't done anything approaching villainy...yet. Still, her gift from Edward felt wonderfully solid in her gloved hand. "Do you know anything about it? Is that why you wished to speak with me?"

"The likes o' me migh' be of help to ye in that regard, yer ladyship," he replied. She thought she detected the slightest sneer at the use of her title.

"I'm doing quite well on my own," she replied tartly. "I've identified the killer—and in fact, I was expecting his arrival and was *not* expecting yours. So if you would return me to my home at once, we can end this little farce without bloodshed." She spoke calmly even as her pulse beat through her chest and into her ears.

He barked a laugh. "Bloodshed, eh, yer ladyship? D'ye think that little toy is a threat to the likes o' One-Eyed Jack?"

Irene was of the opinion that anyone who referred to themselves in the third person was pretentious and overfull of themselves (aside from Her Majesty, of course). Adding that to the fact that he was ridiculing her weapon—which she'd taken care for it *not* to be seen, so how had he perceived it?—made her even more irritated.

For some reason, however, she wasn't frightened.

Concerned, confused...but not frightened. Perhaps that was foolish and she should be terrified, but Irene had lived a long life and had encountered many people in many countries all over the world, in many different instances. She did not believe One-Eyed Jack meant her harm. The look in his eye was one of amusement and derision, not threat or violence.

"Nevertheless, I assure you, it will do the job," she told him, shifting so that the little pistol fell into a shaft of light. "And who, pray, calls you by such a ridiculous moniker? One-Eyed Jack? Is that even a real eyepatch?" She peered at him.

His mustache and beard twitched. "Would ye like to find out, yer ladyship? Go on ahead and take a gander, why don't ye." He gestured to the patch, leaning forward a little.

She scoffed. "Do stop wasting my time. As I've told you, I've already identified the killer, so—"

"An' who is that, yer ladyship? This two-time killer?" He settled back into his corner again.

She straightened and gave him her most imperious look.

"I've no intention of divulging that information—to you, at least. Why, I don't even know who you *are*. Now, either tell me what it is you believe will 'help me' or return me to my home. I've no patience for wasted time."

"All wot ye need to know about One-Eye Jack is 'at he makes no promises he don't keep, and he knows a lot about everyone. Even you, Lady Darling."

For the first time, a little hint of menace crept into his low, gruff voice.

She ignored the dart of fear that stabbed her belly; there was nothing for her to fear, nothing anyone could *know* about anything that should worry her. Lady Darling was a kind but haughty old lady, a bit quirky and eccentric, who preferred to stay with her pets in the country and was in no great hurry to be a grandmother. There was nothing to *know* about her.

She pushed away the memory of Lord Milbright's crumpled body. "Very well, then. Since you *know* all about everyone, what do you know about Matthew Feverley? Better, yet, what do you know about Harold Tripley and why someone would want to kill him?"

"Feverley? Wot's this about Feverley?" Then his eye narrowed with what appeared to be humor, crinkles showing at the corner of it. "Yer thinkin' that bloke Matthew Feverley did it?" he said on something like a guffaw.

Irene bristled. This was really, truly *too much*. She rapped sharply on the roof of the carriage, using the business end of her pistol. "Driver, stop this conveyance at once!" she said in her carrying voice.

The carriage did not stop.

Irene clamped her lips shut as her abductor—yes, she could accurately use that term now—merely eyed her with mockery in his one-sided gaze.

She lifted her pistol and pointed it straight at his chest.

"Return me to my home immediately or pay the price. Mind—you wouldn't be the first man I've shot."

"Is that so," he replied, unconcerned. His eye gleamed. "Very well then. I'll take ye home then, yer ladyship. But then if I do, ye won't be kennin' what the likes o' me knows about yer murder investigation. Yer barkin' up the wrong tree, y'are."

She cocked the pistol. The click sounded ominous—at least to her ears—inside the rumbling carriage. "Then cease bandying about and tell me what you bloody well know."

"'At's just it, yer ladyship, I can't tell ye. I need t'show ye." As if on cue, the carriage rolled to a halt.

Irene looked out the window and her eyes widened. The carriage had stopped in a narrow, dingy alley, Heaven knew where in the city. The only suggestion of illumination came from the moon, gamely trying to shine between the close-set buildings, through the thick clouds of fog. There was an anemic lantern hanging from a recessed door, but its circle of light was hardly the size of a thimble. Something shifted in the darkness and she thought she caught the glint of metal in a shadowy hand before the figure slipped into the black abyss between two buildings.

A glint like that of a knife blade.

Her heart was pounding hard as she turned away from the scene. "What is this nonsense?" she said, keeping her voice steady with an effort. "What have you to show me—a dingy alley and a dead-end street?"

"No' at all, yer ladyship." He shifted and suddenly the carriage door swung open into the night.

Irene was immediately assaulted by a wave of unpleasant-ness: the smell of rot and waste, greasy coal smoke, and stale alcohol.

One-Eyed Jack alighted from the carriage first, and, to her

surprise, offered her a proper hand to assist her in doing the same. Irene hesitated.

She told herself any sane woman would do so.

But the woman who'd clambered up the crow's nest of a spice and silk ship as a girl and darted among the streets of Istanbul and bartered with Japanese merchants in Edo and braved the disdain of the *haute ton* put out her hand and allowed it to be clasped by a large, warm, gloved one.

She didn't look at her captor/companion as she stepped out and down; she was more concerned about ensuring she didn't place a slippered foot in one of the items whose odors proliferated throughout the alley.

"Ah, right then...and see there, yer ladyship, yer faithful servant has made his appearance."

She looked over at the sound of a carriage careening into the narrow alley. Her lips twitched as the conveyance came to a violent halt in the manner she'd been subjected to over the last weeks. It could only be Barth managing the reins.

"Indeed. My servants are quite loyal. And resourceful." A little flush of confidence and warmth filled her chest as the carriage door opened and Josephs and George, the footman—and *Vella* of all people!—appeared.

One-Eyed Jack made a noise that sounded suspiciously like a put-upon sigh.

Irene ignored him. She was, all at once, having a nearly pleasant time. The appearance of her servants had instilled an almost farcical air upon the scene.

Josephs and Vella hurried over, with George, and then Benny, trailing behind.

"Are you quite all right, my lady?" asked Vella while Josephs —who was as broad as One-Eyed Jack, but not nearly as tall— gawked up at her captor.

"Of course," Irene replied. "Mister...er...well, apparently

this individual goes by the rather cumbersome moniker of One-Eyed Jack, and he—"

"*One-Eyed Jack?*" Josephs hissed out a breath that sounded more admiring than it should have done, in Irene's opinion. After all, the man had, for all intents and purposes, abducted his mistress. "You're One-Eyed Jack?" He shifted, and Irene saw that he was attempting to hide behind his coat the pistol he'd been clutching even as he gawped at the man with great regard.

"In the flesh," replied the man with a jaunty bow.

"Well, it's quite a good thing that we've come, then," said Vella. Irene noticed with a start that her housekeeper was holding a knife in the hand hanging alongside her skirt. "You don't want to be associating with the likes of him, my lady."

"Now, Vella, let's not...perhaps you ought to not, er...say such things," Josephs said hastily, still looking up at the man whose single visible eye gleamed dark and cold in the dim light.

"Aye, the fella's got a reputation, don't he?" said Barth, who'd clambered from the carriage and joined them, standing behind the much slighter tiger, Benny. He was holding a large truncheon, leading Irene to have a moment of wonderment as to how her servants had managed to equip themselves like a small army, and in such short order that they'd been able to follow One-Eyed Jack's carriage so quickly.

"A reputation for no-good," Vella said tartly. She jolted and Irene realized that Josephs had nudged his wife in an attempt to shut her up, which might not have been the best decision, considering the long-bladed knife Vella still held.

"I've rather come to that conclusion on my own," Irene said crisply. "But apparently this person has something he wishes to show me that, in his mind"—her tone left no doubt that she wondered at the facility of said mind—"is instructive in my investigation of the murders of Mr. Tripley and Lord Garington. And so I suppose I ought to allow him the opportunity to demonstrate whatever it is to me, considering the amount of trouble he's gone through to do so."

"How very gracious of you, yer ladyship," he said, clearly not meaning a word of it.

"But—"

"Vella, I greatly appreciate your concern," Irene said firmly. "I expect I should feel the same way, were I in your shoes. But I have no reason to believe Mr. One-Eyed Jack"—dear Heavens, what a cumbersome mouthful—"means me any harm. After all, if he did, I—"

"*I ain't in the business o' hurting women,*" growled the topic of conversation. "Even impertinent and obnoxious ones."

Irene and the others turned to look at him.

"Unless they shoot me," he clarified.

Irene swiftly concluded that a single eye glaring menacingly at a person was just as effective—perhaps even more so—than a pair of them doing the same. "I have, as yet, no reason to shoot you. I implore you to do nothing to change my mind. Now, what is it that you are so drattedly determined to demonstrate to me?"

"This way, yer ladyship," said One-Eyed Jack, gesturing toward the recessed door lit by the struggling lantern.

She gave one last quelling look at her platoon of servants, silently telling them to stay put and that she would return, then turned in the direction he pointed. She barely avoided stepping in something soft, dark, and aromatic, and spent the next moments watching the ground for other such pitfalls as she accompanied One-Eyed Jack to the recessed door.

To her surprise, he knocked at the door. For some reason, she'd expected him to open it and brazen his way inside.

A little flap of wood at the top of the door opened and a spare bit of light shined through. The flap closed and the door opened immediately. Her companion gestured her inside.

Irene wasn't nervous; not any longer. There'd been something affronted, even angry, in his tone and expression when he stated he'd never hurt a woman, and she was convinced he was telling the truth. Besides, she still had the small pistol clutched in her hand.

She supposed it was testament to the veracity of his statement that he hadn't attempted to remove it from her possession —or perhaps he was only allowing her to keep it in order to give himself an excuse for any future violence.

Or, perhaps he was even taunting her, tempting her to employ the firearm so that he could (as he would wrongly assume) easily subdue her.

Irene shook her head to clear it. Really, she ought to stop thinking so very hard and in so many different directions all the time. Her attention at this moment ought to be on the murder investigation and nothing else.

The person who'd opened the door for them was very large, exceedingly pale in face, hair, and eyes, and was holding a proportionately large iron bar—presumably as a weapon. The individual's sex was indeterminate, for there wasn't a hint of facial hair and their clothing was loose and simple. A cap covered their head, obscuring any hair that might sprout thereon, but the steady, determined look in their eyes was one that caused the hair at the back of Irene's neck to stand on end. Whoever they were, they were not a person she would want to cross.

They were, however, an excellent guardsman for a door one wished to keep secure, she decided, as the person removed their hat to reveal a puff of pale brown hair, and gave a little bow to her and her companion.

"All in order, here, Brown?" said One-Eyed Jack. "Any problems?"

"No, sir. None at all." Brown's voice was high-pitched and smooth as butter. "M'lady," added the guard, tugging at the puff of hair on their head in a quaintly medieval expression of deference.

"Good evening, Brown," Irene said politely, drawing surprised looks from both of them. "I suppose you're responsible for making certain no one unexpected or unwanted crosses this threshold. How often have you been required to utilize that metal bar? It looks rather lethal, and when in use, I suspect its employment could be rather messy."

Brown looked at her, eyes popping wide, then back to One-Eyed Jack. The latter merely rolled his eye and said, "This is not a social call, yer ladyship. This way, if ye please."

Irene did please—at least for the moment—but she didn't appreciate being rushed along. She'd learned long ago, at the youngest of ages, that every servant, merchant, vendor, laborer, or any other person was worth acknowledging and speaking to. One never knew when one might require their assistance or advice. And aside from that, they were often quite interesting and filled with practical suggestion and experience.

Nonetheless, she kept these thoughts to herself as she accompanied One-Eyed Jack down the narrow corridor. Irene was terrible with directions, so she wasn't quite certain of the layout of the building, especially after they made a turn and then another one, and then went through a door—

"There's no sense in tryin' to remember yer way out, yer ladyship. First, ye ain't a prisoner so ye won't need to escape, and second, d'ye think I'd take ye straight to the place so's ye can find it again?"

Irene once again forbore to comment. Besides, she was becoming impatient.

She could hear, coming from somewhere, the sound of voices and revelry. The essences of cigar and pipe smoke lingered in the air, along with the smell of stale beer. She had the impression that one of the few doors along this corridor might lead to a room where all of this socializing was taking place, but One-Eyed Jack didn't stop at any of them.

At last they came to a set of stairs. One-Eyed Jack gestured her to start up ahead of him, and she complied, setting an efficient pace. At the top, she was only slightly winded and found herself standing on a small threshold, confronted by a heavy door.

A massive lock hung in place, keeping the entrance secure. One-Eyed Jack pulled from his coat pocket a ring of keys, selected one, and fit it into the lock.

"I'm the only one wi' the key, yer ladyship, so don't be getting any ideas."

"I have no idea what sort of...*idea* you think I might be having," she said primly. "Whatever you have in here can't be of that much interest to me."

He didn't respond. Instead, he removed the lock and opened the door, then gestured for her to precede him inside.

The chamber in which she found herself was a surprise. An elegant chandelier of blue and green glass hung from a chain in the center, casting a warm but generous light throughout the space, which smelled faintly of cigar smoke, whisky, and that sharp cedar scent she'd noticed in the carriage. A fireplace took up space on one wall, and a small blaze danced within. A peacock-shaped screen stood on the hearth to protect the floor and its rug from stray sparks and ashes.

The furnishings were as fine as any in the Darling residences, but were of a more masculine, and therefore large and dark, style. Three armchairs, upholstered in rich brown animal hide rather than brocade or silk, angled around a long, low table near the fireplace. The walls were paneled in mahogany from the wainscoting to the floor, and above they were papered in dark green with a subtle print of paisley in a lighter green. There wasn't a fussy pillow or ruffled curtain in sight—although there was a window with its drapery closed tightly. Still, the place looked eminently comfortable and—dare she admit it?—inviting.

A carved wooden sideboard held an array of liquor bottles and glasses. A large desk, just as heavy and masculine as the chairs, but this in dark walnut, was positioned on the wall opposite the curtained window. On another wall was a large cabinet as tall as Irene's shoulder, boasting many drawers. The rug beneath her feet was thick and she was quite certain hailed from Persia, and the painting above the fireplace—a Gainsborough—was surely just as costly.

Irene hid her surprise at finding such a luxurious room attached to a dingy building in a dark, dirty alley. In fact, she was piqued by curiosity, and a reluctant prickle of admiration.

The fact that the chamber didn't appear to be the sort of place a man would keep a person held captive was also a relief.

But she'd already caught him in one lie. And she suspected she might verify at least another—if not an actual *lie*, at least a prevarication—before long. The man must think she was the worst sort of fool.

"I find it quite dishonest for you to suggest you're the only one with a key to this room, my good sir," she said, taking a seat, uninvited, in one of the brown leather chairs. She hoped she could get back up again; it was rather deep and low and she was wearing a corset...and she had a hip. "Certainly you wouldn't allow this chamber to be left unattended—or inaccessible—with this array of gaslights illuminated or a fire blazing. It would be far too dangerous."

He lifted his brow and gave a mocking bow. "Ah, yer ladyship, you've caught me out. 'Tis true that another trusted person has access to this room for that very reason. And for others."

In a breech of etiquette, he had declined to remove his hat, and it remained set low over his brow and the top edge of his eye patch. His overcoat was large and bulky, making it difficult to perceive the shape and true size of his figure. She wondered if that was purposeful.

But now that he was out of the shadows and in a more well-lit room, she could better make out his features—at least, she could see his nose, which had an ungainly hump on its bridge. The remainder of his face, including lips and chin, was obscured by the thick beard and mustache, as well as the shadow from the brim of his low-riding bowler.

"Such an easy admission leaves one wondering what other misleading information you've imparted this evening. But," she went on with a little wave of her hand, "I find it far too tedious to spend any further time on your personal habits, Mr. One-Eyed—oh, devil take it! What a ridiculous, juvenile moniker. I refuse to bumble about with it and I shall simply refer to you as Mr. Jack. Unless you care to share your surname."

His eye danced with humor. "Ye can simply call me Jack, yer ladyship. No need to stand on any ceremony wi' the likes of me. And I won't be tellin' a soul that ye've become so familiar wi' such a low class citizen as myself."

Irene barely held back a smile. The man was preposterous, but she had to admit, this was quite the most enjoyable adventure she'd had in some time (now that she was fairly certain she was in no danger of bodily harm). Still, there was a pressing task at hand—to identify a killer—and despite her fervent wish that this Jack person was correct in that she was barking up the wrong tree with Matthew Feverley, facts were facts.

Mr. Feverley's cufflink had been found beneath the desk at the murder scene and there was no possible way it could have been lost there unless he'd been the killer. And he could very well have been wearing brown gloves last night.

"Very well, then, Jack," she said. "What is it you wished to show me that required such a complicated and dramatic sequence of events?"

He'd walked over to the sideboard. She heard the clink of glass and surmised he was helping himself to a whisky.

But when he came over to her, she saw that he was holding a pair of glasses, each with a finger or so of a clear, amber liquid.

"I've heard Lady Darling has a fondness for a good whiskey," he said, offering her the glass. "This is a particular rye whiskey that I've come to prefer. It comes from Kentucky, a southern state in America."

Once again, she had to hide her surprise.

Instead of informing him that she was quite aware of Kentucky and its special bourbon whiskey, she took the glass and sipped. The strong liquid burned her throat and warmed her belly. It carried the faint sweetness of honey and a subtle floral scent. She didn't think she'd ever tasted a spirit so pleasant.

"Do you approve, your ladyship?" he asked, taking a seat across from her. She noticed now that he held a very large book bound with leather ties. Its covers were thick leather and there were many pages inside. The fact that it was hand-bound suggested that more pages could be added as desired.

"Indeed I do," she replied, taking another sip from her glass. "It's quite satisfactory."

He made a quiet sound of agreement, then set the massive book on the table between them. Without explanation, he opened it and began to leaf through the pages.

Irene attempted to read from upside down, but whoever had scrawled in the book had abominably messy penmanship. She could only presume it was his.

She was, however, able to discern that the book seemed to be some sort of ledger—she'd seen plenty of those sorts of documents in her lifetime. In fact, for a time, her father had given her the responsibility of updating the ledger on his ship. She'd hated every minute of hunching over the book, scrabbling numbers and summing them up, but she'd learned how to do it.

"Here we are, then," Jack murmured, and turned the book around so she could read it.

He didn't have to gesture. The line at the top of the page read *Harry Shaw, Esquire.*

There were a great number of entries beneath his name, and the book, sitting on the table in front of her, was far enough away that she could make out most of the words without using the spectacles she had tucked into her reticule. Jack had terrible penmanship, and although he clearly attempted to keep things neat in this ledger, there were notations and ink splots that suggested impatience and lack of attention.

The list of wagers filled the page and went on to the next one. It was immediately apparent that this was a list of wagers Mr. Shaw had made. Most were on horse and dog races. Some were card games. Others she didn't quite understand, for they were strange notations, but the total at the bottom...

"Good Heavens. Mr. Shaw owes a large sum of money to... you, I presume?" She looked up.

Their eyes met and she felt the shock of intimate connection, and something else. He blinked and brought his attention back to the ledger, where he stabbed his finger at one of the lines. "Aye, to me, indeed. And *me* book ain't the only one wot 'is name is listed so many times," he said, his voice more gruff and coarse than it had been a moment ago. "And 'is ain't the only name in 'ere either."

"Who else is in that book of yours?" Irene settled back in her seat and sipped her whisky. It was bloody tasty, she had to admit. She'd have to ascertain the name of it and how to obtain a bottle for herself.

Jack's response was to collect the book toward himself again and flip through a few more pages. He turned it toward her once again.

"Gerald Chessley," murmured Irene, running her finger down the list of bets. Mr. Chessley had better luck than Mr. Shaw, but not by much, and the size of the figures he wagered were enough to make her eyes widen. "What on earth is this? 'Wager that Lord Garington will sell his prized mare before end of August'? And the amount he's betting is...why, it's mad!" She looked up. "What sort of foolishness is that?"

Jack shrugged, spreading his large hands. He'd removed his gloves when pouring the whisky, and she noticed his hands were rugged and calloused like those of a laborer. "It's none of me concern, yer ladyship. I only just take the bets and hold the book."

"You mean, you encourage these men to waste their money on frivolous, foolish activities," she snapped. Why on earth would someone bet on such a ridiculous thing?

He drew back and the gleam in his eye was no longer filled with humor. "Encourage 'em? There's no need t'encourage those idiot chaps. They do it all on their own. It ain't me fault their money—and which they have plenty of it—falls through their gloves like water. I run a clean bookin' house and club, yer ladyship, and I don't take kind to anyone inferrin' otherwise. I provide an honest service. There are some who ain't so honest. Those are the blokes ye should be getting' all yer ruffles in a bunch over."

She lifted her chin. "I don't approve of gambling and betting. They're foolish and wasteful habits."

Again Jack shrugged. "Gambling—well I can't be disagreeing with ye over that. Betting...well, now, a person can get to be quite skillful at it. A few good, careful bets can set up a bloke right fine, yer ladyship."

"I suspect you're speaking of yourself," she said, reluctantly intrigued.

"I don't gamble. That's a fool's game, and I won't argue wi' ye there. When yer leavin' it all up to chance, well, that's not the sort o' game I play. There's no gambling in me house."

Irene wasn't completely certain of the difference between gambling and betting. So she asked him to explain. She had no qualms about being ignorant over a topic any proper lady was supposed to know nothing about, and if one didn't ask, one couldn't learn.

"Gambling, as I said, is a fool's game. It's all chance and the capriciousness of Lady Luck—what number the dice'll show, whether the marble ends up red instead of black on the wheel, whether a certain card'll be turned up..." There was a flicker of his single set of eyelashes that had her narrowing her own eyes at him.

"Unless someone has secretly set the deck in a certain order," she said, watching him closely.

He merely shrugged, but his mustache twitched. Then he went on. "Gamblin' is pure chance, and then betting...well, that does take skill and a bit o' luck. But a good bettor—such a bloke never makes an unwise wager. One might believe that Mr. Chessley had some reason t' think Lord Garington would need to sell his prized mare in short order, in which case it could very well be a good bet. A logical one, if ye will."

She looked back down at the book. "Well, I suppose he has no chance of winning that one, now that Lord Garington is dead. The viscount won't be selling anything," she said. "And just because Mr. Shaw and Mr. Chessley owe many people a lot of money doesn't mean either of them are a killer. Why would one of them kill Mr. Tripley over that?"

"Per'aps one of'em owed the chap a great amount of blunt and decided he didn't want to pay," commented Jack.

"No..." Irene said, shaking her head. "I think it's something else. He—the killer I mean—had some sort of secret. I believe Mr. Tripley was going to reveal what it was if the killer didn't set things right."

"And how do you know this?" Jack settled back in his chair and eyed her with curiosity. It was striking how heavy the weight of a one-eyed gaze could be on a person.

Somehow, Irene found herself telling Jack about the telephone call overheard by the housekeeper at the Tripley manor. "It seemed Harold Tripley was going to reveal what he knew the next day if the killer didn't set things right. And it seems the killer chose to do away with him instead of setting things right."

Jack made a quiet, interested noise. "The conversation could have been wi' an entirely different person for an entirely different reason," he pointed out—rather logically, Irene had to admit.

"It's possible. But I find it quite suggestive that he'd given a deadline of the next day to the person on the other end of the telephone wire and he was killed that night—the night before the deadline. The timing of it is suspicious."

He made another sound of interest, but this had a bit of disbelief in it. "Anythin' else, yer ladyship?"

"Mr. Chessley witnessed Lord Garington in a heated conversation with Mr. Tripley during the dinner party," Irene told him. She really couldn't say why she felt it necessary to answer his questions and divulge her clues and information, but she didn't question herself too closely. Perhaps it was the whisky that was loosening her tongue. It was going down quite easily.

"And why should a person believe Mr. Chessley? What if the bloke was lyin', to protect himself? What if *he* was overheard by Lord Garington, himself having an altercation with Mr. Tripley? Has that occurred to you, your ladyship?"

"As a matter of fact, it has," she replied tartly.

She didn't feel it necessary to mention that it hadn't occurred to her until just now, just as the words had issued from her lips, that perhaps a suspect in the case of a murder might, possibly, be lying.

A knock on the door had her turning sharply, and grateful for the distraction.

Jack didn't rise, but he did look up. "Come."

The door opened partway. Irene couldn't seen the face or figure of the individual without, but she heard the words spoken. "They're 'ere, guv. The ones wot ye said."

Jack nodded, and the person withdrew, closing the door behind him.

It was at that moment Irene was struck by how blessedly fortunate she was to be an old, widowed lady.

If she was not, her entire reputation would be at stake—no doubt ruined—not only for merely being in the presence of a man like One-Eyed Jack, but for being *alone* with him, in a closed-door room. Not to mention drinking whisky.

Fortunately, no one gave a pin about the reputation of a dried-up dowager marchioness...except perhaps her children. Rose would be having hysterics if she knew her mother was sitting in the study of a...well, whoever or whatever One-Eyed Jack was.

Anyhow, age might have its infirmities, but it certainly did have its benefits as well.

"Somethin' amusing, yer ladyship?" Jack had risen and gone over to pull the draperies open. He paused in this action, as if waiting for her response.

Irene settled back in her chair, thinking that the only thing that could make her more comfortable would be if she didn't have to be swathed into this feminine contraption called fashion. And what a shocking thought—that sitting here in the study of a disreputable person could be comfortable in any way. "I was meditating over the fact that being an old woman has its advantages—namely that I needn't worry over my reputation."

"An old woman, are ye?" Jack said, clearly amused. "Me granny died at the age o' ninety-three, wi' a back as curved as a shepherd's hook. *She* was old." On those words, he yanked the curtains wide.

Instead of an exterior window, Irene found herself facing a pane of glass that looked into a small chamber. It looked precisely how she'd always imagined a gentleman's club would appear: thick with cigar and pipe smoke, comfortable chairs tucked around a card table, smaller tables at the side for drinks, ashtrays, and other refreshments. A life-sized painting of a bare-breasted woman, whose upper thighs and hips were barely covered by a silky, twining scarf-like thing, hung on the wall. Irene did not allow herself to blush, but it was a near thing.

But there *was* something that caused her eyes to widen in shock: the identities of three of the men who sat at a table of five immediately adjacent to the window.

Mr. Shaw. Mr. Chessley. And Mr. Bentley-Bodham.

Just as she realized this, Mr. Bentley-Bodham looked up, directly at the window...directly at her.

Chapter Fourteen

I rene gasped and reared back, out of sight.

Jack gave a little chuckle. "Don't ye worry about that, yer ladyship. They can't see in here through that glass."

"What on earth do you mean?" Irene said.

He shrugged. "It's a little...mm...invention o' mine. It looks like a mirror from that side. I had it made specially."

Irene was fascinated. "How can that be? I can see them just fine. And you say it's like a mirror on the other side?"

He seemed surprised by her admiration. "It ain't magic or anythin'. It's just that the silvering that's put on a glass to make a mirror...well, I found that if ye don't put it on too thick, it lets a bloke see through from the other side an' it looks like a bad mirror from their side.

"How exceedingly clever," Irene said, taking the last sip of her whisky. She set the glass down with regret.

"Another, your ladyship?" asked Jack.

She eyed the empty glass, but, regretfully, declined. She felt pleasantly warm and relaxed, but she didn't want to become too informal and let her guard down too much.

Jack had risen to refill his own glass, and now he went over to the window. She watched as he pushed a small lever over a sort of opening—like a tiny door—in the wall beneath it.

All at once she could hear the voices of the men on the other side of the strange one-sided window...as clearly as if they were in the same room as she!

Her eyes widened and she looked at Jack. "What did you just do? How can I hear them? Are you *spying* on them?"

"I find it comes in handy to hear what a bloke has to say whilst he's drinking and playing cards," was all he said. "Most especially if he wants to place a wager."

"How are you doing that?" she asked, rising to investigate the little opening.

"It's only like a telephone line that's always open," he explained.

"Very clever," she murmured, then returned to her seat. A glass of whisky sat next to it. She flickered a narrow look at him, but he just shrugged again. Well, she didn't have to drink it.

Although she could hear the men speaking in the next room —and there were two others besides her three suspects: Lord Ashton and Mr. Speakes—she didn't pay much attention to them. They were pulling out decks of cards and a jigger of dice and ordering whisky and other libations. From the sounds of them, they'd been enjoying their libations for quite sometime.

"Are Mr. Bentley-Bodham and Mr. Feverley in your book?" she asked.

Jack pulled the ledger back over to himself and flipped through it then handed it back to her.

She perused Mr. Bentley-Bodham's page. It was much shorter and the list of wagers was sparser. Still, she noticed a line that read, "Wager that the Henselm Building will not be finished in time for the wedding dinner of Mr. Cartwright and Miss Lemmons."

She shook her head. Men were very strange.

"And what about Mr. Feverley?" she asked, pushing the book back toward Jack. As she did so, something caught her ear from the conversation of the five men dealing cards in the next room.

"—Garington tragedy," said Mr. Speakes. "Ghastly affair, I'm sure. You were there, I hear, B.B., last night at the Lyceum?"

"Terrible. People screaming bloody murder, running about, shrieking and all," replied Mr. Bentley-Bodham in an affected manner that Irene found quite vexing. "That Lady Darling pushing her way into the thing. Dithering old bat," he said grimly, gesturing with a flick of his wrist for the butler to fill his glass with spirits.

Irene frowned, glaring at the window. She almost wished Mr. Bentley-Bodham could see her so she could express her displeasure.

"Two murders in two nights," said Lord Ashton, puffing hard and fast on a cigar. The smoke billowed out like that from a train engine. "Makes a chap wonder, don't it?"

"Wonder about what?" said Mr. Chessley, his eyes owlishly wide.

"Why, how *I'd* do it if I were so inclined," replied Ashton, a smirking sort of smile curving his mustache. "You were there—both times, weren't you?" He looked at Chessley, then turned to Shaw and Bentley-Bodham. "All of you were, didn't I hear? Imagine that—and you're all here tonight. Did one of you do it?" He laughed, his eyes dancing with delight. "Come now, 'fess up. No one here will tell. What a coup if you did, now, ain't it?"

"'Course not," said Bentley-Bodham as he adjusted his pince-nez in order to stare at Lord Ashton. "Have to be mad to try something like that in a house of people. Even if I wanted to off someone, which I don't, I wouldn't do it like *that*."

"Don't know...I think it could be the biggest bet of all," said Mr. Speakes, grinning as his whisky slopped over the rim of the glass. "What a wager that would be! Could a person pull it off without being caught?

"Sneak into the room, off the man quietly—then go back to his cigars and port." Speakes laughed. "Have to be a cool sort, wouldn't you? Of course it warn't one of you three. Methinks not a one of you have the stones to do a thing like that. Why, you get green around the gills simply placing a bet at Epsom, Chessley."

"'At's true enough," said Shaw, nodding. "You'd have to have a steady hand and a lot of gall to stab a man in the heart whilst his wife's in the next room entertaining the ladies." He laughed and reached for his drink. His eyes were glassy and his hand wavered before his fingers closed around the glass. "Ah, what I wouldn't do to be in the room with the ladies instead. Plenty more to look at than a slew of stuffy neckcloths."

"This is a preposterous conversation!" cried Bentley-Bodham.

"Preposterously intriguing," said Ashton. His eyes had narrowed. "If I were to do away with someone, I'd use a pistol. Keep my distance, right? Wouldn't want to get blood on my clothes—Marbury would have a fit!

"Best valet in London, but the man is like an old biddy with my wardrobe. It gets rather tiresome when a chap wants to have a bit of fun and don't want to worry about his neckcloth getting soot or grease or blood on it, so his valet ain't upset, eh?" He shook his head. "How 'bout you, there, Chessley? How would you do it?"

"Certainly not in a house full of people," replied Chessley.

"But perhaps in a curtained theatre box?" said Speakes, looking at him slyly.

"Nowhere. I wouldn't do it anywhere. I—are we playing cards or what? No, no, we've got too many for whist. I—I think I'll go on home. You four can play." Chessley pushed back from the table so hard his chair tipped, but didn't overturn. "Excuse me."

None of the others watched him go off with his slight limp, but Irene did, speculatively.

"Chessley don't have the nerve," said Ashton casually. "I don't think you do, either, B.B., sad to say. But you..." He lifted his drink in a little salute, pointing a finger at Harry Shaw. "I could see you pulling it off."

Shaw smirked and raised his own glass in return. "I didn't do it, but I'll take it as a compliment, Ashton. Like to think of m'self as the sort who has a cool head. Could have done it if I wanted to—but if I were to off a chap, it wouldn't have been Tripley. No," he said, his face settling into a thoughtful expression. "Not Tripley. He wasn't worth it."

"Who then? Who do you think did it?" Speakes leaned forward, and Irene found herself doing the same from the next room.

"It was a vagrant!" cried Bentley-Bodham. "A-a tramp or someone. They sneaked in the house, looking for something to steal, and when they found Harold Tripley in his study, they had to silence him. Very simple." He tossed back the rest of his drink. "Rather don't like the thought a killer was roaming the house whilst we were eating dinner in the next room." He gave a genteel shudder. "The whole bloody thing is *balderdash*."

"Indeed. It's enough to put a chap off his drink, ain't it?" said Ashton, spewing out a stream of smoke from his cigar. "Still, it don't seem Scotland Yard's got any better idea who did it. And then there's Garington...plenty of people didn't like him much," he said thoughtfully. "Can't say I'm all that sorry he's gone, to be fair. Unpleasant fellow to be sure.

"But doing it at a theatre? Not even in the man's own box! Imagine that. Chumley won't be back there, I'll wager. Heh, now there's a motive for murder: someone wanted Chumley's box. Do away with a chap in it—don't really matter who, now, does it?—get blood all over and scare the ladies, and now the box is yours," said Ashton.

"That's preposterous," said Bentley-Bodham, for the third time. "Over a theatre box?"

"People have killed for less," said Speakes gravely, then ruined it by giggling. "Though I can't think of what at the moment." He giggled again, a high-pitched, raspy sound.

Irene shook her head in disgust. The male species was... something. Especially when members were potted.

"Have ye heard enough?" asked Jack, drawing her attention from the tableau.

"Entirely," she replied. "That was quite instructive, I suppose."

"It sounded no more than crass and childish to me," Jack replied, reaching over to close whatever device had shunted in the sounds from the next room. He drew the curtains closed again, and suddenly the room felt closer and more intimate.

"Quite so," Irene replied. "It gives one rather a different perspective of a few gentlemen now I've seen them in a more... shall we say, free...environment. I can't say it's improved my opinion of any of them, and in fact, I should say it's worsened it."

He sat back down and drew the ledger to him one more time, flipping through the pages. "Matthew Feverley. Your main suspect. Hm." He pushed the book to her and she took it.

The list of wagers on Mr. Feverley's page were short and succinct, and rather benign. She was about to push the book back to Jack when a wager near the top of the page—from some time ago—caught her eye.

She froze, her finger settling over the inked words. *That Miss Rose Colchester will not accept the suit of Lord Martindale.*

Her finger plopped onto the page as she stared down at the

words. Why was Mr. Feverley betting that her daughter would not wed? Of course she had, and to the Earl of Martindale...

"Yer ladyship?"

She looked up, suddenly remembering that Jack was present. "Thank you," she said, shoving the book back toward him with a bit more vehemence than necessary. "I believe I've seen enough tonight. I should like to return home."

She rose from the low chair—not without some difficulty, but she managed it—and marched to the exit. There was only the tiny, subtle niggle of question as to whether Jack would actually allow her to leave, but when he rose to join her and opened the door, she knew her instincts had been correct.

"Do you prefer your own carriage to conduct you home—in its own erratic and energetic fashion, or shall I be arrangin' for transport in a more sedate manner, yer ladyship?" Jack asked as they wended their way through the corridors back to the entrance.

To her surprise, Brown was no longer guarding the door. No one seemed to be, in fact.

Irene smothered a sigh. "I suppose I've no choice other than the former, as harrowing as the journey will likely be. After all, my people have been waiting for me for...good Heavens, over an hour."

"As ye wish, yer ladyship," Jack replied, and with a grand, almost mocking gesture, opened the door and beckoned her out into the bleak, dingy, smelly alley.

To her surprise, she discovered that her army of servants—the Josephses, Barth, George, and Benny—were sitting around a small fire in what looked like a metal washtub. Brown was with them, and the entire lot of them were drinking ale, toasting sausages on long sticks, and having a grand old time of it.

Irene frowned, glancing at Jack. "This is your doing, I suppose."

"I've great respect for brave and loyal servants," he said with a little bow. "Such enterprise ought be rewarded, yer ladyship."

"I cannot argue with that, but now it is time to end the revelry," she said, her voice pitching louder and toward her servants.

They scrambled to comply, and, moments later, she was ensconced in her carriage as it bolted wildly from the alley.

Irene sighed and closed her eyes, curling her fingers on the edge of her seat, hoping she would return home intact.

She'd learned some interesting things tonight, although nothing she'd discovered had done a thing to exonerate Matthew Feverley from being the obvious villain.

In fact, she had even more questions than she'd had before being whisked away in such a presumptuous and peremptory manner...one of which was why the man known as One-Eyed Jack was hiding behind a fake eyepatch and a false nose.

The next morning, Irene woke with the heavy knowledge that she would be doing two—perhaps three—very difficult things between the time she rose from her bed and the time she climbed back into it...which would be long after midnight, since today was the day of the Enfield Ball. She did hope to snatch a nap in there somewhere, but it was unlikely.

The unpleasantness of the first of the tasks, which she would force herself to do immediately after breakfast, made her want to avoid starting the day by lolling in bed.

But Irene was not the sort to procrastinate over difficult tasks. She could blame her father for instilling the sensible habit of getting the worst things out of the way as soon as possible instead of stewing over them. If one stewed and worried over those difficult things, one merely lived in the unpleasantness for even longer.

The sooner started, the sooner finished, Papa would say as he rousted her to muck out the stalls of the cows and chickens they brought onboard the ship with them. That had been one of her first jobs, at age nine. Fortunately, she'd moved on to more interesting (and less pungent) ones over the years.

Today's first task was far less smelly than the mucking-out, though it was certain to be uncomfortable and messy. Still. Her conscience required it to be done.

And so, at half-past eleven, Irene's carriage came to an enthusiastic halt in front of the Tripley home.

As one would expect, the place was shrouded in black—at the windows and draped over the door knocker. Although it had the air of abandonment, Irene knew that Trudy Tripley and her family remained inside, accepting callers bringing condolences, and gifts of food and comfort.

Whether Trudy would accept Irene this morning was uncertain.

Smayle answered the door to Irene's knock.

"Lady Darling," he said, his voice filled with pleasure and bit of surprise.

"Smayle. I'm so very sorry for everything that's happened," she said as he beckoned her into the house. "Do you think Mrs. Tripley will see me? I should very much like to speak with her."

"I will ask her," he replied gravely. "She has not been herself, as one would expect."

"Of course not," Irene agreed.

"But we—the downstairs people—we know what you're doing, Lady Darling, and we are very grateful for it. Even if the mistress can't see her way to it."

"Thank you," Irene replied. "Have there been many callers? And what about her sister? Has she come to stay?"

"Oh, yes. There've been many callers every day. The mistress hasn't seen them all...she's been too overcome. Mr.

Tripley's sisters and brother were here yesterday and will be back tomorrow. Her sister is staying here, but she's gone home this morning to attend to a few things. She'll be back soon. Mrs. Tripley's other sister is on her way from Scotland and should arrive tomorrow. The children are back home as well."

Irene nodded. At least Trudy wasn't required to handle all of this alone. "Shall I wait whilst you see if Mrs. Tripley is at home to me? It might be best if we spoke privately."

Smayle settled her in a small sitting room, and moments after he left the room, a maid came in with a tray of tea.

Irene helped herself to a cup and waited for well over ten minutes. At last the door opened.

Trudy Tripley came in alone. She appeared as haggard as one would expect, given the tragedy she'd experienced. Irene set down her tea and rose, for the moment holding back her instinct to rush to embrace the woman.

"Trudy," she said.

"Irene." Her voice was choked and she reached out with a hand to steady herself against the back of a chair. "W-why are you here?"

Her words sounded more confused than angry or vexed. Irene took it as a sign to approach.

"Why don't you sit with me and we can talk about it," Irene said, putting an arm around the woman who seemed to have become much more frail over the last two days.

"I..." Trudy couldn't seem to summon the energy to form words.

"I'm so very sorry about what happened to Harold," Irene said, helping the woman to sit on the divan. "If there is anything I can do..."

Trudy shook her head, her eyes dazed. "I simply can't believe he's gone. That someone...someone did such a thing. You were here," she said, a bit more emotion coloring her voice. "You saw it. You saw...him."

Irene nodded. "It was terrible. The most terrible thing one could imagine happening."

"I just don't know w-who...I-I'm afraid to stay here, you see. I'm afraid someone will come in...and...and—"

"Shh," Irene said, patting the quaking woman on the back. "You're safe, Trudy. No one is going to come in and hurt you. Lots of people are here with you, staying in the house with you. But if you'd like a place to go, a safe place, you can certainly stay with me at the dowager house. I've plenty of room."

Trudy looked at her, then away, her eyes downcast. "I was angry with you that night," she murmured. "I said a terrible thing about—about—"

"Never mind that," Irene said. "It's forgotten. It didn't mean anything. You were shocked and devastated."

"I-I was. I didn't know...I don't know what to think." She'd been holding back her emotions, but now they burst forth in a flow of wild tears and wracking sobs.

Irene pulled her into an embrace and offered a handkerchief to replace the soaked one Trudy had been using. "It's horrible, and so difficult right now," she said. "But we're going to find out who did this wicked, wicked thing, Trudy. We are going to find out who did it."

And if it was Matthew Feverley, Irene was going to take that young man to task like she'd never done to another person...and then turn him over to the authorities. He'd hang for it and she would be sad over it, but that was justice.

"They don't know who did it," Trudy said, pulling away and dabbing at her streaming eyes. "They think...Scotland Yard, I mean...they say it was someone *here*. Someone wh-who was at the dinner party. But how could that be? How could it be one of *them*?"

"It had to be one of the gentlemen," Irene told her. "No one else could have done it. And I've been asking around, investigating. I'm going to find out who did it, Trudy. I promise."

"What do you mean?" For the first time, the haziness ebbed from Trudy's eyes and she focused on Irene.

"I'm detecting, like Sherlock Holmes," Irene said. "I'm following clues and making deductions. I want to find out who did this, and I think—well, I *know* I'm smarter than that Inspector Burgess. Would it be possible for me to ask you some questions? It might help me to solve this crime."

"Questions? Like...like the inspector? Oh, but he's asked me so many questions...it's all such a mess inside my head." Trudy didn't burst into sobs this time, but tears rolled freely down her cheeks. "I just can't think...I just want to go away from here."

"Of course you do, dear. Anyone would after what you've been through." Irene realized she wasn't going to get any information from the widow. "Would you mind terribly if I looked through Mr. Tripley's desk? Just to see if there is anything there that might help me determine who would have wanted to hurt him."

"What? Look around Mr. Tripley's desk? But...but..." Trudy dithered and sobbed and wavered and wailed, but in the end, she agreed that Irene could look around.

Irene would have done so regardless—for she was quite certain Smayle would have allowed her to do so—but it was nice to have the widow's permission.

Even though she was anxious to search Harold Tripley's study, Irene sat with Trudy and managed to get her to drink a bit of strong tea with extra sugar and a small chopped-egg sandwich. She suspected the poor woman hadn't eaten much of anything the past few days, and had probably slept little.

Grief, she well knew, took a terrible toll in those first few days and weeks. One had no choice but to get through it, somehow, and eventually those terrible days grew fewer and farther between...but they never went completely away. She could tell Trudy that things would get better, assure her that the pain would ebb—eventually—but the poor woman wasn't ready to hear that. And so she sat with her for a little while longer before ringing for Smayle.

The butler came in, assessed the scene, and immediately turned round to call for Mrs. Tripley's daughter to help her up to her room.

Irene spoke to him in the corridor. "Mrs. Tripley has given me permission to search through Mr. Tripley's study and desk."

Smayle' wiry eyebrows bounced up and then down, but he said nothing other than, "Of course, my lady. Allow me to show you the way."

Irene was fully aware that Scotland Yard had done their own search and that it was unlikely she'd find anything important, but she couldn't resist the chance to take a look for herself. There was always the possibility she'd find something they missed or something they didn't realize was important. After all, Inspector Burgess hadn't seen the cufflink.

The thought of the cufflink reminded Irene of another of the unpleasant tasks ahead of her today, but she put it out of her mind for now.

She walked into the study and was assaulted by the memory of doing so...had it only been three days ago? It seemed much longer.

She walked over to the desk, allowing her mind to take her back to that moment when she first noticed Harold Tripley's shoes akilter on the floor.

She moved closer, as if in a dream, remembering the way she'd seen him sprawled, the way the bloom of blood on his shirt told her he was quite dead, the curtain cord draped over his throat...

She remembered the buzz of voices in the room, the way her heart thudded hard in her ears, the little shrieks from the ladies at her pronouncement...the way Mr. Bentley-Bodham strode over, ridiculing her statement that Mr. Tripley was murdered... the way Mr. Feverley helped her to keep everyone clear and to seat Mrs. Tripley....

Had Mr. Feverley come close enough to the desk for him to lose his cufflink then, innocently? She narrowed her eyes, thinking, remembering the movements...but she couldn't remember him drawing near enough to have dropped the cufflink. No, he had definitely stayed in the front of the desk, with his back to it and the dead body. Still...one should be certain.

"Smayle," she said, turning to where the butler (most correctly) waited in the doorway. "Could you bring the maid who found the cufflink? I'd like to see if she can tell me precisely where it was discovered."

"Of course, my lady," he said, and withdrew.

It wasn't an excuse to have him leave; Irene had nothing to hide. Still, she felt mildly less exposed as she began to open the drawers of Mr. Tripley's desk.

Of course she had no idea what she was looking for but she assumed if there was something to find, she would recognize it.

She did. At least, she thought it was something important.

Irene lifted the paper she'd discovered in one of the drawers and held it at arm's length in an attempt to read it without digging out her reading spectacles. Yes, she'd been correct. It was a betting slip, a wager that had been marked *paid*.

The paid notation was signed with a now-familiar flourish that was clearly a J, not an F.

Harold Tripley wagers that Miss Ferndale's wedding to Lord Leavington will not come off.

She frowned, studying the betting slip. The amount of money on the wager was enough to make her eyes widen.

She tucked the betting slip into her reticule, uncertain what, if anything, it meant...but the connection to One-Eyed Jack was clear. Further investigation revealed nothing more of interest and the rather mundane facts that Mr. Tripley was not the most literate of letter-writers, he was right-handed, and he kept a number of different types of tobacco in various tins inside his desk drawers.

Just as she was closing the last of the drawers, Irene heard Smayle at the door.

"Now come on in here, Charlotte. Lady Darling can be a bit intimidating, but she is quite nice."

Putting on her least intimidating expression, Irene turned to see the butler urging a young, neatly-dressed and -coiffed maid over the threshold.

"M-my lady," said the girl, curtsying before she'd even come into the room.

"What's your name, pet?" Irene asked.

"Ch-Charlotte," she replied, curtsying again.

"All right, then, Charlotte...that happens to be the name of one of my closest friends," Irene said, giving her a smile. "I think it's a lovely name. Now, why don't you come over here and if you will, please show me exactly—or as close as you can," she added hastily when she saw the girl's expression seize up into one of horror, "as near as you can remember, where you found the ruby and mother-of-pearl cufflink—the morning after the murder, was it?" Irene instantly regretted using the word "murder" but it was too late.

The girl, who'd blanched at the "m" word, looked worriedly at Smayle. He nodded with gentle encouragement then gave her a firm prod toward the desk.

"Only...my lady...I don't remember exactly," she said. "I was using the carpet sweep, you see, my lady, and suddenly there was an awful sort of clinking and clanking, and so I stopped it right away and I bent down to see what it was that was making all the ruckus inside, you see." Apparently, once the girl got to talking, she was quite loquacious—which Irene appreciated. She felt that all the details were of importance in a murder investigation.

"All right then, do you remember where the carpet sweeper was when you heard the sounds?" Irene asked.

"Only, I was pushing it under the desk, you see, my lady. Right there, just along the edge." She pointed to the left side of the kneehole of the desk. "Back in there, I heard it, you see."

"Very good," Irene said, bending as much as she comfortably could do to look at the area. Yes, she could see how it was possible that the cufflink could have fallen off during the altercation and then landed there—or even bounced off the front of Mr. Tripley's person and tumbled down under the desk. She did not, however, see how Matthew Feverley could have lost it innocently, even whilst standing in front of the desk.

She sighed and straightened. This was good information. Unfortunately, her lack of confidence in Inspector Burgess was bolstered after examining this scene, for he clearly had only looked in the area where Mr. Tripley's body had lain and not any further than his own skinny nose.

"Is there anything else you noticed that was odd or out of place, Charlotte?"

The maid curtsied again. "No, my lady. Only, there was nothing else except...well, except the knowing what happened there. Right there." Charlotte shuddered and pointed with a shaky finger. "It were awful, my lady. It really were the most awful thing, to know that the master was done away with right there, and he lay there and bled onto the floor and all of it." Apparently now that she had delivered the pertinent information, any last bit of nerves had been replaced by the relish of recounting the horror of the situation, as inaccurate as it was (Mr. Tripley had not bled enough to bleed onto the floor).

"It was a ghastly thing," Irene agreed. "Thank you very much, Charlotte. I'm certain Mrs. Tripley is quite pleased with your work and attention to detail. You are dismissed, thank you.

"Smayle, I believe it would be instructive for me to speak with Mrs. Tripley once more before I take my leave. I've found something important that I need to ask her about."

Smayle appeared uncertain about this implied request, but Irene donned her most intimidating expression and, after a bare moment of hesitation, he nodded and replied, "Of course, my lady."

It took some time, again, but Trudy Tripley did join Irene in the parlor once more. Her appearance wasn't the least bit improved from their first interaction. In fact, she appeared not only distressed, but also slightly vexed.

"Irene, I simply *cannot* do this," she said, fairly swooning into a chair. "I realize you think you're a real Sherlock Holmes sort of person, and I am quite appreciative of your intentions, but it's simply too *much* for me—"

"I only have one question," Irene said. Which was a lie, but she'd decided that whilst playing detective, it was fair to cheat and lie since her ultimate goal was to identify and apprehend a murderer...and so lying and cheating were small-scale transgressions in comparison.

"What is it?" Trudy asked wearily. "I can't imagine what you could have found that will help identify who took my Harold from me. It's simply...*untenable*."

"Were you or Harold particularly close with Miss Ferndale or Lord Leavington?" Irene had thought about the best way to broach the subject of the bet slip and had decided on this approach. "I understand that Miss Ferndale abruptly canceled her wedding to Lord Leavington. Was there any reason Mr.

Tripley might have been...well...pleased about such a development?"

"Why, what an absurd question," said Trudy, straightening her shoulders and looking at Irene in an affronted manner. "What on earth does that have to do with *anything*? What precisely are you implying, Irene?"

Irene sighed. "I'm not implying anything, Trudy. I'm simply trying to determine why your husband would have bet a large sum of money that Miss Ferndale and Lord Leavington would not wed." She'd already been digging in her reticule, and now she withdrew the betting slip. She handed it to Trudy.

The other woman hesitated, then took the paper. "What is this?" she said, in a tone that suggested she understood what she held, but was still confused about its relevance. "I don't understand. What does this have to do with Harold's *murder*?"

Irene shook her head. "I don't know," she said with great feeling. "I truly don't know. But it seems an odd thing for Mr. Tripley to wager on, and..." She hesitated, then went on, "...it seems that several of the gentlemen who were here at the dinner party also frequent the club where this wager was made."

Trudy looked down at the betting slip again, then handed it back to Irene. She seemed more subdued now. "I don't know why he would have made such a wager, and for that amount of money. Why, that's more than we paid Mr. Dicksee for my portrait." Her voice wavered, then steadied. "We hardly knew Miss Ferndale—only enough to speak briefly at social gatherings."

"And Lord Leavington?"

Trudy shook her head. "Why, I hardly knew him at all. I should only barely recognize him if I were to be in the same room."

"What about Mr. Tripley? Did he know Lord Leavington?"

Trudy shook her head again. "He never spoke about him

except...well..." She tilted her head and furrowed her brow as if something had suddenly struck her. "Why, someone...there *was* someone...oh, my head is so utterly muddled..."

"There was someone...someone who knew Leavington well? Someone who, perhaps, didn't care for Leavington?" Irene had no idea what path to take, but these seemed reasonable questions. She felt as if she were on the verge of something important...if only Trudy could settle her mind and think!

"Yes, there was someone, someone who didn't have nice things to say about Leavington. Harold told me, now I think of it. Harold mentioned it...good Heavens, I'm remembering now." Her eyes went wide and they focused on Irene, and the top of Irene's scalp began to prickle. "They...now who was it? I simply *can't* remember. But it was someone who disliked Leavington quite a bit. Claimed he'd—oh! He'd...er...stepped in on him with Miss Ferndale! That's what it was!" For the first time since her husband's body was discovered, Trudy Tripley seemed alert and aware. "Whoever it was—drat it, Irene, I simply *can't* put a finger on it—was rather put out that Lord Leavington made inroads with Miss Ferndale and was going to marry her."

Irene gritted her teeth. Why could Trudy not remember who it was her husband had been speaking of? How could she forget? She didn't know why, but she knew this was important.

"Please try and think, Trudy," Irene implored, doing her best not to sound vexed or impatient. "It could be related to your husband's murder."

"But how? Why? How could the fact that Miss Ferndale and Lord Leavington didn't get married have *anything* to do with Harold *being stabbed in his own study?*" Trudy's voice rose to a shriek and she burst into tears. "I simply don't know why you're asking these horrid questions!"

The door to the parlor opened and Irene recognized the woman who rushed in—Trudy's sister.

"I think my sister has had enough visiting for today, Lady Darling," she said in a tone that brooked no disobedience but was still deferent enough that Irene, who was of much higher rank than Mrs. Conning, was not offended.

"Yes, of course," she said, rising. There was nothing more she could do here, but at least she had the niggling of a suspicion settling in the back of her mind.

Somehow, for some reason, she had become certain the aborted wedding of Lord Leavington to Miss Ferndale was related to Harold Tripley's murder. Why or how, she didn't know, but it seemed the thought was hovering just out of reach...

She made her excuses and was showing herself down the stairs and to the main entrance when she heard someone addressing her.

She turned, looking up. At the top of the stairs, on the landing, stood Trudy's sister.

"Lady Darling, my sister says she's just remembered whatever it was you wanted to know," she said. Her voice was cool, as one might be when one's sister has been utterly disrupted and upset over questions related to her husband's murder, but she went on, "She says she remembers who Harold had said was upset with Lord Leavington. It was Lord Garington."

Chapter Fifteen

W ell, that wasn't very helpful at all, was it, Irene thought, rather vexedly, as she climbed into her carriage.

Lord Garington was dead, so he couldn't be the culprit, now could he?

Irene pondered, then her head jolted sharply backward when the carriage took off. She really did need to speak very clearly and firmly to Barth again about his driving habits.

She sighed, settling back into her seat. She wished she had some time to think, but she had asked Barth to bring her to a second destination—the next in her list of unpleasant tasks.

The carriage pulled up in front of the Feverley house and Irene alighted. She squared her shoulders and approached the entrance, wishing once again that she'd re-equipped herself with the extremely useful appendage of a walking stick. For some reason, she felt it would be a steadying sort of thing for what she was about to do.

"I'm sorry, my lady. Mrs. Feverley is not home at the moment," said Franklin, the butler, as he gestured her into the house. He would not leave a marchioness standing outside the door, even if she wasn't going to stay.

"I should like to speak with Mr. Matthew Feverley," Irene said, stifling the rush of relief that she didn't have to speak to the mother of the man she believed murdered two people.

Franklin did not react to this irregular request other than the most subtle widening of his eyes. "I do not believe Mr. Feverley is home either, Lady Darling. Perhaps you will wait whilst I ascertain whether he is available."

"Of course," she replied, and began to show herself to the parlor where, only two days ago, she'd spoken with the amiable and easy-going young man. It was worrisome that, at that time, he'd seemed so interested in and so wryly supportive of her plans to detect the killer.

Of course he had...if he was, indeed, the murderer. He'd want to know what she was thinking and deducing in order to stay one step ahead of her, knowing how able, intelligent, and efficient she was. Anyone would do the same.

Irene sighed and sank down onto the divan in the sitting room. She simply couldn't get it into her head that Matthew Feverley could have done such a thing. It seemed so out of his calm, even, amiable nature.

She tilted her head sharply as the thought struck her, and she stilled as she allowed the wisp of an idea to weave through her mind.

Out of his nature.

That *was* something to think about, wasn't it?

There was no doubt, no argument, that whoever had stabbed Mr. Tripley and cut the throat of Lord Garington had done so at great risk of discovery. They had been bold, wild actions. Whoever had conducted those heinous activities had to have been desperate, quick-witted, and willing to think and act quickly and rashly in order to do such horrendous things.

Matthew Feverley had always struck her as the sort of person who was not at all rash, not at all the sort of person who risked himself, or who was bold or wild. He'd seemed steady, thoughtful, a bit ironic and even dryly amusing, but not impetuous or bold.

She supposed that a person who was backed into a corner, so to speak, or at the end of one's rope, could be driven to take such a great risk to protect their life and secrets....

But even so, wouldn't they attempt to eliminate those who meant to expose them in a more measured, careful manner than slitting their throat in a theatre filled with people...then *climbing* from one box to the other to escape?

As she sat in the sitting room, Irene realized she'd been missing a salient point.

Whoever had slit Lord Garington's throat had not only thought to switch their gloves with his, but they'd also climbed from one box to the other. A person who did that had to be physically able to do so, quickly and easily.

It could *not* have been, she thought suddenly, with that same prickling at the top of her scalp, someone who had a pronounced limp—which implied a weak, disabled leg that might not have the strength or agility to help climb from one side to the other.

It would have been extremely difficult for Mr. Chessley to have moved quickly and ably from one box to the other after taking the life of Lord Garington.

Did that strike him from her list?

If not, it certainly dropped him to the bottom of it, Irene thought grimly. Which mean that Matthew Feverley was still at the very top of it, devil take it—all because of that bloody cufflink.

The door of the sitting room opened, and Franklin came in. He wore an apologetic expression, his hands clasped at his front.

"Lady Darling, I regret to inform you that Mr. Matthew is not in residence at this time. May I leave your regards for him?"

Irene rose, unwilling to admit the relief that she wouldn't have to confront Mr. Feverley quite yet over the evidence against him. However, she was perplexed that he had not yet responded to her summons of the day before. "No, thank you, Franklin, that won't be necessary. I expect I shall see him at the Enfield Ball tonight."

Franklin's very slight, almost imperceptible reaction indicated that even the downstairs people were aware of how scandalous it was going to be if Lady Darling should attend the very first Enfield Ball since Lord Milbright's death.

Irene merely gave him a steady look that suggested he ought to keep his thoughts to himself, and said, "I should like to speak with Mr. Feverley's valet, if you please."

Franklin's eyes widened, but she didn't react. "My lady?"

"If you please, Franklin." She gave him her "imperious marchioness" as she sat back down, clearly indicating her intention to remain until her request was granted.

He wavered for a moment, then hurried from the room.

It wasn't long at all before a man of about thirty came into the room. Irene recognized him as the valet, both by the way he held himself—with confidence, being a high-ranking servant—and his attire, which was not livery but a coat and simply-tied neckcloth. He was followed by Franklin, who hovered in the doorway as the younger man approached Irene.

"Lady Darling, I understand you wished to speak with me. I'm Marcus, Mr. Matthew's valet." He bowed.

Now she rose and showed him the cufflink she'd withdrawn from her reticule. "Does this belong to Mr. Matthew Feverley?"

He hardly needed to look at it, resting in the palm of her gloved hand. "It does, my lady. He arrived home the night...the —er—other night with only one cufflink. He hadn't noticed it was missing, as I recall." He gave her a curious look. "May I ask where you found it?"

She looked at him soberly. "Regrettably, somewhere it shouldn't have been, Marcus." She slipped the cufflink back into her bag. "Unfortunately, at this time, I cannot return it to him."

His eyes widened and now he appeared shocked. "My lady?"

"Thank you very much, Marcus, and Franklin," she said, her heart sinking. She had had one last bit of hope that the piece of jewelry would turn out not to belong to the amiable young man. "If you will excuse me, I shall take my leave." Without further ado, she swept from the sitting room.

Irene settled in the carriage and found herself gripping the edge of her seat as the vehicle launched into the street. Devil take it, she was going to *have* to speak with Barth about it. The conduct of her driver was truly getting to be quite untenable. She simply could not—

The carriage gave a sudden swing to the side, throwing Irene hard against the wall, then the vehicle bolted forward. She heard a shout outside, but by the time she looked out the window, all she could discern were houses rushing past. What on *earth?*

She found herself holding on for dear life as the vehicle charged down the street as if it were being chased by the hound of the Baskervilles.

Irene managed to steady herself long enough to rap on the ceiling as she shouted, "Barth! Stop this at once! Halt this carriage *immediately!*"

The vehicle didn't even slow as it took another corner so rapidly and wildly that Irene felt the wheels on the right lift and then thud to the ground as it righted itself, then went on at the same breakneck speed.

By now, her shock and vexation had turned to real fear, and

her mind scrambled to determine what to do, how to stop this, and what had happened. She knew Barth was not simply being an irresponsible driver; something was very wrong.

She tried to look out the window to see whether he'd been injured or perhaps even knocked from his perch, and the horses had been spooked and gone wild without their driver, but the carriage was barreling so wildly down the road she kept being thrown from one side to the other.

Then all at once, the carriage jolted to a violent halt. Panting, Irene pulled herself back up onto the bench seat and assessed the damage to her person. She would have bruises for certain. A little shaky, she started to reach toward the door, but suddenly it swung open of its own volition.

A figure stood there, seeming to fill the doorway. It—he?—was wearing a hat and a mask that obstructed his face. A black coat, gloves, and boots covered the rest of his person. The only thing she could see was the shadowy glitter of malevolent eyes behind the holes of the mask. They were so recessed, she couldn't perceive their true color.

The person thrust a cane at her and it came nearly to her bosom. Irene's breath caught in an emotion between fear and affront. How dare he?

"Who are you and what do you want?" she said in a voice that was steady, albeit a bit breathless. Her fingers had closed around the reticule dangling from her wrist, which was unusually heavy due to the small pistol she had neglected to remove after last night's events.

Or perhaps it had been intentional that she had not removed it. After all, she was hunting a man who'd killed two people.

"What have you done with my driver?" she went on, realizing that was the only explanation for what had occurred. Something had happened to Barth, and now they were—as she noted by glancing beyond the shadowy figure—in a narrow, dingy alley very similar to the one to which she'd been taken last night.

"You are interfering in things that are none of your concern," said the figure in a low, raspy voice. The cane end thrust closer to her but stopped short from actually touching her bosom—lucky for him. "Keep your nose out of other people's business...or you'll be next."

By now she'd closed her fingers around the little pistol, and she yanked it from the small bag. Unfortunately, it caught on the edge of the drawstring opening, and so her smooth flourish of drawing the weapon was hindered and she nearly lost her grip on it.

But she managed to drag it free after only a hitch, and suddenly she was pointing the barrel at the person—man—in front of her. "Who are you? What do you think you're doing, threatening me? Are you the one who killed Harold Tripley? I demand you reveal yourself—"

All at once, he was gone. The door slammed closed and Irene bolted toward it.

Bolting was her intention, but not what actually occurred, for her clothing—as usual—hindered any sudden or agile movements. Not to mention the very weak pair of knees she was relying on for leverage and balance.

She turned the handle and pushed at the door, but, though it rattled in its frame, it wouldn't open. He'd somehow wedged the dratted thing closed!

Irene swore like a sailor—quite literally, for she'd had the best of role models—and began to shake the handle of the door in hopes of jolting loose whatever held it in place. When that didn't work, she began to shout and pound on the window...then stopped because she felt utterly foolish.

She took the pistol and was just about to shoot at the door when it flew open. (Thank Heavens she'd hesitated.)

"Lady Darling!"

It was Barth, and he was an utter wreck. His face was covered with blood that had dried down the side of it. His eyes were wild and his hair on end. He was panting, out of breath, but managed to gasp, "My lady...are you hurt?"

"I am unhurt. But you—what on earth happened to you? Are you quite all right?"

"The bloke hit me, he did, and pushed me off'n the seat," Barth told her, his voice and eyes as wild as his driving skills. "I held on, milady, I did, and he drove off, tryin' to knock me over, off, to the ground. I held on, milady," he said again, earnestly, "though me head was bleedin' and all. But then he went round a corner and knocked me off good, he did, and I fell...but then I run after you, I did."

"Good Heavens," she said, truly astonished. "What a brave and strong young man you are," she told him.

...And, at that moment, decided she would never say another word about his driving skills.

Nearly eight hours later, Barth carefully navigated the carriage up Enfield House's driveway—which was clogged to a standstill with other similar vehicles. There hadn't been a jolt or a jerk, or even a quick turn since Irene and Priscilla had been assisted inside a short time ago. Irene hoped this was a permanent development.

After her harrowing experience with being kidnapped for the second time in less than twenty-four hours, she'd returned home, bedraggled and more unsteady than she'd like to admit, and calmly related to the Josephs what had occurred.

After receiving their utterly horrified exclamations of shock and concern, and assuring them that not only was she completely fine but insisting that Barth was a true hero and ought to be treated as such, Irene locked herself in her private sitting room with her three pets and proceeded to go to pieces.

The going to pieces was short-lived, mainly because Irene was more angry than frightened over what had happened—and because Beatrice decided she was entitled to the small tray of tea sandwiches Vella had brought in. Once she rescued the sandwiches, Irene dried her eyes and had a good, long think as she nibbled on sustenance.

Then she had an equally good, long soak in her bathing tub whilst continuing to review the details of the unpleasant event. She determined several things:

First, that even though this was the second time she'd been abducted in less than twenty-four hours, the culprit was not the same person; that is, One-Eyed Jack had not been the man standing in the doorway of her carriage. That man's boots had been too fine and highly polished—and too small—to have belonged to the betting club owner.

Second, and most obvious, it was clear that her second abductor was the person who'd killed Harold Tripley and Lord Garington.

Third, and also quite obvious, the killer's actions today were just as risky and impetuous as the two murders he'd conducted... perhaps even more so.

One thing was certain, whoever he was—and she was beginning to think she actually, finally, *did* know the identity of the villain; it had been a grave mistake, him confronting her as he had done—he was feeling anxious and threatened by her activities.

That alone was cause for a bit of smug contemplation.

Now, Irene looked across the carriage at Priscilla, who quivered with such excitement and nerves that her trembling was noticeable even in the dim light of the vehicle.

This was to be the largest, most important social event she'd attended thus far, and the girl clearly had astronomical expectations. The feathers in her coiffure vibrated wildly and she kept patting at her hair and readjusting her shawl whilst attempting to peer at her reflection in the carriage window.

Once the carriage came to a gentle halt at the entrance to Enfield House, she and Priscilla were helped out of the carriage by the Enfields' footman. They took a moment to smooth and readjust their gowns before starting up the short flight of stairs into the grand foyer of the mansion.

Monsieur Claude had shown his genius once again in the evening gown he'd created for Irene. It consisted of a dark sage green underskirt of satin with an airy black chiffon overskirt that gave the appearance of nothing more than a light wafting of smoke overlying the gown. The bodice was created from black and sage green chiffon twisted around and across the bosom in a sort of X that was sewn into the sage-green satin in the back. Irene had argued with Monsieur Claude about how much of her fifty-year-old décolletage to reveal, but the monsieur had had his way.

"You still have the beautiful breasts, my lady, and they must be shown to their advantage," he told her without the least bit of remorse as he tugged the neckline lower during the final fitting.

"You haven't seen them without a corset holding them up," Irene had returned crossly. "When left unfettered, they dangle nearly to my belly! And when I sleep, they're *always* getting in the way."

Monsieur Claude laughed and brushed her off, saying, "I have seen plenty of younger breasts—in their forties or even thirties—swinging and swaying and dangling far more wildly than yours, my lovely madame."

Irene didn't believe him, but she had no choice in the matter. When one put oneself in the fashionable hands of Monsieur Claude, those hands were in complete control and brooked no argument.

As Irene stepped over the threshold of the entrance to Enfield House, she took an assessment of herself and her nerves. She felt nothing but a sense of expectation and anticipation, as well as determination, and she smiled inside.

She might be an old woman by any standard, but with age came experience, confidence, and brashness.

"The Most Honorable Dowager Marchioness of Darling," announced the butler in ringing tones.

Irene held her head high, fixed a cool, confident smile on her face, and scanned the room as she stepped over the threshold.

She'd fully expected what happened next: the buzz of conversation swept to a halt, beginning from the front of the ballroom and rippling to the back in a fan-like motion that was actually visible as heads turned to look. The silence settled and held for hardly any longer than an instant, then all at once it hissed and rumbled, exploding to life as fans flew up to hide mouths and to stifle conversation, commentary, and cattiness.

Irene couldn't help but notice the shock on Lady Pelicourt's face. Her lips had gone prune-like and she turned to speak to her daughter, who wore the same expression.

Due to the circumstances of Irene's introduction, no one was paying any attention when Miss Priscilla Bedwith was announced in her wake. But there was nothing Irene could have —or would have—done about that.

"Lady Enfield," she said, moving forward to her hostess with both hands extended in greeting. "How good of you to have me and my ward, Miss Bedwith."

"Lady Darling," Ellen replied. Her voice was cool and remote, but when she took Irene's gloved hands in hers, she gave them a quick, double squeeze. There was a flicker of warmth and then humor in her eyes before her lashes swept down to hide it. "I daresay one must let bygones be bygones." She'd lifted her face so her voice would carry to the many cocked ears that hovered nearby.

"Indeed... I feel precisely the same way," replied Irene in the same projecting, but cool, voice as she squeezed Ellen's hands in return. "Forgive and forget, and move on."

Then she stepped away and swept around to observe the room.

The buzz of conversation had not waned, and did not, as Irene walked regally down the four steps into the gallery that led to the ballroom, which had been decorated to evoke a sort of glittery, elegant fairy garden.

Strips of sparkling silver, pink, and green fabric hung from the ceiling at varying lengths, gleaming and shining as they wafted gently in the air. Countless potted plants—ferns, small trees, roses and other colorful flowers—had been arranged to create a garden-like atmosphere. The tables were clothed in shades of green with more potted flowers as centerpieces. Archways twined with greenery offered multiple entrances to the dance floor, which was fenced off from the rest of the room by the potted plants and temporary fencing. Lights twinkled all over—dozens, perhaps hundreds—of glass vessels (jars, bottles, tumblers), each with a burning candle inside, hung from the ceiling, dangled from holders, or sat on tables throughout the room. Garden benches decorated the edges of the space, offering comfortable seating for those who chose not to dance.

It was gorgeous—a befitting return of the Enfield Ball. Irene noticed that the small balcony from which Lord Milbright had fallen was blocked from entrance by a large topiary and a small bench. There was only one way up to it, although there was another door at the rear—that was not an exit; it led to a small closet.

The location where Lord Milbright's body had landed on the floor was now occupied by a three-level water fountain.

Irene could heard the strains of a string quintet's exertions over the gossipy exchanges that were happening like little whirling dervishes all around her. She kept the smile on her face, and when she reached the bottom of the steps, waited for Priscilla to join her.

The girl was already babbling. "My lady, I can hardly believe—that was—"

"Ah, quite so—and there is Mrs. Merryweather," said Irene, interrupting what would likely have been either an unnecessary comment regarding the reaction to her entrance, or something equally inane. "She is also a friend of your mother's, and her daughters are quite pleasant. As one of her daughters is married and the other is not, but is your age, I think it would be an excellent decision to converse with them for a bit. They know many of the eligible young men here, including having two brothers who are bachelors."

Quite frankly, Irene wanted nothing more than to disengage herself temporarily from Priscilla—once she was assured that the girl was ensconced in a proper social situation, of course—so that she could pursue her own agenda. She hoped Matthew Feverley would be in attendance; even though he decried social engagements, surely his mother would insist he attend tonight's event. Mr. Shaw, Mr. Chessley, and Mr. Bentley-Bodham would also very likely be here as well. No one would miss this event. She wanted to speak to them again in an attempt to assess their physical capability for climbing from one theatre box to the other, as well as to compare their figures with that of the man who'd overtaken her carriage earlier today.

Irene also wanted to find out more about Miss Ferndale and Lord Leavington's aborted wedding.

"Delia!" she said with a smile, sweeping toward Mrs. Merryweather for an embrace.

"Irene, darling," replied the woman, then she added quietly into her ear, "That was quite well done. Your grand entrance, I mean to say. I confess, I wasn't quite certain what to expect. We'd heard you'd been invited. No one was certain whether you'd attend. You were *brilliant.*"

Irene smiled at her friend. "Why thank you, and Lady Enfield was quite gracious to include us. What a pleasure to see you tonight, Delia. You look tremendously well."

"Oh, you're too kind. I understand you've had some unpleasant experiences over the last few days," Delia Merryweather murmured, then stepped back. Her eyes held interest and concern. "Ghastly events. Two murders, and you were there for both of them? First Harold Tripley and then Lord Garington? How shocking and horrible."

"Sadly, yes, I was," Irene replied, then, as etiquette dictated, turned to Delia's daughters. "Dear Patricia, how marriage does seem to agree with you!" She allowed her gaze to dip briefly to the slight roundness of the young woman's belly—which wasn't really noticeable unless one knew to look, but her cheeks were slightly fuller and a woman could tell when another woman was blooming with child. But even Irene wasn't so bold as to mention such a condition in a public setting. "And Melanie... what a lovely frock. Do I detect the hand of Monsieur Claude therein?"

"You do, Lady Darling, and thank you for the reference," replied Melanie Merryweather with a little curtsy.

"Thank you, Lady Darling, I do find marriage to be quite pleasant," said Patricia, her cheeks flushing with pleasure at

Irene's subtle nod to her condition even as a hand smoothed over her middle. She curtsied as well.

"May I present Miss Priscilla Bedwith. Priscilla, please meet a friend of mine and your mother's, Mrs. Merryweather, and her daughters, Mrs. Bluestone and Miss Melanie Merryweather," Irene said.

After another series of curtsies, the three younger women began to chat politely. Delia drew Irene aside.

"What a horrible thing to have happen to Harold Tripley," she said in an undertone. "Poor Trudy. I can't imagine who or why one would do such a thing—and in someone's *own home!* Who could have done it? I mean to say, must we all be concerned about some random thief breaking into our houses and killing us in our beds?"

"I highly doubt that, because I am quite certain the killer was an invited guest to the dinner party," Irene told her even as her eyes scanned the room. She caught sight of Mr. Chessley as he disappeared down the hall. As she knew well the layout of the Enfield residence, she suspected he was heading to the rooms put aside for men to play cards or billiards.

"Do you mean to say, someone who was at the *dinner* did it?" Delia Merryweather goggled at her even as she managed to keep her voice down.

"I mean to say exactly that. It was one of four men—Lord Garington was a suspect before he—er—right." Irene winced a little as she realized how callous she might sound. "You heard about what happened to him?"

"At the Lyceum of all places! How ghastly," Delia replied, her eyes wide with sincere horror rather than salaciousness. "In Lord Chumley's box, I hear. Is it true someone actually *cut his throat?*"

"Yes, unfortunately, that is correct."

"But how do you know so much about it?" Delia asked.

They were standing close together because the room was very crowded around the edges, leaving space for the decor and the fenced-off dance floor. As this was the first Enfield Ball in four years, of course *everyone* was there, so the place was an utter crush of people in between tables, garden benches, potted trees, and the archways and fence.

"I've been investigating the deaths," Irene told her. "Like Sherlock Holmes." And if it weren't for a bloody misplaced cufflink, she was certain she'd already have identified the culprit. But the cufflink simply wouldn't leave her *be* to follow her instincts regarding the killer.

"*Investigating?* Why, what do you mean?" Delia goggled at her, but there was a flare of admiration along with shock.

"I was present at both instances, and I simply feel so terribly for poor Trudy that I knew I *had* to do something," Irene said, waving it off. "Now, forgive me for changing the subject, but I simply *must* hear the details about what happened with poor Miss Ferndale's wedding. I understand she called it off quite suddenly."

"And only the day before the ceremony was to take place," Delia said, her eyes slitted with speculation. "No one really knows what happened, but Lord Leavington was left flat-footed and, by all accounts, was quite shocked by it all.

"I understand he took himself off to the country—but whether it was out of shame or the devastation of a broken heart, one isn't quite certain. I had thought they were quite happy together, and very much in love," Delia added wistfully. "I simply cannot *imagine* what could have happened to change her mind."

"Is she here tonight?" Irene said, looking around.

"Oh, no. No one has seen her since it all happened. I understand she went off to Paris the day after—which would have been the day of her wedding. Poor girl. She really is quite a sweet, lovely thing. Her parents must be devastated."

"Was Lord Leavington particular friends with Mr. Tripley?" Irene asked.

"Harold Tripley? Why, I have no idea. Why do you ask?"

Irene shrugged. "No particular reason. What about Lord Garington? Did they socialize, he and Lord Leavington?"

"Why, I don't quite know," replied Delia. "Quite frankly, I tried to avoid Garington as much as possible, so I haven't any idea. Mr. Merryweather disliked him as well. He had this sort of...*thing* about him." She shuddered, unable to put into words what were obviously unpleasant feelings...but Irene understood. "Does this have something to do with...what happened? But how could it?"

"I don't know," Irene answered. "At least, I'm not certain, but—oh, I see the twins across the way. Please excuse me, Delia dear, so I can greet them. Monsieur Claude has put us all—my daughters and me, I mean to say—in different shades of green, and I want to see how they look." Irene waved in the direction of where Rose and Violet stood.

They weren't looking toward her, and Irene was glad for that. She had no intention of speaking with them—at the moment at least.

Confident that Priscilla was in good hands with Delia and her daughters, Irene slipped away.

She was on the trail of a killer...

And suddenly, *there he was*.

The man she knew in her heart who'd done it, damn the bloody cufflink. She knew who'd killed two people and abducted her last night and it wasn't Matthew Feverley.

She saw him—the killer—through the crowd and began to push her way in his direction. She wasn't certain what she was going to do when she got to him, but she'd figure it out. After all, as she'd previously pointed out, she had a loud, carrying voice. She also had a pistol in her reticule, much to the dismay of her maid.

He must have felt her attention on him, for he suddenly looked in her direction. Their eyes met.

His widened with comprehension, and suddenly, he was gone, lost in the crowd.

~

Priscilla couldn't stop gawking at the beautiful ballroom. She'd never seen anything so gorgeous as this fairy garden-themed decor.

Her companions, the Merryweather sisters, seemed equally appreciative of the beautiful environment, and they chatted, gushing about it, quite a bit. Neither of the Merryweathers had been out during the last Enfield Ball, so they'd had no idea to expect such elegance and glamor.

"Hm," said Melanie Merryweather, her eyes narrowing thoughtfully as she looked across the room. "I don't believe I've ever seen that gentleman before. Do you know who he is, Patty? He's the dark one with the mustache speaking to Wessley and Lady Pengelley."

Priscilla's heart gave a little lurch and she swiveled to look before she caught herself. Yes, it was Hugh—Mr. Bafferty—about whom Melanie (she'd insisted Priscilla call her by her familiar name, and Priscilla had been pleased to suggest the same in return) was referring.

"Why, no, I don't think I've ever seen him before," said the older sister, Mrs. Bluestone, with great curiosity in her voice. "I wonder who he is, to be so familiar with the duke. Oh, Lady Pengelley does look particularly well tonight doesn't she?"

"She's about to become engaged to a young and handsome duke, so one would expect so," Melanie said with a grin. "That wedding will be quite an affair! I do hope we're invited."

Priscilla noted that her companion didn't seem to feel any grudge or envy toward Lady Pengelley, and she chalked that up to Melanie Merryweather not being nearly as determined to improve her rank as she herself was.

Then, pleased to be able to offer her companions a bit of valuable information, she said, "That gentleman is Mr. Hugh Bafferty. I know him quite well, for our estates in Yorkshire are adjacent."

"You do?" Melanie's eyes widened, sparkling. "Eek—he's looking over here right now!" She squelched a little sound of excitement and swiftly turned away so as not to be caught gaping. "He's quite handsome. And he is friends with the duke.... Do you think you could make us an introduction?"

"Of course," Priscilla replied, knowing that any introduction she would make of Melanie Merryweather to Mr. Bafferty would be in vain. Melanie was not at all the type of woman who would attract Hugh—Mr. Bafferty's—affections.

"He's coming this way," said Mrs. Bluestone in an undertone as she fanned herself whilst looking in the opposite direction.

Priscilla's heart was beating quite rapidly for some reason that made absolutely no sense. She resisted the urge to pat her hair or smooth her gown. It was quite the most lovely frock she'd ever owned, or had ever dreamed of owning. Lady Darling had been quite right that Monsieur Claude was a genius, and the buttercup yellow made her look rosy and glowing. She knew she'd never looked better.

"Get your dance card ready, Mellie," murmured Mrs. Bluestone, giving her sister a little nudge and a wink.

Priscilla tamped back a prickle of annoyance that the sisters would assume Mr. Bafferty would invite Melanie to dance. He certainly might do so out of politeness or obligation, but it was rather poor of them to expect it.

She was pretending not to watch Mr. Bafferty make his way over to them when a deep voice spoke behind her. "Miss Bedwith. You're looking quite ravishing this evening."

She turned to find Mr. Shaw at her elbow, and had to force herself not to take a step backward. She had not forgotten the way he made her feel the night at the theatre—standing so close, and leering down at her décolletage as he'd done. At least tonight he didn't smell as strongly of spirits. But he was still... well, there was something about him that put her off.

"Good evening, Mr. Shaw. Do you know Miss Merryweather and Mrs. Bluestone?" she said, stepping away from him and automatically attempting to deflect any of his attentions onto her companions.

"Of course I know Miss Merryweather. And Mrs. Bluestone, how good to see you again. Is your husband here this evening?" Mr. Shaw seemed particularly affable, but he was still standing so close to Priscilla that she felt crowded.

"Oh, yes, I do believe he is in the card room, Mr. Shaw," replied the elder Merryweather sister with a smile. It seemed she didn't feel the same dislike that Priscilla did for the gentleman.

"Excellent. I suppose I shall see him there...perhaps after Miss Bedwith has agreed to take a turn around the dance floor with me?" He smiled at her and somehow managed to keep his eyes above her chin, though she suspected it was an effort.

"Oh, how kind of you to ask, Mr. Shaw, but I've already promised this dance to Mr. Bafferty," she said, just as Hugh came into earshot. She caught her old friend's eye pleadingly as he approached and said, "Mr. Bafferty, have you come to claim our dance?"

To his credit he didn't flicker an eyelash. Instead he gave her a smile that was warm enough to make her stomach do a little flip as she remembered those lips touching hers—*stop that, Pris!* she told herself fiercely—and replied, "If you'd honor me so, Miss Bedwith. But first, perhaps you could introduce me to your friends." His smile shifted to include both Merryweather sisters, and Priscilla found herself having to suppress another prickle of vexation.

"Yes, of course, Mr. Bafferty." She conducted the introductions quickly, then turned to him. "I've been simply clamoring to get on the dance floor. Mr. Shaw, please excuse us—I do hate to miss the rest of this piece."

She hadn't realized it was a waltz.

And then, all at once, she was in Hugh's arms...just as she had been that fateful night.

The night she couldn't put out of her mind no matter how hard she tried.

"Miss Bedwith, I cannot keep my thoughts to myself on how gloriously beautiful you are, always...but particularly tonight," he said. "I'm surely the envy of every other man here at the moment."

"Oh." Priscilla flushed. She was so extremely aware of the strength of his fingers as he clasped them around hers, and the light, steady pressure of his hand at the center of her back as he guided her through the steps...the dark, steady eyes as they looked down at her.

One-two-three, *one*-two-three.

"Thank you. I can't thank you enough for...er...going along with me," she told him, trying to suppress a sudden rush of nerves.

It was just that she'd never actually *waltzed* with Hugh Bafferty before. The country dances they'd attended had been far more informal, with line dances and square dances.

She'd never felt the strength and authority of his arms, guiding her through the steps...the solidness of his stature, squared off to hers...the ease of his footfalls...the proximity of his person...the scent of his hair...

"It is truly my greatest pleasure, Miss Bedwith." He was looking down at her with a crooked smile that somehow seemed a little sad. "If only it weren't simply that you needed rescuing."

"Oh." Her cheeks rushed with heat. How easily he'd seen through her. "It's only that Mr. Shaw is...well, he's rather insistent and I...well, I appreciate your gallantry."

"Priscilla, if you don't know by now that I would do anything for you—including rescuing you from an over-ardent suitor or pulling you from a pond or anything else your heart desires—I fear you will *never* understand. Nonetheless, I am happy to take you on a turn around the dance floor and deposit you safely distant from Harry Shaw if that is what will make you happy."

With that, he lifted his eyes from hers and trained them over her shoulder as he spun her gently around another couple (where had he learned to dance like this?) and navigated them smoothly to the edge of the dance floor.

Priscilla was aware of a strange, bereft feeling as he guided her through one of the archways from the dance floor back into the crowd, as he'd promised—directly opposite from the area where she'd left Mr. Shaw and, thankfully, out of his line of sight.

"I trust you will have a pleasant evening, Miss Bedwith. I thoroughly enjoyed our dance. I certainly wish there could be more of them. Good evening." Mr. Bafferty bowed and then disappeared into the crowd.

She stared after him, shocked by his sudden exit, completely discomfited by his parting words...and feeling strangely abandoned.

"Miss Bedwith," said a posh voice behind her.

She turned, still hazy with confusion over her sudden abandonment, and discovered one of the gentlemen from the dinner party at the Tripley household.

It was Mr.... Hm. Good Heavens, what *was* his name?

"Yes?" she said, forcing a smile. She couldn't remember his name, but she dared not admit that she'd forgotten him when he'd addressed her so familiarly. What a breach of etiquette that would be! After all, she'd sat at the same table with him for dinner only three nights ago. "Are you...are you having quite an engaging evening?"

"Yes, of course. Miss Bedwith, I should very much like to speak with you, if I may?" He smiled charmingly at her and offered an arm. "Never fear—I shan't take you off onto the terrace or into the gardens and sally your virtue or ruin your reputation," he said with a wider smile and a warm chuckle. "One is certainly aware of the influence of your sponsor, and one wouldn't wish to upset her, would one?"

"No, of course not," she said, still unable to remember his name. Nonetheless, he was certainly well turned-out, and she *had* met him before, and he most definitely knew that Lady Darling was her chaperone...surely there could be no harm in allowing him to speak to her. She smiled, fluttering her lashes. He was also, probably, a very eligible bachelor...one who was far more suitable than a simple country squire with a small estate in Yorkshire, whether it abutted her own lands or not.

"Capital. Perhaps we should go this way—it's quite easier than shoving one's way through the crush, isn't it?" He gestured to a doorway that led out of the ballroom and into a corridor.

Priscilla allowed him to take her arm and lead her into the hallway.

The corridor was quite empty and silent, and the grip on her arm where he held her was far too tight.

Suddenly something painful was pressing into her side.

She looked down and realized it was the tip of a knife.

Chapter Sixteen

Irene skimmed her way through the crowd so quickly no one tried to stop her to speak. If she heard a person call after her, "Lady Darling!" she simply ignored it and went on.

Although she was determined to confront the killer, she also wanted to find Mr. Feverley. She suspected if he was anywhere, it was in with the gentlemen playing cards or billiards in one of the smaller chambers, since he was not the sort of man who liked to be in the thick of social things...rather like herself, she supposed.

Before she faced the murderer, she quite needed to speak with Mr. Feverley about the dratted cufflink. The bloody, stupid cufflink that had, so far, completely muddled up her deductions.

If it weren't for that, she'd had no question about her conclusions.

She shrugged, throwing off her frustration. She was close. She knew she was. If she could just find Mr. Feverley...

As if conjured, suddenly, there he was, just across the room at a table. Playing cards.

"*Mother!* What are you doing?"

Irene nearly jumped a foot. "Janey," she said, turning to face her youngest daughter as her heart settled back into place. And her husband as well. "Charles. How nice to see you. Both of you look wonderful," she added with great sincerity. They really would make beautiful babies.

"Thank you, Mama. What are you doing, lurking about the card and billiard room? Are you still *detecting*?" Jane asked, her eyes sparkling with excitement and interest. "Oh, don't worry—I've told Charles all about it. He's forbidden me from being your Watson, but he wants to know about it all anyhow. And, I must say, your gown is absolutely *gorgeous*."

Irene winced and glanced at Charles Kearnley, who wore a bemused smile.

"You do look exceptionally lovely, Lady Irene," he said as Irene fumbled her own response, "Er...well, I—"

"Mama, I *know* you were snooping about. Have you found him yet? The killer?"

Jane's voice was a trifle too loud and Irene winced again, then batted her hand in the air to suggest that she speak more quietly. "Very nearly. I mean to say, yes, except for one little problem." That dratted cufflink. "Incidentally, what do either of you know about Miss Ferndale and Lord Leavington's aborted wedding?"

Charles and Jane exchanged glances, then looked back at her. "I've heard some things," Jane said, subdued now. The sparkle had left her eyes. "My maid—you know Gussie—well, she knows Lydia's—Miss Ferndale's—maid and she told me, in the strictest of confidences what Lydia's maid—"

Charles cleared his throat loudly and gave his wife a look.

Jane looked up at him and patted his arm, smiling affection-ately. "I'm only telling my mother—and you, of course—I haven't even told the twins—and she won't tell a soul, will you, Mama?"

"Of course not," Irene said. "But I begin to believe there might be a connection between the wedding that didn't happen and the death of Mr. Tripley. You see," she said, drawing closer to both of the young people, "Mr. Tripley wagered a significant amount of money that the wedding wouldn't take place. And then the wedding was canceled and he collected the money from the wager he won. And now he's dead...and so is Lord Garington, who was my prime suspect."

"Garington," said Charles wearing a disgusted expression. "Truth is, not many people are upset about his demise. Not that one would wish death—especially murder—on a chap, of course, but he wasn't well-liked and he was not the sort of fellow one liked to associate with. He was...well," he looked down at Jane and something passed between them. Then he went on, "I shall only say that there was a moment when I thought I might have had to call him out."

Irene looked at her daughter, and then her son by law, and then back again, shocked and then furious. "Do you mean to suggest that Lord Garington did or said something...inappropriate? To you, Janey?" It was a good thing the man was dead, or she might have been tempted to do away with him herself. Irene was no stranger to men who thought they could do what they wanted to a woman.

Jane's cheeks were pink and she wore an uncharacteristically reticent expression. "It's water under the bridge, Mama, and my lovely, heroic, gallant Charles took care of matters quite handily. Garington had quite the black eye."

"He's lucky it wasn't more than that," Charles growled.

Irene's hackles were still raised, but she nodded. It seemed Charles Kearnley had, indeed, taken care of matters. He was not the sort to shrink from doing what was right. God bless him for protecting her daughter.

"What did Gussie tell you about Miss Ferndale, then,

Jane?" Irene felt as if she truly were on the verge of discovering something important, especially now with the knowledge of Lord Garington's perfidy.

Jane glanced once more at Charles, then moved close enough to speak directly into Irene's ear. She smelled like sweet tea roses and face powder. "It seems Miss Ferndale was compromised by...by someone—I don't know who; the maid didn't say— and he...well, this someone threatened to tell Lord Leavington about it."

"And so she saved her reputation by calling off the wedding before he could do so," Irene said thoughtfully. "Could it have been Lord Garington who compromised her? Since he seems to...have that inclination." She had to tamp back a rush of fury again, thinking about her poor Janey.

Jane had stepped back a bit, but still kept her voice low. "Garington had attempted to court her, but her interest didn't last long. And then she met Lord Leavington." Her expression was sad. "Everyone thought it was a love match. It certainly seemed to be." She was leaning back into her husband's torso, and he'd slipped an arm around her. "It was so shocking and sad when she called it off."

Irene nodded thoughtfully. "And Harold Tripley made a nice sum of money over an event that everyone expected to happen, but didn't," she murmured, mostly to herself. "And now he's dead. And so is Lord Garington."

There *had* to be a connection, didn't there? It seemed too coincidental otherwise.

Then it hit her. She gasped and said, "What if someone made the wager and then took steps to make *certain* the outcome he sought occurred?"

"That is quite a brilliant theory, but Harold Tripley? Hmph. Can't see him doing such a thing as compromising a woman, or even threatening to expose her over such a secret," said Charles thoughtfully. "He was a good chap. Not the sort. Never heard a thing against him, though he did like the races and a few wagers here and there. Honest man, he was."

"Maybe someone else made the same wager..." said Irene. "And cheated."

She had been looking into the billiard room from where they stood in the hall, mostly staring off into the distance as she thought about all of these considerations. As she did so, she caught sight of a gentleman, lining up his cue, bending over the billiard table to take a shot.

And then it struck her.

She gasped so loudly Jane and Charles started and looked at her in concern.

"Mother?"

"Charles, is it possible that a man might lose a cufflink whilst playing billiards? Perhaps if it's loose and he brushes his sleeve against the edge of the table?"

"Certainly could happen. A chap might even take off his coat when playing—if there are no ladies about, I mean to say," he added with a smile at his wife. "It would be quite simple for a cufflink to get dislodged, especially when making a difficult shot."

"Thank you, thank you, *thank you!*" Irene beamed up at him, then surged onto her tiptoes and planted a kiss on his cheek. She got a brush of whiskers and managed to make him blush. "You've just cleared things up for me. Now, I must visit the ladies resting room, and you two ought to go back into the dance and take a turn about the floor."

Jane and Charles didn't argue; they seemed more than willing to slip into each others' arms and waltz across the room. Love matches were still relatively rare in the *ton*, and demonstrating one's affection for one's spouse was also rare. But Irene's children had no qualms about either, and that, she decided, was something that made her very proud. Love was, after all, a powerful and good thing.

"Off with you," she said again, waving at them to go. She really did intend to visit the ladies resting room, but of course after that, she was going to find and confront the man who had killed Harold Tripley and Lord Garington.

Now that she understood what happened with the cufflink, it all made terrible sense.

Irene freshened up, and decided she'd best check in on her other responsibility—Priscilla—before facing down a murderer. Hopefully, the young woman had come to her senses and realized she had no chance with Wessley, and that Mr. Bafferty not only loved her, but would be an excellent husband.

But when Irene returned to the ballroom, she didn't see Priscilla anywhere. She took the risk of beginning to circle the room whilst watching the dancers (spotting Jane and Charles, as well as Rose and Violet), knowing that people would—and did—stop her to speak with them, slowing her progress.

She'd only made it a third of the way around when a large person stepped in front of her.

"Lady Darling." It was the Wall of Man, Mr. Finley Marshall himself.

"Good evening, Mr. Marshall," she said, barely stopping in time to keep from treading on his boots. "I didn't expect to see you here tonight." She lifted her chin, giving him a close, thoughtful look.

He was just as tall and vexingly imposing as she'd remembered, and his well-shaped bald head shined smoothly in the light from all the tiny candles. His dark mustache and short, compact beard—which were graying heavily at the edges—were neat and smooth. He was attired in very proper evening wear, but gave off the impression he wished he wasn't.

"This was not an event I was eager to attend," he said in a

dry tone that brought a smile to her lips. "But I'm told I should... well, blast it—that I ought to attempt to...er...invite your ladyship to the dance floor."

Irene's brows rose, and she looked off to the side, where she spotted Miss Adina Trewlove watching them. The girl wore a determined expression. "I see. Sadly, I'm rather engaged elsewhere at the moment, Mr. Marshall. I seem to have misplaced my ward, Miss Bedwith."

He glanced over at his niece, then drew in a deep breath, squared his shoulders, and turned back to Irene. "Perhaps a brief turn around the dance floor would accomplish two things: first, it will satisfy my niece that I've fulfilled my social obligations—which I detest greatly—and second, it will give you the opportunity to look for Miss Bedwith out there. You will be delivered to the other side of the room more efficiently than the manner in which you've been traveling."

As she couldn't argue with either of those points, Irene inclined her head and took his arm when he offered it.

It was surprisingly firm and warm beneath her fingers—his arm—and Irene felt a little quiver of awareness...a sensation she hadn't experienced for more than nine years. It made her feel unexpectedly warm—although that might just have been one of those strange heat waves that flashed over her at random moments.

Mr. Marshall was a barely adequate dancer, which probably explained his reluctance to participate in these sorts of social obligations. Fortunately, the piece was a waltz, which was a fairly simple step—as long as one didn't attempt to get fancy by swirling vigorously around other couples on the dance floor.

Mr. Marshall did none of that. He simply moved them through the steps rather like Irene imagined one of Jules Verne's automatons would do if they were programmed to waltz.

He smelled of some pleasant, subtle scent, and he managed

not to step on any of her toes—which Irene greatly appreciated, for he was not a slight man. Edward had not been a practiced dancer either, and he had trod on her slippers so often that she eventually refused to dance anything but a very slow and sedate waltz with him.

"Did your valet nix the eyepatch tonight, Mr. Marshall?" she said, looking up at him with a little smile. "I can see why— that sort of accessory doesn't quite do at a ball, does it?"

A little furrow appeared between his brows. "I beg your pardon, Lady Darling...an eyepatch? If you're making some subtle social—or fashionable—reference, it's quite beyond me."

She studied him closely as they turned, rather mechanically, through the *one*-two-three count. "You know perfectly well I'm referring to your little masquerade last night, Mr. Marshall. Or shall I call you Jack?"

The furrow grew deeper while his brows somehow winged up around it. "I don't mean to be obtuse, Lady Darling, but I simply don't know what you mean. Who is Jack?"

"He is a man—certainly not a gentleman—known as One-Eyed Jack," she said, still watching him closely. She'd been certain—well, *fairly* certain—the man who abducted her last night had been completely swathed in disguise, with his ridiculous eyepatch, unruly beard and mustache, and low riding bowler hat. She was a close reader of Sherlock Holmes stories, after all, and Watson was always being fooled by his friend's disguises. Irene was determined not to be a Watson.

Besides, Jack had been about the same height and build as Finley Marshall, at least as far as she could tell, and there was something about Jack who'd reminded her of him...

"I see," he replied in a tone that suggested he very much did not. "That would explain the—er—eyepatch."

Though she continued to examine him closely and to watch

his expression, Irene observed nothing to indicate he was prevaricating.

So he *wasn't* One-Eyed Jack?

How curious.

"Shall I leave you here, then, my lady?" he said, and Irene realized they'd made their way across the dance floor and she hadn't given one look for Miss Bedwith anywhere. She'd been too occupied by the man in front of her, drat it. "Have you located your ward?"

Irene opened her mouth to reply in the negative, then froze in shock. Good Heavens.

There she was, standing on the very balcony from where Lord Milbright had fallen. Priscilla appeared utterly ill-at-ease, even terrified.

"What on earth is she—" Irene took two steps in that direction and then she noticed the man standing behind Priscilla, mostly in shadows.

It was the murderer.

Chapter Seventeen

Any last niggle of doubt as to whether Irene was correct in her deductions evaporated.

The killer met Irene's eyes, staring down at her from his position on the balcony. He made a slight gesture with his head—an invitation?—then stepped back into the shadows, taking a glassy-eyed, silent Priscilla with him.

A multitude of questions threatened to paralyze her (What was he doing on the balcony? How did he get up there? Why did he have Priscilla?)—but the answers didn't really matter at the moment. It was clear Priscilla was in danger.

Irene began to shove her way through the crush, vaguely aware of miffed and questioning comments in her wake, including a familiar male one that belonged to the Wall of Man.

She ignored them all, for her focus was getting to Priscilla before anything happened to her. Oh, bloody *hell*—she'd messed this up badly, hadn't she? What was she going to tell Mrs. Bedwith if something happened to her daughter?

Irene was nearly to the stairs that led to the balcony. It appeared that the killer and his hostage had somehow circumvented the bench positioned there at the base of the steps. Her heart was pounding but she was, somehow, calm and determined. No one else seemed to have noticed the two people on the balcony, and that was probably a good thing.

She darted around Mr. Fleming, who stood near the burbling water fountain, and noticed he was holding a walking stick.

"May I borrow this?" she said, and took it from his hand before he could react. A walking stick and the little pistol she had not yet removed from her reticule would be quite useful in confronting a killer. She ignored Mr. Fleming's outraged cry.

"Lady Darling!"

She ignored the Wall of Man, who sounded as if he were right on her heels, and skirted the bench at the bottom of the balcony stairs.

The last time she'd climbed these steps had been four years ago. She pushed away the memory and steadied her mind.

Although previously, no one had seemed to notice Priscilla up on the balcony, by now, people had caught sight of Irene as she climbed the steps. Lady Darling was always noticeable, and she'd left a trail of outrage and vexation behind her.

At the top of the stairs, she found herself in the small space where she and Lady Enfield had had their infamous altercation.

The killer was at the back of the promontory, out of sight from the crowd below. He was positioned near the small door that used to lead to the servants' hall, but now ended only in a closet.

Irene realized that he likely intended to use that door as an escape route, and she smiled to herself. The only way off this balcony was in front of her and down the stairs. She still couldn't fathom why he'd come up here at all.

She had the walking stick in her hand as she faced him, and used it to appear to prop herself up. It wouldn't hurt to seem less able than she was, and besides, she was a bit out of breath from her activities, including the ascending the stairs so rapidly.

"Let Miss Bedwith go, Mr. Bentley-Bodham. She's done nothing to you and it's the two of us who need to speak."

Priscilla was struggling not to cry, but, Irene noted with satisfaction, she wasn't swooning or otherwise collapsing. The glassiness had faded from her eyes, and her hopeful gaze was now fixed on Irene.

"Oh, I won't be doing that, Lady Darling. I do think Miss Bedwith is going to be with me for the foreseeable future." He shifted so she could see the knife he had positioned at Priscilla's side.

Did the man not realize how many layers of corset and crinoline were beneath a woman's gown? It would be no small feat to shove a knife far enough through boning, thick seams and layers of heavy material into Priscilla's flesh, no matter how sharp it was. Irene relaxed a bit more. Really, Mr. Bentley-Bodham was simply not the smartest person she'd ever met— either that, or he had no experience with a woman's undergarments. It was shocking he'd (so far) gotten away with every terrible thing he'd done.

"Perhaps you'd like to take her place? We're heading to the Continent, you know, where I can disappear forever." He'd always had a sort of sleek, polished, posh demeanor, but, despite his threats, he now came across as a desperate, frightened little man. His eyes darted about, and his lips were moist from where he'd licked them.

This change in his persona was certainly because he knew she knew he was an evil, sniveling, cheating coward. She could see him for what he really was. And, of course, because she was a woman, and she—like her namesake in *A Scandal in Bohemia* —had taken the upper hand in the matter.

"Of course I would," she replied, leaning more heavily on

the cane. She was vaguely aware that the buzz of conversation from below had filtered into silence, and realized she was living a moment of *déjà vu* from four years ago, when she'd been part of a different confrontation on this very balcony. "But first, we ought to talk about what you've done, oughtn't we?"

Everyone was holding their collective breath, watching from below.

Irene smiled then turned like an actor onstage so that she partially faced him but also cheated out toward the people—her audience—below. She spoke, projecting her voice so that all could hear.

"Mr. Bentley-Bodham, I know what you've done. And I know why. I also know that you have no escape. It was incredibly foolish of you to allow yourself to be trapped up here. I'm not certain why you even climbed these stairs...but then again, you're not nearly as intelligent as you think, are you?

"After all, a mere woman is standing in front of you, and she is about to explain to an entire crowd of people why you stabbed and killed Harold Tripley in his own home, and why you cut the throat of Lord Garington and escaped by climbing from one theatre box to the next. Incidentally, it was that activity that first put me looking in your direction. You were the only one of my suspects—well, very nearly," —she thought of Mr. Feverley, but he'd never *truly* been a suspect— "who could have successfully done so."

Gasps filled the air as her words sank in, and then everything turned quiet again. Even the musicians had stopped playing and the servants had ceased serving. Everyone waited to hear what she had to say.

"The reason you did these things, Mr. Bentley-Bodham? Very simple: you're a cheat. You cheat at everything—cards for certain, and anything else you can fix. You've been fixing wagers at mens' clubs for years, making quite a bit of money doing so.

"You happened to fix a big, very lucrative wager—I shan't mention it in deference to the privacy of the individuals involved, but you know to what I am referring—and when Mr. Tripley, one of your fellow bettors, discovered what you'd done, he confronted you. You see, Harold Tripley was not a cheat or a reprobate or an evil-minded person like you are, Mr. Bentley-Bodham.

"He was an honest man who was horrified when he learned what you'd done—not only because of the money involved, but because of the reputations of those who were part of the wager in the first place. He gave you a chance to come clean, and instead of doing so, you chose to silence him."

Irene paused for effect as the truth of her words filtered through the crowd, expressed by murmurs and quiet gasps. She looked out over her audience and nodded. "Yes, and why did this so-called gentleman kill Lord Garington as well? Because, I believe, he was involved with the set-up of the wager and you were afraid he would be frightened enough to confess once he realized you'd been the one to kill Mr. Tripley."

"You're a stupid woman," snapped Mr. Bentley-Bodham. "It wasn't like that at all. Garington is the one who told me how to do it, and he tried to convince Tripley to keep his mouth shut. When I realized Tripley was about to blather to all and sundry, I had to take care of the matter. And then *Garington* wanted *money* from me to keep quiet about it! Of course I couldn't allow that."

"And there you have it, ladies and gentlemen," said Irene to the audience. She was rather enjoying herself now. "A confession from a killer, right here at the Enfield Ball."

"It matters not a whit," snarled Bentley-Bodham. "I'll be off and away before anyone can stop me anyhow. There are many places in this world to hide, and I've got plenty of money."

Still holding Priscilla, still with the knife blade positioned at her side, he edged closer to the door at the back of the balcony. Irene found it exceedingly regrettable that those on the ground below wouldn't be able to see his expression when he opened what he assumed was an escape route.

"It's been quite lovely chatting to you, Lady Darling," he sneered, and gave Priscilla a little shake as he shoved her toward the door while keeping the knife in place. "If you wish this young woman to be left unharmed, you'll stand away. Open it, girl!"

Irene took this opportunity to move more toward the right side of the tiny balcony. The stairs were on this side, and she knew precisely how many steps it would take to cross from where he stood to the stairs.

Nine.

A shaking Priscilla finally managed to open the door, and Mr. Bentley-Bodham stood there, stupefied, as he faced the small, empty closet Lady Enfield had installed just about four years ago.

"As I said, Mr. Bentley-Bodham...you are quite trapped up here. And so you really ought to release Miss Bedwith before someone gets hurt."

"Of course I shan't," he said, and thrust the knife into the girl's side.

Screams and shouts rose from below. Priscilla gasped and swooned, collapsing in his single-armed grip, then tumbled to the floor when he lost his hold on her.

Mr. Bentley-Bodham whirled toward Irene, the knife glinting in his hand. But she was ready for him. The walking stick she'd borrowed from Mr. Fleming whipped up, smacking into her would-be assailant's knife hand, and the blade spun away. She whipped the stick back around, catching him in the upper arm and causing him to stagger in the direction of the stairs. He gaped at her and turned, stumbling, as he attempted to run away.

Irene had expected this—but she had not expected to see the Wall of Man standing there, halfway up the stairway like a bloody sentry, drat it. Even so, she lunged toward her opponent and slammed the tip of the walking stick onto the floor...right in the escapee's path.

Mr. Bentley-Bodham tripped over the angled stick and stumbled, losing his balance and flying toward the stairs.

He hit the top one with a thud, and then began to roll down...stopped by the Wall of Man.

Irene, who'd immediately dashed toward Priscilla, looked up from where she'd been kneeling next to the girl. As she'd expected, the knife had made no real inroads through the layers of fabric and Priscilla was completely unhurt.

"Thank you, Mr. Marshall," she said, noticing that the man's foot was positioned on Mr. Bentley-Bodham's person, holding the panting man in place with perhaps more force than was strictly required.

"What is it you're wanting me to do with the bloke, your ladyship?" he asked calmly in a room of dead silence.

"I haven't any strong feelings about what happens to him next," she said, helping Priscilla to her feet. This activity, along with the young woman waving to the watchers below, produced a round of loud applause.

When the clapping died down, Irene went on, "Although a person might think that Mr. Matthew Feverley would wish to have a few personal words with Mr. Bentley-Bodham."

"And why is that, Lady Darling?" asked Mr. Marshall, as if delivering a line they'd previously practiced.

She managed to suppress a grin. "Well, you see...Mr. Bentley-Bodham attempted to incriminate Mr. Feverley as the killer by dropping his cufflink at the scene of the crime. Imagine how frustrated he must have been when Scotland Yard managed *not* to find the perfect clue he'd left for them."

"He did *what*?" cried a voice from the crowd. It wasn't Mr. Feverley; it was his mother, outraged—as only a mother could be when one of her chicks is threatened. "Why, I'd like to have words with him myself!" She began to shove her way through the crowd. Even from her perch on the balcony, Irene could see Mrs. Feverley's eyes lit with fire.

"You might perhaps have to stand in line," said Irene wryly, for she'd noticed Mr. Bafferty had burst from the crowd and was charging up the stairs toward the pinioned murderer.

Mr. Marshall staved off the incensed young man, but Irene noticed that, when Mr. Marshall dragged Mr. Bentley-Bodham to his feet, he accidentally dropped the man back onto the steps...and Mr. Bafferty's leg moved sharply. She heard a sickening thud, then a groan and then the thump as the killer's head clumped back to the floor. She was required to suppress another grin.

"Hugh," Priscilla cried in a sort of strangled whisper, detaching herself from Irene to rush toward the young man.

Irene watched, smiling smugly.

Not only had she caught a killer, but she'd also arranged for a marriage.

It was all in a day's work.

Chapter Eighteen

"It's absolutely inconceivable that the first Enfield Ball in four years ended in very nearly the same way the last one did," Rose said, giving her mother a stare that was, quite frankly, an accusing glare. "In a scandalous scene happening on the balcony, ending with a man falling from it!"

"Well, *I* certainly didn't intend for it to happen that way," Irene told her, stroking Beatrice's exposed pink tummy as the little dog snored in her lap, legs splayed wide. Mr. Timms sat on the back of the chair behind her, preening and squawking randomly. "It wasn't *my* fault Mr. Bentley-Bodham—oh for pity's sake, that is simply too many syllables and he doesn't deserve the respect of a title. I declare that he shall be referred to as B.B. from now on." She picked up the whisky she had insisted on Josephs pouring for her the moment she walked in the door, and took a healthy sip.

She and her daughters, their husbands, her ward, Mr. Bafferty, and the Josephses were all ensconced in the parlor—along with Watson, Mr. Timms and Beatrice, of course. These were all the people she cared about and loved the most. Even

Priscilla Bedwith, who had finally come to her senses about Hugh Bafferty.

The Enfield Ball had, as Rose suggested, ended rather abruptly with the Scene on the Balcony, Reprised, and everyone had filtered off to go home quite a bit earlier than one would have expected.

Lady Enfield had been overheard saying, "I promise it shan't be another four years before I host a ball, but, good Heavens, this is becoming quite a disruptive custom." Irene had grinned to herself. She was looking forward to the two of them privately reviewing the situation very soon. (She was certain it would involve whisky, detailed confidences, and much laughter. She was quite looking forward to having her friend again.)

"As I was saying," Irene went on imperiously, "it wasn't my fault B.B. was stupid and short-sighted enough to position himself up there. One wonders what on *earth* he was thinking."

"I believe... I believe he was trying to catch sight of you, Lady Darling," said Priscilla in a quiet voice. She was sitting very close to Mr. Bafferty on one of the divans. He had been holding her hand, and neither of them had attempted to leave the other's side since the ball. "He was unable to spot you otherwise."

As Irene had thought of doing the same—climbing to the balcony—in order to espy Priscilla, she nodded. "Yes, I suppose that does make sense. Well, he certainly made an erroneous decision."

"I do wish you would clear up a few things, Lady Irene, if you would," said David, who was the Viscount of Willowby and Violet's husband. He was using the informal address Irene had insisted all of her children's spouses use. Irene liked him quite a bit, even if she did consider him a tad boring. Nonetheless, he was a good husband to her daughter. "How is it that you came to settle on Mr.—er, B.B. as the culprit? From what Vi tells me you had an array of suspects, but none of them were obvious."

"*You* suspected Matthew—I mean Mr. Feverley," said Rose, looking a little haughtily at her mother. "I can't imagine why."

"I explained why," Irene said patiently. "Because his cufflink was found at the murder scene, and there was no possibility it could have been there if the killer hadn't dropped it. That turned out to be true, because Mr. Feverley had been playing billiards with B.B. and he must have lost his cufflink then. Our killer noticed it and decided it would make a perfect clue, and a way to frame someone else for his deed."

"So he dropped it there after he killed Mr. Tripley?" asked Violet.

Irene noticed that David had been extra solicitous with his wife tonight, and her suspicions that she was about to become a grandmother in about six or seven months' time were strengthened.

"I think he actually dropped it afterward, when we all gathered in the study. I was standing near Mr. Tripley's, er, body— that term simply sounds so cold and disrespectful, but it is, nonetheless, accurate—and B.B. attempted to come close in order to, apparently, ascertain whether I was capable of discerning a murder when I saw one. He really was quite an arse," she said with feeling, ignoring the smothered gasps from Violet and Rose, and the stifled laugh from Jane. She scoffed at them, winked at her sons by law, and took another sip. She was feeling pleasantly warm and relaxed, having successfully accomplished the two tasks she'd taken on.

"That proximity gave B.B. the opportunity to toss the cufflink to the floor. As it happened, it must have bounced and fallen under the desk, where Inspector Burgess inconveniently neglected to look. I say inconveniently because had *he* found the cufflink, and I hadn't been made aware of it by the maid, I would not have been distracted by such a red herring."

"Quite so, Lady Irene. I'm certain of it," said Charles. He was still grinning over her use of the word 'arse.' "But how *did* you come to settle on B.B.—I say, that *is* a much easier way to refer to him, isn't it?"

"One of the first things that strongly suggested B.B. as the culprit had to do with the murder of Lord Garington. I knew the killer had climbed from Lord Chumley's box into the one being used by the Wall of—I mean to say, Miss Trewlove and Mr. Marshall. Whoever did that had to have been athletic and agile.

"Mr. Chessley has a fairly prominent limp, and Mr. Shaw was extremely inebriated that night—so much so that he was swaying on his feet. I concluded that neither of them would have been able to make such a climb successfully.

"That left Mr. Feverley, who—regardless of what some people might think, I did *not* ever suspect, although things did look rather grim for him for a time—could easily have made the climb, and B.B., which narrowed things quite a bit.

"And then I discovered that at men's clubs there are betting books that list wagers made, and winnings paid, and that sometimes the wagers could be over rather strange and off-putting things. I shan't go into any details, but suffice it to say, I hope that none of my sons by law partake of the game, hoping to make money off a person's tragedy, loss, or difficulty." She looked at each of the three in turn, and was pleased to see nothing but agreement in their eyes.

"Quite so," said David vehemently.

"Indeed," added Charles.

"Of course not," said Lawrence, Rose's husband.

"Excellent. Anyhow," Irene went on, then paused when she glanced at Vella. She seemed to be quite interested in how Irene was going to continue this story. Vella grinned at her and lifted her brows in question.

Indeed. Irene hadn't quite considered the fact that her daughters might be a bit put-out by the fact that she'd been abducted—twice!—without her telling them. She would simply have to gloss over those details and hope they never found out. Especially Jane. She had a feeling Jane would be the most vexed, mainly because she hadn't been abducted too.

To that end, Irene also had a moment of gratitude that she hadn't been required tonight, after all, to remove and brandish the pistol that was still in her reticule. She did not want to have to explain *that* to her girls.

"Anyhow, earlier today, I discovered a paid betting slip in Harold Tripley's desk—I had permission from Mrs. Tripley to snoop, Jane,"—she gave her youngest child a quelling look—"and the slip was for a wager that the Ferndale-Leavington wedding would not take place. It was for a large sum of money. And so that is when I began to think about people who would make bets about something that could potentially be influenced.

"Something happened to induce Miss Ferndale to call off the wedding. What if that something had been manufactured in order that another person would make a lot of money? And perhaps—and we may never know for certain—the person making the bet was going to be sharing his winnings with someone else, someone who did *not* want their name on the bet? Someone known for cheating...

"And perhaps that person who did not want their name on the bet had somehow influenced or maneuvered the wedding to be called off. Again," Irene said forcefully as Jane sat up straight and gave her a sudden, understanding, and nervous look, "we may never know precisely who or how. And perhaps it is best that we don't, since it's likely been difficult enough for Miss Ferndale over the loss of her wedding."

"Quite so," said Charles fervently. "Ought to respect the girl's privacy." Irene saw him tighten his fingers over Jane's and she suppressed another pang of fury toward Lord Garington.

"And since everyone I'd spoken to about the suspects mentioned that B.B. cheated at cards, well, it followed that he could cheat at something else as well. And so I had mostly settled on him except for that little problem of the cufflink, which you, Charles, assisted me in solving."

"Any time, dear Lady Irene," he said, smiling and flashing two dimples. When he did that, Irene could certainly sympathize with why Jane had fallen for him.

"And there you have it all," Irene said, grinning. "My first murder case solved, and my latest matchmaking venture complete." She lifted her glass toward Priscilla and Mr. Bafferty, who smiled and flushed as they looked at each other with moony eyes.

"Your *first* case?" Rose said, giving her a narrow look. "Surely you don't mean to suggest you'd do it again, Mother."

"I most certainly would. I was brilliant at it, you must admit." Irene grinned as she looked at her over the rim of her glass.

"But Mother, what will people *think*?" said Violet, sitting up straight.

"I don't think people will think much at all, dear," Irene said, settling back into her seat and cuddling her poodle close. "After all, I am the eccentric Dowager Marchioness of Darling. But if they do, I have one thing they don't have."

"What is that?" Jane asked.

"Old age. When you get to be my age, you don't care what *anyone* thinks of you...and so you can do whatever you like!"

And Irene certainly intended to do just that.

Also by Colleen Gleason

Lady Darling Mysteries
Lady Darling Inquires After a Killer

The Gardella Vampire Hunters
Victoria

The Rest Falls Away

Rises the Night

The Bleeding Dusk

When Twilight Burns

As Shadows Fade

Macey/Max Denton

Roaring Midnight

Raging Dawn

Roaring Shadows

Raging Winter

Roaring Dawn

The Draculia Vampires
Dark Rogue: The Vampire Voss

Dark Saint: The Vampire Dimitri

Dark Vixen: The Vampire Narcise

Vampire at Sea: Tales from the Draculia Vampires

~

Wicks Hollow Series

Ghost Story Romance & Mystery

Sinister Summer

Sinister Secrets

Sinister Shadows

Sinister Sanctuary

Sinister Stage

Sinister Lang Syne

Three Tomes Bookshop

Paranormal Women's Fiction

Tomes, Scones & Crones

Purses, Curses & Hearses

Stakes, Cakes and Mandrakes

Hexes, Exes and Codexes

~

Stoker & Holmes Books

(for ages 12-adult)

The Clockwork Scarab

The Spiritglass Charade

The Chess Queen Enigma

The Carnelian Crow

The Zeppelin Deception

~

The Phyllida Bright Mysteries

(writing as Colleen Cambridge)

Murder at Mallowan Hall

A Trace of Poison

Murder by Invitation Only

Murder Takes the Stage

Two Truths & a Murder (November 2025)

The An American in Paris Mysteries

(writing as Colleen Cambridge)

Mastering the Art of French Murder

A Murder Most French

A Fashionably French Murder

In the Spirit of French Murder (May 2026)

About the Author

Colleen Gleason is an award-winning, New York Times and USA Today best-selling author. She's written more than forty novels in a variety of genres—truly, something for everyone!

She loves to hear from readers, so feel free to find her online.

Subscribe to Colleen's non-spam newsletter for other updates, news, sneak peeks, and special offers!
http://cgbks.com/news

Connect with Colleen online:
www.colleengleason.com
books@colleengleason.com

www.ingramcontent.com/pod-product-compliance
Lightning Source LLC
Chambersburg PA
CBHW020356110726
47899CB00006B/1731